The Unlikely Hero of ROOM 13B

ALSO BY TERESA TOTEN

The Unlikely Hero of Room 13B

TERESA TOTEN

DOUBLEDAY CANADA

Doubleday Canada and colophon are registered trademarks of Random House of Canada Limited

Library and Archives Canada Cataloguing in Publication

Toten, Teresa, 1955-, author
The unlikely hero of Room 13B / Teresa Toten.

Issued in print and electronic formats.
ISBN 978-0-385-67834-6 (pbk.).— ISBN 978-0-385-67835-3 (epub)

I. Title.

PS8589.O6759U65 2013   jC813'.54   C2013-902630-4
                                          C2013-903037-9

This book is a work of fiction. Names, characters, places and incidents are products of the author's imagination or are used fictitiously. Any resemblance to actual events or locales or persons, living or dead, is entirely coincidental.

The author gratefully acknowledges the support of the Access Copyright Foundation Research Grants.

Cover image © Mstewart/Dreamstime.com
Cover design: Jennifer Lum

Printed and bound in the USA

Published in Canada by Doubleday Canada,
a division of Random House of Canada Limited

www.randomhouse.ca

10 9 8 7 6 5 4 3 2 1

To all those who think they are alone

If you can fill the unforgiving minute
With sixty seconds' worth of distance run,
Yours is the Earth and everything that's in it,
And—which is more—you'll be a Man, my son!

Rudyard Kipling, "If"

CHAPTER ONE

The boy inhaled as the door opened. It was as if he knew. The girl stepped into the room, and within the space of a heartbeat, he was lost.

The girl made her way towards the semicircle of chairs, not smiling exactly, but not hesitating either. She was older for sure. Probably. So it was hopeless, of course. She sat down directly across from him, at her end of the semicircle. Without looking up, she crossed her genius, perfect legs and flipped a long black braid behind her. By the time he exhaled, the boy was in love.

It was like he had drowned in a wave of *want*.

Without even knowing how he knew, he somehow did know that if *she* wanted, he would give the girl everything. Hers for the taking as of that moment were his iPad 3 (especially since he himself was no longer allowed to use it), his first-edition copy of J.D. Salinger's *Nine Stories*, his Xbox, his autographed Doc Halladay baseball *and* his most prized Orcs from the Warhammer Fantasy Battle game—the classic eighth edition, not the other poseur stuff. For *her* he would master his most troublesome rituals and offer up what was left of his sanity.

"Greetings, Robyn, and welcome!" said Dr. Chuck Mutinda, nodding first at her and then into a raggedy file folder. This simultaneously shattered and enhanced the moment. The boy now knew her name.

Robyn.

"Thank you," the girl said to her feet, and the boy stopped breathing altogether, so hypnotic was the sound of her voice.

The girl's eyes were blue. Up until that very second, the boy had never noticed the colour of anyone's eyes, could not have told you the colour of his mother's eyes. But Robyn's eyes . . . well, they were the shade of an angry sky rimmed by thick lashes the colour of soot. Her beauty—which, shockingly, no one in the room felt compelled to jump up and comment on—was ravishing. Everything in him felt tossed and trampled.

He ached deep inside just looking at her, but he could not look away.

So *this* was what *that* was like?

"Robyn Plummer is a slightly late addition to our merry band, having recently completed the residential program at Rogers Memorial Hospital."

Residential. His heart stopped then started up again. He focused on his breath the way Chuck had tried to teach him to do—except that he'd never really paid attention, so it didn't help. *Residential.* They were all freaked by the mere possibility of *residential*.

"Welcome, Robyn, to room 13B and the Young Adult OCD Support Group. 'Course," Chuck explained, "there is no room 13A, which makes a 13B a bit superfluous. And you will have no doubt also noticed that there is no thirteenth floor on the elevator. We have to get off on fourteen to get to this floor."

"Yeah, man, what's with that? I spent half an hour riding the damn elevator my first time here. I thought it was some psycho test," said Peter Kolchak, slouching into his chair. A couple of the kids snorted in agreement.

"So," continued Chuck, ignoring the interruption, "in some blessed existential way we, uh, don't exist." He said this as he said almost everything, with the faintest hint of a Jamaican lilt. He was long parted from that country, but not yet from the singsong rhythms of its language. He returned to the file. "Robyn is sixteen and . . ."

Sixteen! The boy seized on the number. Sixteen was bad. It was an even number, and therefore had to be sterilized. And it was very bad as an age. *Sixteen*—he repeated it fifteen times and tapped it out thirty-three times until it felt "just right." Okay, so it could have been worse. And then he realized it *was*. There was also the height thing. You could tell even when she was sitting. The height—*her* height—could be and certainly would be a barrier. Robyn was unusually tall for a sixteen-year-old goddess, and he, sadly, irrefutably, was quite short for a boy of almost fifteen. Too young, too short—definitely obstacles.

But these too were surmountable.

The boy would grow, and fast, now that he had a goal. He'd just never had a goal before, not really, or at least not one that he could remember. He would start right away, immediately, this instant. The boy began listing his brand-new goals as Chuck introduced everyone to Robyn. He wrote them in bullet points with his right index finger into the shielded palm of his left hand.

- Grow immediately.
- Find courage.

- Keep courage.
- Get normal.
- Marry Robyn Plummer.

That should do it.

The boy straightened up hard into his chair. The chewed-up plastic bit into his shoulder blades. It was almost his turn.

"And beside Elizabeth Mendoza is—"

"Pretty Boy Ross," said Peter, who had been providing a running commentary throughout Chuck's intros. Peter was sitting beside Robyn and facing her all the while, moving ever so slightly closer. *Pretty? What the hell?* Peter was going to be a problem. Or maybe he just needed a meds adjustment. With some in the group it was hard to tell.

Chuck raised an eyebrow, which was about as threatening as Chuck got. "And beside Elizabeth is our youngest member, Adam Spencer Ross."

Noooo...!

Did he actually say that? Between Chuck and Peter, Adam sounded like the group's pet bunny. Elizabeth was only a few months older, for God's sake! Chuck had said the same stuff last week during the first round of intros. Somehow, it hadn't sounded as gormless then. Adam would normally tap or count the tiles, but since, as of seven minutes ago, he was a man with a goal, he didn't. Besides, they were all looking at him. So Adam Spencer Ross rolled dice he didn't even know he possessed. He sat up straighter and presented Robyn with his finest "Whaddya gonna do?" smile.

And then a miracle happened.

She smiled back.

His feet got hot. Robyn had not smiled back at the others—who, he had already determined last week, were *way* more nuts than he was. Adam had tracked her reaction to each intro as he'd listed his newly revised life goals. With years of multi-tasking of a very high order behind him, he could tap, count *and* pay attention to critical information.

"And finally, back to our newest member, Robyn Plummer ..." Chuck's Rasta dreadlocks seemed to wave at her while he searched through his notes. "Robyn is in grade 11 at Chapel High."

That's it! Game over! Confirmed as dead-in-the-water! Grade 11 was deep into high school. It was practically *out* of high school! Juniors dated college boys, sometimes. Even he knew that. Peter Kolchak, who was still ogling her, was in college, or would have been if he hadn't flamed out. Adam was in grade 10. This was Montague and Capulet territory. That he was in the gifted program at St. Mary's was no bonus. He got angry with his mother all over again. She had point-blank refused to let him skip from grade 3 to grade 4, even though the nuns had suggested it rather strongly (for nuns, that is). He and Robyn would have been in the exact same year if it weren't for his mother. Adam tapped his right foot twenty-nine times in three sets ending with three middle-finger taps for good measure. It was barely perceptible even in this room of experts. The annoyance with his mother receded. She meant well and he did love her, after all, whatever colour her eyes were.

Robyn folded her hands neatly in her lap. They jutted out of a forest green school blazer. The uniform jacket was too small and the school kilt too short. This was more about neglect than an effort to look cool. Adam would swear to it. Except for shiny perfect lips, her brilliant face shone without a trace of makeup, but bright blue nail polish gleamed on every fingernail. Ten little robin's eggs. *Robyn's* eggs. He knew with impenetrable certainty that this was the reason she had chosen that colour. He *got* it. It was yet another reason, in the head-spinningly fast accumulation of reasons, why they should be together, forever.

Chuck was in serious overdrive in his signature laid-back kind of way. He was going around the room again. There was muttering.

Adam had missed something.

"Trust me, people, studies show that this can be very freeing. Try it on for size. Just pick a character. It's like you can be more true to you, somehow, if you're someone else."

Huh?

Chuck looked like he didn't care one way or the other. But Adam knew better. He'd already been going to one-on-one therapy for almost a year before Chuck suggested that it was time to join the group. Dr. Charles Mutinda cared plenty.

Chuck had asked everyone to pick a *nom de guerre*, as he called it, for this and all future sessions. They would leave their doubt-ridden, shell-shocked and agonizing selves at the door and become instead all-powerful beings. Adam got excited despite himself. *He* would cease to be, becoming the Venerable Lord Kroak or Grimgor Ironhide! Yes! Why not?

But by the third pick a clear trend was forming: except for Elizabeth Mendoza, who claimed a reality TV star named Snooki, the rest of them called in comic superheroes. In fact, the group was loosely forming into either DC's Justice League or Marvel's Avengers, with just a hint of X-Men. Connie Brenner chose Wonder Woman, lining up in the Justice League camp, while Peter

Kolchak called in Wolverine. Kyle Gallagher said he wanted to be Iron Man, while Tyrone Cappell said he'd like to be Green Lantern if that was all right with everyone.

"Naw you don't, Cappell!" snorted the newly christened Wolverine. "Haven't you heard? Green Lantern's a fag—I mean, gay."

Green Lantern seemed to ponder this for a moment and then stammered, "Uh, y-yeah, so Green Lantern would in fact be especially perfect."

"Oh. Right, yeah. Cool. Whatever," said Wolverine.

Jacob Rubenstein, who sat on the other side of Robyn, chose Captain America and couldn't stop smiling. Chuck interjected to tell everyone that Nicolas Redmond, the massive brooding fellow sitting not so much in the semicircle as behind it, had chosen the Mighty Thor. "Right, Nick?"

The storm cloud growled his assent.

Adam smiled at the Viking like an idiot. He couldn't help it. "Hey, man, Thor's the best!" The newly anointed Viking glared at him. Didn't matter. Adam loved the anguished Thor comics. He had a million copies perfectly stacked in order of issue in his closet. Nicolas Redmond was a perfect Thor.

Then it was *her* turn.

"Robyn," she whispered. "If you don't mind, I choose Robin. Not my name but like the . . . well, you know." Each consonant and vowel shimmered with pain.

And even though he had never noticed girls before, not at all—okay a bit and sort of, but not *really*—Adam knew he had to save her, must save her, or die trying. He loved her deeply, wildly and more intensely than he would have believed possible even minutes ago. Robyn, *his* Robyn, needed someone larger than life—a victor, a knight—and *he* would be it. For her, Adam would be and *could* be normal and fearless. He *so* wanted to be fearless. He could do it. He would be *her* superhero.

That's it!

They were all looking at him now, including Thor and Robyn. Her smile sweetened, Adam was sure of that too. He felt himself grow. It all made perfect sense. The universe was unfolding exactly as it should.

"Batman," he said in a strong, clear voice. Adam Spencer Ross would be her Batman.

CHAPTER TWO

"**S**o, my man, did you do your homework?"

Adam and Chuck were about three-quarters of the way through their monthly session when Chuck began threading a fountain pen in and around the fingers of his right hand. The pen-flipping became hypnotic. Did Chuck know that? He had to. Chuck knew everything.

All Adam had to do for his one-on-one homework was the List. But he usually didn't, couldn't or wouldn't, and he didn't know why. Chuck also assigned homework in Group. Most of it was from an OCD handbook that they'd had to buy before Group started. Adam didn't do that either. It was crazy. He did *all* his school homework. He was probably the only kid at St. Mary's to do so. He did it in record time in the school library using their computers. And he did it *perfectly*. But Chuck's stuff?

Nope.

Until today.

Adam had *goals* now.

"Yes, sir. Yeah, I did."

Chuck raised his left eyebrow and then his right. He hated being called *sir*.

"Hey, there's a first time for everything, right?" offered Adam.

Chuck's eyebrows were also hypnotic. He could raise them independently of each other, which is a superior trick when you think about it. When Chuck lifted his right one it meant he was sort of pissed or frustrated, like he was with Wolverine that last Group. The left one raised meant he was surprised or questioning, like he was now.

Adam was supposed to keep a weekly Tens List, a State of the Union–type thing, and bring it in for review. Chuck had assigned it about four months ago, and Adam had finally done his first one today, on the way over. But the thing was, at least he'd done it. And he would do one *every single week* from now on *and* bring them all in. If doing psycho homework would put him on the fast track to being fixed, then move over, Adam was boarding that bus. Robyn was waiting.

"Can we review it together?" asked Chuck.

"No! Uh, I mean, no. We . . . Not this time, if that's okay. Okay?" Adam's heart was racing. It went to the starting block as soon as Chuck said the word *review*. Of course the therapist would want to "review" the List, discuss it, pick it apart. Hell, it freaked him out that Chuck was even going to *read* it.

Chuck slid his glasses farther down his nose and peered over the rims. The glasses were massive wire-rimmed aviators from the 1980s. The man was a walking time capsule.

Adam sighed, relenting, and handed Chuck a piece of paper that had been folded over so many times it looked like a runner-up in a demented origami contest. The therapist began the process of unfolding the paper and reading it while Adam paced inside himself. He knew the List by heart. He'd rewritten it several times in his head before committing pencil to paper. It was not perfect.

September 12   **THE LIST**   Adam Spencer Ross

Meds: Anafranil 25 mg 1 x per day
Ativan as needed 4-6 per week

Primary presenting compulsions: Ordering, Counting,
Magical Thinking re: Clearing Rituals

1. I believe that I fell in love with Robyn Plummer last
   Monday. This feeling is extremely uncomfortable. I would
   stop it if I could.
2. I believe that I should have been allowed to skip grade 4.
   I would be in grade 11 now and my entire life would be
   different. Better. Somehow.
3. I believe that playing Warhammer games all these years
   with Stones (Ben Stone) has probably kept both our
   heads above water, but just barely.
4. I believe that my four-year-old half-brother, "Sweetie," loves
   me more than all the adults in our lives put together. This
   does not stop him from being a considerable pain.
5. I believe that Group is mucho-weirdo (except for Robyn).
   I can't see how it's going to help anything, but the superhero stuff is not half bad.
6. I believe that even numbers are complicated and can on
   specific (although not predictable) occasions have toxic
   negative ions attached to them.
7. I believe that I am a liar because I have to hide all the
   things I have to hide. It's hard to remember where one lie
   ends and another one begins. I believe lying that much
   changes you, makes you sick.

Chuck didn't flinch while he read, but Adam's heart remained in the starting block waiting for the pistol to go off, waiting for signs of disgust.

On your marks!

Without looking up, Chuck asked Adam whether he'd been working on his breathing exercises. Adam said he had.

Get set!

"Really?" Left eyebrow raised. "Then you had better do one now, because I can hear you escalating from across the room."

Go!

And off his heart went. Chuck *knew!* He had to know. He knew what a liar Adam was, and would condemn him accordingly because he deserved to be—

"Adam?" Chuck spoke so softly, Adam wasn't sure that he'd heard his name.

"Yes, sir?"

"Everybody lies, son. Everybody."

Chuck had gotten into his head and pulled that one out. Adam's heart slowed to a jog. He nodded.

"And don't call me sir," he said before returning to the List. "I'll knock that out of you if it's the last thing I do."

8. I believe that I am having trouble with the Robyn feelings. They are so big. Is this normal? Do they go away eventually, some of the time, ever? It's like drowning in electricity.

9. I believe that my mom may be getting a little weirder. But it's so hard to tell, you know?

10. I believe that I am going to do all the OCD homework

stuff, including this List thing, from now on because I have to get better for Robyn. I also believe that because of Robyn, Group won't suck as much.

"Big step, Adam. Good job!" Chuck refolded the note. "We won't review. We won't ever delve into a List if you're not ready. So take that pressure off yourself, okay? Just do them."

"Yeah, sure." Adam nodded and looked up at the clock. He would've agreed to a circumcision just to get himself out of that beige-on-beige office. It was over fifty minutes. *Time to go.*

"Just one point, though—okay? One small check-in?"

Adam nodded. Fifty-three minutes. *On your mark!* "Yes, sir."

"Your mother?"

Get set!

"Yeah, she got weird."

The left eyebrow rose.

"Er, she got weird*er* a couple of days ago." Adam looked away from Chuck. "She was ripping up a letter or an envelope or something when I got home from school. It was like she was hyperventilating. We both pretended that I didn't see. She didn't talk for the rest of the night."

Chuck wrote stuff down. Fifty-five minutes. They were over their time. There was probably some poor schmuck dousing himself with hand sanitizer in the waiting room. "It's usually something to do with the divorce, money, my dad . . . what the hell, pick one, eh? No biggie, right?"

"Right." Chuck closed the file folder and nodded. "Good. I think the medication level is working for us. I'm still surprised the Anafranil is symptom-free, but given all the trouble we were having with the newer class of drugs, I'm relieved. Sometimes old school is best school, right?"

Adam nodded as if he were paying attention.

"Be precise in the List, okay? It's critical now that you're responsible for your own dosage. But it's all good. So over the next month: breathing, the List, exercise, and you're on your way."

On his way. It was all worth it if he was *on his way.*

To what?

To being fixed. To being *normal.*

Adam got up, distracted by the possibilities, and absently shook his therapist's hand. "Thank you." He was on his way to normal. He was on his way to Robyn. *Robyn.* Her lips turned up at the ends. Those pillowy, perfect, shiny lips. From now on, Adam was going to run home every week, or at least walk briskly. No more buses or cabs, anywhere anytime. Between the exercise, doing all the assignments, the breathing thing, going to Group and one-on-one, hell, he'd be cured by the end of the month.

"And, Adam?" Chuck called just as he reached for the door. "I'm sure you're right about the letter—that it's nothing—but try to keep me up on your mom's stuff, okay?"

Adam turned the knob.

"It's important."

"Yeah, for sure." Adam exhaled and opened the door. "You got it," he lied.

CHAPTER THREE

Adam thought about Robyn non-stop all week, and every week for three weeks straight. Big love and his OCD made that pretty much inevitable. If he were an artist, he would have drawn her. If he were a writer, he would have written about her. If he were allowed a smartphone, or even a regular PC, he would have scrolled and dug and searched. But he wasn't so he didn't and he didn't so he couldn't.

Adam had gotten into a bit of thing last year, scrolling endlessly for hours, counting the blink of the cursor, images, words, the letter *m*, among other things. It took longer and longer for it to feel "just right." Therefore, change of meds and no more personal devices. Now he just *thought*. They couldn't take away his thoughts, though most of the time he wished they could.

Adam thought about her smile, her voice, her legs, her black hair and her sky-blue eyes. It was a checklist: *eyes, legs, smile, voice, legs, hair, eyes* . . . He thought about her so much that he'd been semi-mute during the last two Groups. Both sessions were painful, except for the looking-at-her part. And he wasn't the only awkward one. Four sessions in and everyone still seemed weirdly shy or something. So far, Group had all the esteem-building properties of your first middle-school dance—the one that was held in the *small* gym. Wolverine was the only one who consistently stepped up to the plate. Problem was, he stayed there *and* emitted a full-on masculinity vibe while whinging about his bat-shit hypochondria. "Did you know that almost one hundred superbly conditioned young male athletes die every single year from hidden cardiovascular diseases like hypertrophic cardiomyopathy? I'm sure I should be on some kind of diuretic." He just *had* to be crazier than Adam. Unfortunately, Wolverine also moved and looked like the hockey player he'd been before he'd convinced himself that the off-gassing in the ice rink would kill him. Worse yet, Adam was convinced that Robyn was in Wolverine's sightline. Even worser, he was tall.

Today would be different. "My kid's a talker," Adam's mom always used to say. "He could talk a cat out of his pyjamas." It was time. He would say stuff. For sure.

Adam used his walk over from school as a time to test-drive topics. Walking took twenty minutes longer than the bus, but the added exercise had the advantage of making him feel righteous, *plus* he could scroll through possible talking points along the way. On the one hand, he wanted to be helpful. So far, Green Lantern rarely said anything and Captain America looked seriously preoccupied. Thor could only be counted on to growl randomly when he wasn't catching up on his sleep. Even Snooki and Wonder Woman were pretty much comatose, and Adam would've pegged the both of them as talkers. This left the therapist in a lurch with Wolverine. Adam was uncomfortable with lurches and very uncomfortable with Wolverine.

He liked Chuck. They all liked Chuck, and not simply because he was the only psychiatrist in the city who specialized in adolescent OCD issues. Adam had to make this work for Chuck. And he had to do it while looking tough and tall and badass.

He considered bringing up the letter. The new one that had come last week. It was for sure some twisted thing because it had freaked out his mom even though she'd tried to keep it a secret again. But it was his mother's letter, so this was complex. It was *her* problem, right? But the letter had upset her, and therefore it had upset him, so in the end it was *his* problem. *No.* He knew things like that now, the whole separating-of-issues issue. Still, Adam worried. But at least now he knew that he shouldn't. He also knew better than to discuss anything that had to do with his mother. A badass does not talk about his mom.

So he had come up with five mom-free potential topics by the time he got to the clinic.

Wonder Woman, Wolverine and Robyn were in the lobby waiting for the ancient elevator.

"Hey, Batman!" the girls called out at the same time. Wolverine nodded, barely.

"Hey, guys. Connie—I mean, Wonder Woman—Robyn, Wolverine."

Wonder Woman gave him a tight smile and returned to tracking the elevator indicator. It was on the fourteenth floor. It would take more than forever to descend. Wonder Woman was perspiring. Adam stepped in behind her, noticed little beads of sweat forming on the back of her neck. Even more telling, she was straining to maintain a breathing pattern. In for five beats, hold for three, out for six.

Adam's stomach pitched in an instant recognition of fear.

"So what's up, Batman?" said Robyn.

Even her voice made him crazed. He turned and caught her smiling right smack at him with that shiny, fabulous mouth.

"Not much. You?"

Adam needed to walk right up to her, throw his arms around her, kiss her and claim her in front of everybody. Now *that* would be badass. Instead he glanced back at Wonder Woman. She was examining the floor indicator as if it held the key to the universe. The elevator descended to the eleventh floor, then the tenth. Her skin was slick and clammy.

"Hey, you know what, guys?" he chirped. His voice was definitely chirpy. Adam cleared his throat and tried for a lower register. "As of last week, I have this serious new get-into-superhero-shape resolution."

Ninth floor, eighth floor—she was going to puke, he could feel it.

"Like, I'm trying not to eat so much crap, you know? I even made my mom make a quinoa salad." *Damn.* He said *mom* and *quinoa* in the same sentence! Adam's "badass" cred lay in shreds at his feet and still he persisted. "And I'm up for the physical stuff too. Like, uh, I'm walking everywhere, trying out a little jogging here and there. So thing is, I'm going to take the stairs—any joiners?" He sounded like SpongeBob SquarePants.

Fourth floor . . . third floor.

Robyn looked at him like she'd never seen him before.

"Anybody?"

Second floor.

"I'm in!" said Wonder Woman, heading straight for the stairwell. The elevator doors opened.

Wolverine put his foot on the elevator's frayed green carpet and held the doors open. "Really? I mean, it's thirteen god-damned floors!"

Robyn turned to Adam and winked. "I'm in too, Batman. It'll be a thing—we get all fit and fierce, right?"

Wolverine snorted and stepped back. "Stupidest idea in the history of stupid ideas. Fine, let's go," he muttered. "Probably filthy in there, teeming with fungicidal bacteria and God knows what . . ."

They were dying by the fifth floor—which was fifty-two steps, but who's counting? Wolverine kept taking his pulse and complaining that he was going into arrhythmia. "I can feel my heart fluttering." Thankfully, the former jock was too winded to talk by the ninth floor, one hundred and four steps. There were thirteen steps per floor; it was nice that they were odd numbers.

"Okay," said Adam, who was somehow in the lead. "We'll take a break every other floor. See, good thing we're doing this. I gotta say, we suck. But we'll be superheroes by Christmas!" God, he was doing the SpongeBob thing again.

"We are pretty pathetic," said Robyn, holding on to the railing.

Wonder Woman mouthed a silent *thanks* every time they paused. The rest pretended not to see.

They were late.

"Okay, so here they are!" Chuck called from his chair in the centre of the semicircle. "A little late from crime-fighting, no doubt! Greetings, Batman, Wonder Woman, Robyn and . . . uh, Wolverine?"

"We walked," heaved Wolverine.

"Thirteen floors?" squealed Snooki. "Did the elevator go out? That clunky piece of . . ."

Wonder Woman looked alarmed as she took her place beside Snooki. Was she worried about where this was going?

"No," said Robyn, panting as she sat down. "Batman thought we needed to get in better shape."

Everyone else was already there and in their customary seats. Adam glanced at the clock. It was 4:33 p.m. Only in a room full of hard-core OCDers would three minutes be considered late.

They would start the stairs earlier next week.

After the customary circle greeting, Iron Man launched into a long and convoluted story about the people he felt he had involuntarily yet irrevocably harmed that week. This kind of stuff represented a tight turning circle for the group and for Chuck. You can't constantly be reassuring OCD kids, because that's a bottomless pit, but on the other hand, Iron Man was in such obvious pain that everyone ended up doing some heavy lifting in the soothing department. And then they were off. They spoke, cajoled and complained. All of them except for Thor, but even he stayed awake for the entire session.

"You know, Iron Man, you may want to check your Cipralex or whatever you're on. The dose, I mean." Everyone turned to Adam as he inhaled. "I'm just saying, because sometimes if the rituals ramp up for, like, no reason, it's usually because I've messed up the doses. It happens." He exhaled slowly. "Look, I'm your man for screwing up meds. But that's going to stop right here with you guys, all of it, you know. Week by week, ritual by ritual. I'm going to figure it out here. *We* figure it out here."

"Right on!" said Captain America, and then, because it was Captain America, he repeated it three more times. Wolverine looked like he was going to hurl, but the rest of the group pondered this as one, especially those on multiple meds.

"Batman may have a point," said Chuck. Adam could tell that Iron Man was replaying and rewinding his meds consumption even while Chuck spoke. "Iron Man, I want you to start a dosage journal this week. Every day list your symptoms to meds, intake and timing. I'll review it next week and you can decide whether you want to share or not. Paper and pen, not digital. What do you say?"

"Sure." Iron Man nodded, relief oozing out of every pore.

Thor glared at Adam. But maybe it wasn't so much of a glare as it was . . . well, something else. The Viking never failed to terrify without saying a word. It didn't matter. Adam still liked him best.

Wonder Woman spoke up next. She confessed to an uptick in the food issues as well as sizable uptick in the claustrophobic issues. On the food front, what little she ate had to be green and eaten in order of how dark green it was. Snooki assured her that it was only because school had started full-on and admitted that she was having a bit of trouble around the eating thing as well. Even Robyn chimed in on that one, but she swore she wasn't purging. Purging? What the hell? She'd been a puker?

And so it went. Everyone except for Thor said something, admitted something, opened up and shared some little secret. Or . . .

They could all be lying.

Adam knew he was.

CHAPTER FOUR

When Group finally ended, Adam helped Chuck stack chairs for precisely seven minutes, which he figured gave Robyn plenty of lead time. He praised Chuck for a great session—"Now you're cooking!"—and took off barrelling down the hall and then the stairwell.

Adam had decided to follow her. Again.

He had followed Robyn last week, and the week before too, cursing his cowardice from an estimated forty-one paces behind. Today, though, he would have to say something or he'd completely creep himself out.

Robyn cut through the Pleasantville Cemetery each time. The cemetery was like a massive park plopped right in the middle of the city. She went in through the Bayfield gates, three blocks from the clinic, and came out the other side through the Main Street gates. Adam had decided that when she stopped this week—because she stopped every week—he'd accidentally bump into her.

The love of his life seemed to hover near a bunch of graves by a monster willow tree. Last week when Robyn left the cemetery, Adam had run back to where she'd paused. He couldn't tell, given his obligatory safe stalking distance, which grave it was that had held her attention. There was a killer statue of a winged angel crying over the headstone of a Lieutenant Archibald-Lewis, who died when he was nineteen in 1918. Actually, the whole perimeter around the old willow was ringed with stone angels of various shapes and sizes, the lieutenant's being the largest. They were all crying, or so it seemed to Adam. And most of the headstones had an inscription, poem or Bible verse carved into them. It was nice. Adam liked reading them. The lieutenant's read: *Until the day breaks and the shadows flee away.* Poor guy. Still, it probably wasn't him.

Right beside the lieutenant there were two were massive plinth-like things with a ton of people's names engraved on all four sides of their bases. But most of those people were seriously old when they died, *and* they'd died a long time ago. The first monument was a column with an urn stuck on top and the second was a plain pink granite obelisk that pierced the sky. Well inside the angel ring was a huge pockmarked grey headstone covered with an elaborate carving of a cross entwined with roses. That was for a Marnie Wetherall, 1935–1939: *Until we walk in the clouds together.* Four years old, that sucked bad. But Adam didn't think it was her either.

Adam figured that Robyn had stopped in front of a headstone of polished black granite. The mammoth stone swallowed up the light. It was a brooding thing, all modern and sharp angles. The dates made the woman buried there thirty-six years old when she died, but the last name was different. Robyn's was Plummer and this woman was *Jennifer Roehampton, May 7, 1971–October 14, 2008.* And nothing else. The black granite was free of poetry frag- ments. There were no biblical offerings, no soothing sentiments.

It made him sad.

Today he entered the Bayfield gates like a superhero. Adam stopped short near the cluster of headstones by the big willow. Sure enough, there she was.

Okay.

Before he could talk himself out of it, and while he was still blinded by determination, he marched straight to the willow. He stopped on the path right behind her. Robyn stood with her head down in front of the black granite.

Adam cleared his throat as quietly as possible. "Hey, wow, is that you, Robyn? Wow, eh?" Three weeks in front of the mirror and that was his best game-opener? Batman would've coughed up a fur ball before spitting out anything that lame.

Robyn smiled as soon as she saw him. "Hey, Batman . . . uh, Adam. I mean, um, Adam-Batman." She stepped away from the headstone. Her eyes grew lighter as they settled into the surprise of seeing him. "What are you doing here?"

"Uh . . ." Right. He hadn't actually got that far in his prep efforts. There was a lot to learn. "On my way home?" Sadly, that came out as more of a question from a too-short, too-young kid than an answer from a superhero, but Robyn didn't seem to notice.

"Wow, me too," she said.

Adam looked pointedly at the black headstone.

Robyn pointedly didn't notice. Instead, she locked onto his school jacket.

"St. Mary's?" she asked.

She was so crazy beautiful, so heart-hurtingly, breath-stoppingly beautiful. This was nuts. She was beyond him.

Didn't matter. She was everything.

"St. Mary's is a Catholic school, right?"

"You bet!" he said with supremo dork-like enthusiasm. What if she hated Catholics?

"So you're Catholic?"

He gulped and nodded.

"I'm kind of nothing, but I'm fascinated by Catholicism," she said. "I want to learn all about it."

"Me too." What was *that*? He'd just said he was one, for God's sake!

Miraculously, Robyn Plummer smiled again. That was the fourth and a half time she had smiled at him since they'd met. His ears got hot.

"I mean, I'll tell you anything you want to know, whenever you want to know it."

"Promise?" Her cheeks reddened just enough to connect all her freckles.

"Promise," he said.

He would slay a dragon for her.

"That was nice what you did back there." Robyn crooked her head in the direction of the clinic.

"What? Iron Man and the meds? Naw, I just guessed—"

"No." She turned but did not step towards him. "I mean, that was good too, but I was talking about Wonder Woman, the elevator. Nice catch." Robyn smiled and looked sad at the same time.

He would slay a *million* dragons for her.

Adam had never felt more alive than in that cemetery at that very moment. His world shifted. *She* and *he* were talking. *She* and *he* were possible. Maybe. If he didn't blow it. *Don't blow it, don't blow it, don't* . . .

And then he almost did.

CHAPTER FIVE

So *now* what? It was one thing to have a life-shifting moment in a graveyard but quite another to humiliate yourself in mid-shift. The problem was that Robyn was so close and so . . .

Intense urges helicoptered inside him. Things were happening to his body. *That* thing. Adam was going to humiliate himself any second. What to do? Before any of his rituals came galloping to the rescue and hijacked everything, he remembered what he'd heard the guys at school say: *Cross your legs and think of Sister Mary-Margaret—man, she's better than a cold shower.* Adam couldn't very well cross his legs, but thinking about St. Mary's assistant head did the trick.

Eventually.

Adam tried arranging his face into its best neutral, non-threatening, absolutely unsexual expression.

Robyn looked perplexed. Okay, so he might need more bathroom-mirror time refining that one.

"Uh." She raised an index finger. "I just need a minute, okay?" She turned back to the black granite stone.

Robyn touched it tenderly, although that could have been his imagination, since he really couldn't see. He shifted to the right, gaining a critical sight advantage in doing so. She bowed her head. Eyes closed. Adam couldn't really see that part either, but he figured it was a good guess. She made the sign of the cross, sort of, and genuflected, mostly. *That* he could see. The sign of the cross missed a gesture, and the knee did not touch the ground. Everything was just a little off. Adam had plenty of opportunity to observe this, since Robyn continued with the ritual crossing and almost-kneeling another three times. She got it wrong each time.

There it was. Adam could be a value-added kind of guy. Robyn didn't know what she was doing. She *needed* him.

As soon as she began to turn back, Adam snapped his head straight up to avoid being caught ogling her. He was going for a contemplation of the heavens through the willow's gnarled old branches.

"Wow," said Robyn, craning her neck as well. "Wow, wow, would ya look at that! Amazing." They both levelled their gaze. "It's so beautiful. How did you know? There's more to you than meets the eye, Pretty Boy."

Did she wink?

Did he blush?

Lazy shafts of light snuck in between the branches and backlit Robyn. It looked like she was posing for a movie trailer.

He needed to kiss her.

"Yes, there is," he agreed. "*A lot more* than meets the eye." Okay, that was scary. Where did it come from? Adam didn't even know he could say stuff like that. He was a stranger to himself. The biggest brand-new item was this whole need-of-her thing. The need was so big and raw and . . . *big.* He'd never felt *this*, whatever *this* was, before. And now he was feeling it way too many times, like right this second, *again*. He decided to sit with it for a bit, like he did with some of the other urges, the OCD ones. Adam exhaled and waited for it to pass.

It didn't.

What would she taste like? His mom usually tasted like Starbucks bold coffee, while his stepmother, Brenda, left an unmistakable imprint of Crest Cinnamon Rush toothpaste. Sweetie—Brenda and his dad's kid—tended to smell and taste like a Labrador puppy. And his father . . . well, his father was more into stiff hugs than kisses, so who knew.

He should say something. Was it his turn? But he couldn't. He was still grappling with the visibility of his urge. Adam had to use all of his concentration to think about Sister Mary-Margaret.

They both waited for him to say something.

He *should* flirt.

If only he knew how.

If Adam had still had access to a computer, he'd have been up all night googling and therefore counting through "how to flirt" or "pick up chicks" sites, which was precisely why he *didn't* have access to a computer. He winced remembering sixteen-hour searches, counting, tabulating and reordering plague paraphernalia sites: smallpox, the Spanish flu, the Black Death, bird flu, SARS, swine flu and West Nile, and then counting, always counting. He'd stopped eating and sleeping. The computers at both homes had been removed, and they'd watched him at school. Okay, so it was a dark time, but that was then.

Right now he'd settle for saying *something*. Maybe he could ask about the gravestone? But at that moment, Robyn tugged at her skirt, which was definitely not regulation, and the ability to form words deserted him. There wasn't a single girl in any school who could match her grade-A, never-ending legs. Somehow the black oxfords and sloppy, dark green knee socks made her naked knees and thighs even more fabulous. God.

"Uh, Batman?"

"You're doing it wrong," he blurted.

"Oh?" She blushed and then recovered nicely. "Really? What exactly? The whole meta-life thing? Or my legs, which you can't seem to stop staring at?"

Adam's face caught fire. "No, no, your ritual there, with the sign of the cross. Uh, it's incorrect." Adam knew just enough to guess that this wouldn't pass for flirting, but he lumbered on nonetheless.

Robyn looked at him all expectant-like, her eyes a calm grey-blue shade. "Oh yeah? Which part?"

"If you're going for Catholic, you're not quite there." Adam walked over and sat on top of Marnie Wetherall, 1935–1939. "Assume the position."

Robyn glanced at the gravestone.

"What? Do you think Marnie would mind?"

"No." She shook her head. "She was just a kid. I bet she's glad for the company."

"Okay, then," he said. "Assume the position. Uh, I mean the prayer position."

They were both at eye level now.

"Follow me. We'll say it together."

She nodded.

"Index finger and thumb touch. Bring that gesture to your forehead."

She did, and with a solemnity that made him tumble ever deeper into the deepest kind of hopeless love.

"In the name of the Father," they both said.

"Now to the centre of your chest," he instructed.

"And the son," they said.

"To the left shoulder."

"The holy . . ."

Robyn looked surprised. This was the gesture she had been missing.

"And back to the right shoulder."

"Ghost," they said.

"Hands together for . . ."

"Amen." They smiled.

"Okay." She nodded. "That felt right, good. So the genuflect?"

"Knee's gotta hit the ground, or Sister Katherine will appear out of nowhere and nail you in the back of the head. It's all the way, all the time, unless you're in a wheelchair."

"Got it," she said. "Thanks. I know I've got a lot to learn. I've just started with the Catholic thing because it feels right, you know? It's been really, incredibly . . ."

"Soothing?"

"Yeah, but in a good clean way, *not* in an OCD kind of way. I mean it."

Adam nodded, pretending to believe her.

They headed for the Main Street gates. "Are all your friends Catholic?" she asked.

"No," he said. "The guys at school are kinda Catholic because you have to be, and most of them are harmless, but I don't have, like, a ton of friends. Let's face it, I take a lot of work, and there's a lot to hide." *Way too much info, dred dork!* Adam regrouped. "My best friend is Ben Stone, but he's kinda Jewish. We have this fierce brother-type bond over Warhammer Fantasy Battle games. I find *that* soothing. But *not* in an OCD kind of way, of course."

She hit him in the arm, but she smiled as she did it, so it was a clearly superior moment. When they finally reached the elaborate iron gates, they both hesitated.

Now what?

Adam lived at the opposite end of the cemetery and three blocks north. He *should* come clean right now, confess, start fresh. One shouldn't lie to one's beloved before she officially becomes one's beloved.

Robyn finally broke the silence. "Well, Batman-Adam, I head left on Main and then onto Palmerston. Halfway down Palmerston and I'm home. How about you?"

"Uh . . . I turn right," he said. It was the God's honest truth, or was going to be. Adam would have to turn right and walk all the way around the cemetery back to where he'd started and go home that way. It would take him an extra forty minutes. He would be late.

"So, uh, see you next Monday, Batman."

"You betcha." *You betcha? Really? Again with the SpongeBob routine.*

Adam watched her walk away, rooted to the cement. Robyn walked great. When she hit the street she turned around and waved. "And thanks for the tips, Batman!"

"Anytime!" he yelled.

He would measure, of course, as soon as he got home, but it wasn't necessary. He had grown at least an inch.

CHAPTER SIX

He paused at the door. Nothing prevented Adam from entering 97 Chatsworth—nothing physical or emotional, obsessive or otherwise. He now knew that it was the power of wanting the *in* to be different that held him captive on the *out*.

Chuck had given him a stack of photocopied articles about this phenomenon and Adam had read them all. This surreal wanting happened to all kinds of people, especially war veterans, especially the young ones who got their legs blown off. There's like this time of twilight when you're awake but not. You're in the right-before-you're-awake part. In this part, you know you've got to throw off the warm covers, go to the bathroom, pee and brush the fur off your teeth. And then you're in the completely-awake part, and you remember you can't. You remember you're never getting up and peeing again. But the next night you go through the same thing again, and the next night and the next. That story killed him. Adam would have cried if he could have. He hadn't cried since his dad left seven years ago, but for sure he would have if he could have.

For weeks now—maybe since the letters started coming—
Adam would unlock the door, willing a different *in*, but it was not
like he was incapable of entering. As of this moment, approximately 21 percent of all thresholds presented problems of varying
intensity for him. Actually, it was 22 percent, but that was an un-
acceptably even number given the 2 *and* the 2.

The problem ranged from minor, almost negligible issues with
the large biology lab and English class doors at St. Mary's, to doors
that needed small hand movements to clear him in, like the
entrance to the Phipps' Family Pharmacy, to a few entrances that
now involved fairly extensive ritual clearing, and finally to some
no-go's, where entry was simply not possible. For this last type of
threshold there was no relief in rituals, no matter how elaborate
or repeated. Crossing such a barrier would cause his disintegration
or, worse, would make him responsible for the mortal endanger-
ment of his mother, or Sweetie, or his father, or Brenda, or
Chuck . . . and the list spiraled ever outwards to include bus drivers
and 7-Eleven checkout clerks.

Of course he knew that this was not true.

But it didn't stop him from believing it.

So far, only the south entrance of the Hudson Street subway
was a no-go.

But *it* was gathering.

He finally opened the door. And there it was, that twilight
thing where he believed that his hallway looked like it had when
he was a kid, when his dad lived here. But like the war vets, he was
fully awake by the time he entered and shut the door behind him.

Semi-neat piles of junk lined both walls, but there was still a
visible pathway. Not so bad, right? Once he was in and faced with
reality, his house became almost the inverse of the twilight-dream

thing. In many ways, the stairs and the hallway—hell, the rest of the house—looked the same as they always had. Today looked like yesterday, which looked like last week, last month and last year. It was one of those tricks-of-the-eye things . . . no wait, that was a *trompe l'oeil*. It was a trick of the mind, that's what it was.

He had a lot of those.

The exact same thing happened when his best friend Ben Stone gained a whack of weight. Ben came from a *big* family, so it shouldn't have been a surprise. When Adam used to see him every day, Ben always looked exactly the same. But now that they could hang out only every couple of weeks or so, and couldn't even Skype, Adam was stunned to realize that he had a fat friend. Overnight, Ben had gone from a Cornish hen to a Butterball turkey. Adam's mom's junk was like that too, morphing from neat little piles into . . . well, what it was now. It was as if Adam could conjure up his house when it was normalish or as it was on that day, and nothing in between. But there had to be an in-between. There had to have been a time when only the dining room was unusable. Then the chairs, the credenza and so on. Next went the garage, slowly filling to the ceiling with plastic see-through boxes of Christmas lights, impressive-looking power tools, brooms, shovels and exercise equipment. Then some of that *stuff* marched into the basement and procreated and its offspring marched right back up to the second floor. Now his mom's bedroom and en suite were infiltrated. The sweet little two-bedroom on 97 Chatsworth Avenue just got incrementally crazier.

And still he didn't understand how.

Other than the two of them, no one had set foot in the place in over a year. His mom discouraged him from bringing over any friends—not that there was a lineup, but it meant that Adam could only go over to Ben's house, and Ben now lived clear across the city. The journey was epic on public transit, though sometimes he'd guilt Brenda into taking him when he was at his dad's.

His mom did not drive. Not anymore.

Yet Mrs. Carmella Ross was a highly competent and caring woman. Everyone said so. *She's decent through and through*, they said. And it was true. Mrs. Ross was a nurse-supervisor at the Glen Oaks Hospital, an important position of authority. His mother dealt with all manner of conflicts and crises, from minor scheduling snafus to the manic helplessness of the dispossessed and the dangerous. She was good at all of it. People admired her. *If you want something done, and done right, give it to Carmella.*

That very same competent Carmella sat outside for hours with her son, hustling the neighbours into buying his homemade lemonade and/or mudpies. "Mudpies! Get your fresh mudpies! Three for a buck, get 'em while you can!" Mrs. Polanski, who lived across the street, bought two dollars' worth one year. His mom never missed a teacher conference. She clapped too loudly at each of his Christmas pageant performances and cursed out the track officials when he invariably came in fourth in all of his junior marathon events. "You were robbed by that McQuarry kid! Those nuns were looking the other way, I'd swear to it in front of Father Rick and the Pope himself!" And when he was finally diagnosed almost three years ago, Carmella Ross practically lived in the headmaster's office, advocating for him, and in her bedroom, crying for him. When Adam called her on it, racked with guilt, she blew him off. "Get off it, kid!" she snorted. "Relax! It's all good. At least you snapped me right out of the divorce dumps. Hell, I gotta thank you!"

His mother was fierce.

Until she wasn't.

Adam picked his way up the stairs. Without even seeing them, he shoved some puzzle boxes closer to the wall. The chaos ended abruptly at his room. Adam's room looked like it was occupied by a prissy monk with a soft spot for Warhammer miniatures and angelfish. He walked over to his perfect thirty-five-gallon tank. All three of his angels, Burt, Peter and Steven, immediately swam up to welcome him.

"Hi, guys!" He reached for the fish food and crumbled a teeny amount over the water as a treat for the boys. Well, maybe not all boys—Steven had given birth to babies last spring, but Burt and Peter ate them. Adam was going to wait to see if it happened again before doing anything as drastic as changing anybody's name.

The aquarium often calmed him, what with the fish zipping around and the bubbles and the soothing whirr of the water filter. Not today, though. Adam's heart was still prickly. "Love hurts, man," he whispered to Steven, who had returned to him after nibbling some fish flakes. Steven nodded.

Adam had finished his homework at school, as he did on most Mondays or Group days, and he wasn't on dinner duty tonight, so he had loads of free time looming in front of him. He was considering cleaning out his clean fish tank when he heard his mom come home.

"Adam? Hi, honey! Are you up there?"

"Hey, Mom!" Adam waved to the boys and raced down the ever-narrowing stairway.

Mrs. Ross kissed the top of his head, then stepped back and looked at him. "You growing?" Before he could answer, she proudly pointed to a brown shopping bag.

"Look, I braved the elements—this beautiful autumn day, in other words—and went clear across the city to bring us this!"

Adam recognized the bag. "You went to the Hungarian restaurant!"

Mrs. Ross reached into the bag and retrieved a large aluminum takeout container. "Ta-da! Mrs. Novak's world-famous Hungarian goulash and buttered egg noodles. Nothing's too good for my favourite son!" she said, as she always said.

"Hey, lady, I'm your *only* son!" he said, as he always said.

Mother and son went to the kitchen, which was still *almost* normal. They whipped out the necessary plates and cups and cutlery, and tucked into their feast. He poured her a glass of red wine, and she poured him a glass of Tropicana orange juice, pulp-free. She talked about work; he talked about school. Carmella mentioned that she might be up for a promotion by the end of the year, and Adam said that Group, in the end, might work out after all. And during that whole time, they told each other everything except for the parts that they didn't. Mother and son were as honest as two people lying to each other could be.

And then the phone rang.

CHAPTER SEVEN

"Yes, hello, Brenda." His mom sighed and leaned against the wall. "I'm sorry to hear that."

"Yes, he is, but I just got in and we haven't even . . ."

"Yes, yes, I appreciate that—more than most, as you well realize—but today was his Group day and . . ." Mrs. Ross turned to Adam while nodding into the phone.

I already did my homework, he mouthed.

His mom's shoulders slumped. The fight was lost. "Brenda, you know I love Sweetie . . ."

"Okay, I can't stand the thought of him suffering like that. If Adam agrees, let us finish dinner and then you can come and pick him up. Hang on." She put her hand over the receiver. "You okay with that?"

Adam nodded.

"Do you have anything you've got to be in early for tomorrow?"

He thought for a moment. He and Eric Yashinsky, an almost-friend, were due in the physics lab at 7:45 a.m., sharp. Both boys had been offered a special opportunity to take Advanced Placement Physics in grade 10, but because of scheduling difficulties it had to be at that unholy hour twice a week, and the days were never fixed.

"Physics," he said.

His mom smiled and years fell away. "Lucky you, Brenda—it's a physics day. You'll have to drive him in at dawn."

"Yeah." She nodded. "Seven forty-five sharp or Sister Mary-Margaret will come after you with a lecture and rosary in hand. We can't have Adam squandering God-given opportunities."

His mom glanced at the wall clock. "Okay, give us another thirty or forty minutes to finish up dinner. Yeah. Okay. No, it's okay . . . Yeah, I know." More nodding. "Believe me, I know." Sigh. "Bye."

Adam opened up the containers. "Sweetie's in a state?"

His mother ladled out the goulash. "Yeah, and like I said, I get it. Well, not whatever is cranking that little boy—you never got into 'states'—but I get where she's at. What I don't get—" Mrs. Ross plopped some glistening butter noodles on top of the goulash. That's the way they both liked it. "What I don't get is what you bring to the party. No offence."

Adam frowned and started swirling his noodles. "Is it possible . . . I mean, does what Sweetie . . . ? Did I make him nuts? Is it because of me, because I'm the way I am?"

Carmella grabbed her son's hand with an urgency that surprised them both. "No! Don't say that! Don't you dare think that about you or him!" She let go. "Besides, that kid is not nuts—he's a sweetie! You *know* that. Look, he's wired up a little too tight is all, and Brenda frets about him too much. He'll toughen up, mark my words."

"But he could have got the wiring from me."

"Right, Einstein. Who's the science genius in this room? You know how this goes. Same dad, different mother—you don't enter the picture. You don't even get to be in the picture, my gorgeous, genius boy. Sweetie doesn't even have your father's traits. Your dad's an ass and the kid is adorable."

"Mom."

"Well, it's true."

"Which part?"

"Both." Carmella smiled. "Not only that, but I've never seen one breathing being devoted to another as much that kid of theirs is to you. I guess what you bring to the party, come to think of it, is some kind of weird 'feel better' gift for Sweetie."

They finished their goulash side by side, in semi-comfortable silence.

Brenda honked the horn while Adam was throwing socks into his backpack. Because he spent so much time at his father's house and had a lot of his stuff there already, he could get ready in seconds. He glanced at his watch: twenty-five minutes. It must be a bad one.

She honked again—politely, though. Brenda was nothing if not well-mannered. The new Mrs. Ross wouldn't dream of entering the house, because she had been asked not to by the old Mrs. Ross. That had more to do with the state of 97 Chatsworth than any natural hostility between the women, because truth be told, there wasn't much.

The two Mrs. Rosses were mirror opposites. It was like his dad went for a total purge, with Brenda being the anti-Carmella. Adam's stepmother was blonde, pristine and polite against Carmella's dark and compelling exuberance. Carmella's house was aggressive chaos. Brenda's was an homage to *Architectural Digest*, each room patiently waiting for its photo shoot. He had to hand it to his dad, though: both women were attractive even on their most harried days. Their appearance was noted at every parent function at St. Mary's. Adam looked very much like his mother, yet also like his father. This meant that he "fit" seamlessly into both houses, and neither.

What remained exactly the same was that Mr. Ross was ever-absent, off on far-flung engineering projects or holed up in his downtown office. If anything, his absences grew longer as his home life, which now included two complicated sons, grew more ... well, complicated. He was not, as Brenda and even his mom on occasion knew, an uncaring man. Just a missing one.

As soon as Adam set foot outside, the back door to the Mercedes flew open. Wendell "Sweetie" Ross launched himself out of his booster seat and straight into his brother's arms like a rocket. Even fully braced, Adam was almost knocked over.

"Adam! Adam! Adam!"

"Batman," whispered Adam. "Remember? I'm Batman now."

"Oh yeah! I just forgot, Batman. I won't ever never forget again, Batman. Okay, Batman?"

Adam hugged him back. "Okay, little guy. Don't sweat it." He felt his brother's thumping little heart beating way too fast. "It's cool."

Ironically, it was Adam's mom who was responsible for dubbing Wendell "Sweetie." Carmella Ross called everyone "sweetie"; it unburdened her from the task of remembering names, especially at work. In Sweetie's case, however, as she often said, "It pains me to admit it, but that little dumpling really is a *Sweetie.*" Everyone else agreed, including his pediatrician, nursery school teachers *and* Sweetie, who began referring to himself as such as soon as he was able to form words. Now, at almost five, there was no disabusing him of it. Sweetie *was* Sweetie and that's all there was to it. He clung tightly to Adam as if to secure him until they reached the safety of the car.

"Hey, Brenda."

"Thank you, Adam."

"Batman!" corrected Sweetie from the back seat.

"Moms are exempt," Adam said.

"Exempt," Sweetie parroted, and Adam knew he would store the word away and bring it out for rehearsals until he figured out how to use it correctly.

"I mean it. Thanks for this," Brenda said as they drove away. "I know we're both a pain, but look . . ." She gestured to the back seat with her head and lowered her voice. "It's instant. An hour ago, I could barely reach him."

Sweetie had launched into a rousing if garbled rendition of "Puff, the Magic Dragon." Carmella had sung it to Adam as soon as she'd brought him home from the hospital, and Adam had sung it to his brother as soon as Brenda and Dad had brought *him* home from the hospital. It was their go-to song, the one that Adam would sing when Sweetie was in need of industrial-strength comforting. *"A dragon lives forever but not so little boys. Painted wings and la, la, la . . ."*

"Is Dad home?" Adam asked above the singing.

Brenda shook her head. "Argentina. But he'll be back for your double birthdays next week. Your father thought that you would both enjoy the chef's special magic at La Tourangelle for your birthday dinners. Wait until you see your *C-A-K-E-S!*"

Only perfection for the perfectionist, Adam thought but did not say.

"We're going to a really, really pretty restaurant! I saw it. I'm going to have oysters! Do you know what oysters are? I'm going to have three. And your mom, Mrs. Carmella Ross, is coming, and Ben too, but that's a surprise."

"Sweetie!" Brenda groaned.

"Sorry," came a small voice from the back seat.

"That's okay," said Adam. "You know I'll forget by the time we get home, uh, your home."

"*Our* home, Adam," said Brenda.

Adam tossed his backpack onto one of the twin beds in Sweetie's room. Adam still had his very own room there, but as soon as Sweetie had learned how to walk, he'd also learned how to sneak into his brother's double bed, hog all the covers, smoosh them into himself and toss about the whole night long. Sleep was impossible. One day when Sweetie was older, Adam would reclaim that room. Until then, he settled for having a twin bed all to himself.

Sweetie hopped onto his own bed, folded his hands neatly in his lap and waited. Adam sat across from him, mirroring him exactly—except, of course, that Adam's feet touched the floor.

"Okay, so what's up, little guy?"

Sweetie took that as his cue to propel himself towards his brother and snuggle into him.

"Bad, eh?"

He could feel rather than see Sweetie nod slowly. "The scary bits are biting me."

"Got it," said Adam. None of them could ever figure out what the triggers were. What was it that set Sweetie off? "Right, so let's think about something awesome, okay?" More nodding, less tentative now. "Let's bring out the big guns!" He put his arm around his brother. Again, he felt the little heart thumping much too fast. "Only the prime numbers will do in a situation like this. Seventeen is cool, as is thirty-nine, and neither of us much likes going near the two hundreds, right?" Sweetie shook his head. He couldn't count to the two hundreds, didn't much know what they were, but if his brother said that they didn't like them, then they didn't like them. "Okay, so let's both of us think about the real beauty in the bunch, one of our favourite truly superior prime numbers. Let's think about the number *eleven*! Got it? The one and the one? You love eleven. See it?"

Sweetie nodded enthusiastically now.

"Even better, let's load it up and go for broke. Let's do *one hundred and eleven*! That's a one and a one and a one."

"Wow, yeah! That's an eleven with a friend. Yeah! One, one, one, it's very pretty. I love one hundred eleven a lot! I can see all those ones."

Adam felt Sweetie relax into him, felt his heart slow. It was different with him. Sweetie just liked to pick a number and think about it, but it had to be "pretty." Adam had tried to teach Dad and Brenda about the numbers. But they couldn't do it—didn't get it or maybe didn't believe.

But Adam did.

His brother got lost in all those ones for a while.

"Better, Sweetie?"

His brother sighed and melted into him. "I'm all better now. You fixed it."

At least he could do this. At least there was this.

"I'm glad, Sweetie," Adam whispered, and he hugged the little body even tighter. "I'm glad."

CHAPTER EIGHT

A dam and the climbers sat panting in their chairs for a full five minutes before the rest of Group got there and a full minute and a half before Chuck arrived.

"Hey, my stair-climbing superheroes, how's it going?" he asked as he shuffled through the door. "Are there more of you this week?"

It was true. Green Lantern and Iron Man had joined Wonder Woman, Robyn, Wolverine and Batman in their accidental fitness quest. Snooki had threatened to as well, but couldn't that day because she was squeezing in an extra tanning appointment before the meeting.

Chuck took off his faded corduroy jacket and carefully draped it across the back of his chair. He laid down his repurposed file folders just so on the empty chair beside him and painstakingly sorted through them looking for last week's notes. Chuck did this with a nuclear absorption while the rest of Group dribbled in.

Adam, meanwhile, tried to settle into inconspicuous gazing at the ravishing Robyn. She had on a new school jacket. It fit better.

Still the same skirt, though, and still heart-thumpingly too short. He was numb with emotion.

"You okay, Dark Knight?" Chuck took off his aviators and squinted at Adam.

Robyn glanced at Chuck and then resumed examining the floor.

"Me? Yeah, sure. I mean, still out of shape, but I'm good. Well, you know, for being whack and all."

"Cool." Chuck shook his head. "You guys are something else."

Chuck was cool. Adam promised himself that he would talk about Robyn at their next one-on-one. *Robyn*. She still hadn't looked up. He was getting *uncomfortable* again. Just looking at her across the semicircle made him hotter than a match. He counted the ceiling tiles, thought about Sister Mary-Margaret and then returned to the task at hand.

Chuck's continuing preoccupation with his notes gave Adam just enough time to sort out his thoughts and start figuring out what to say during Group. He needed some kind of edge. Maybe it *was* time to talk about the letters. His mom had received yet another one yesterday afternoon. How many was that? They were starting to infiltrate the house somehow. Adam knew it was bad even as she turned her back to him and ripped it up. She couldn't hide the colour draining from her hands while she shoved the pieces deep into the garbage pail.

Sick stuff was attached to those paper shreds, and it got sicker each time his mom brushed him off. Whatever was in those letters was scaring the crap out of her and had set off the tripwire to his not-so-free-floating anxiety. Adam had spent all of last night rearranging his Warhammer figures. There was, of course, an exacting ritual to the rearranging. Each Orc had to be in the correct formation on his shelves, and he also had to replace them all in a particular way, circling down from above, counter-clockwise, thirteen times. If he did it wrong, he would have to start again. It was virtually impossible to do right.

Adam owned almost three hundred miniatures.

It took hours.

Adam hadn't had to "arrange" for months. He was angry with himself, with the situation . . . with his mom, but he knew he couldn't talk about the letters here. The letters were like the inside of the house. Secret. There would be consequences. His mom had laid it out hard a couple of years ago. Talking about the house would be a betrayal. If he betrayed her, they would take her away. Period.

Yes, the compulsions *were* escalating. But just a bit, nothing to worry about, not yet. And yes, it was annoying that the threshold to the large biology lab had amped up from a negligible clearing to a semi-full ritual. But that was sort of nothing. In fact, maybe he could talk about that. Maybe it would help to get support from his support group, because that's why one went to a support group, right? Except he would sound way more nuts than he wanted to sound. No one else had a threshold thing as far as he could tell. Everyone in Group seemed shocked by the new uncovering of someone else's way-weird ritual, each one of which was entirely different from their own way-weird rituals. Thresholds? Too weird. What would Robyn think?

Adam tapped his right foot on the front leg of his chair for three sets of thirty-seven. He tapped invisibly while everyone settled in and started up. Wolverine whispered something to Robyn. It made her smile, sort of. This called for seven sets up to eleven. *One, three, five, seven, nine, eleven.* He didn't have a chance. Even though he'd swear that Peter Kolchak was crazier on his best day than Adam was on his worst, Wolverine had that thing that some guys had, the thing that makes you move as if you're used to being liked. The way he'd just leaned into Robyn assuming she'd *like* what he whispered to her.

What would that be like? How do you get that? And yet . . .

The smile that she had just offered Adam was bigger than the one she'd offered Wolverine a second ago. Adam knew this because he'd counted it out in taps. Wolverine had got two taps, no teeth showing, while her smile for Adam had clocked in at over three beats with a flash of white.

Captain America came in and punched Adam's arm. "Batman, my man! How's it hanging? How's it hanging?"

What did that even mean? Jacob was seriously in over his head with his Captain America persona. The guy was normally a nervous, tidy fellow with energetic checking and repeat issues, not an arm-punching, how's-it-hanging type.

"Cool, Captain America. You?"

Jacob puffed up, delighted that someone had finally remembered to call him by his superhero name. "Cool, man. Cool."

Adam watched Robyn as Robyn sort of watched everyone. Something was up.

Snooki came in looking like a shiny nutmeg and Thor stormed in five minutes late, managing to make them all feel guilty for being on time. The Viking settled into his accustomed seat behind rather than beside Chuck, and glowered his customary glower—or was it dialled down a bit?

As the session got under way, Thor's eyes remained relatively calm even as Wonder Woman went on at mind-numbing length about her food or lack thereof. Food discussions seemed to set Thor's teeth on edge and Adam was right with him on that one.

"I know I should lay off the laxatives—that way lies madness, et cetera, et cetera—but since I bought the bottle, I felt I had to empty it. Every damn ritual comes with its own instruction manual, right?"

Snooki put a comforting hand on Wonder Woman's arm. Snooki was a "patter"—every group had one. That's what Robyn said. Robyn had been to a lot of groups.

"But I won't do it again," Wonder Woman promised.

To who, exactly?

"I mean it. I learned my lesson, guys. I don't need a full-fledged eating disorder layered on top of the claustrophobia and, and other stuff. So I'm back to chewing a hundred times for each bite. Dinner takes almost two hours, but see, that works because ..."

Forget it. Thor and Adam folded their arms across their chests. Try as he might, Adam couldn't come up with anything remotely sympathetic to say. Skinny girls worrying about getting skinnier totally perplexed him. He *hated* being perplexed, especially in Group. There was enough perplexing *outside* Group.

Green Lantern, thank God, had a superior story about having to keep driving back to a school crosswalk several times a day, all week, because he was convinced that he had run over someone last Tuesday. Classic—now this was something Adam could get into. Green Lantern listened to newscasts on the radio and TV, read all the local papers and scoured the Internet, searching for a report of an accident on the corner of Chestnut and Walmer. Nothing. Far from calming him, the lack of reportage just made him escalate. Adam had never had this particular experience—he couldn't drive, after all—but he could completely understand the supremely logical compulsion to return to the scene of the imaginary accident over and over again. He so *got* that one. Adam suggested that, for starters, Green Lantern might want to journal every revisit or *thought* about revisit and assign it a number value, just like it said in the manual (well, on the back cover of the manual anyway). And that act alone might help a bit. Just because Adam didn't do any of the assignments didn't mean they shouldn't be done. Green Lantern looked genuinely relieved.

Robyn didn't. Something was up for sure. She was avoiding eye contact and her vibe was off. She didn't even look like herself, although Adam didn't understand how exactly. He wasn't good with girls' faces. If he ruled the world, girls would say every single thing that was on their minds. He sucked at guessing, and that whole reading-between-the-lines thing was so beyond him, he couldn't get there with a map.

Thirty-seven minutes in and, aside from that lone smile, Robyn had not looked at him once. What was the matter? Something was. He was screwed. She *hated* him. Completely understandable, of course, but why?

Wolverine took the floor and began laboriously listing the reasons why he thought he had congestive heart failure. "I have undefined fatigue, you know?" The guy should have sounded like the douchebag he was, but somehow he didn't. It was unbearable.

Adam crossed his legs, caught himself and readjusted immediately. That was no way to *man up*. He was crossing his legs the way girls do. He examined Thor, who was glowering at Wolverine, or maybe that was just Thor's "listening" face.

"It's chronic, of course, and eventually fatal." Wolverine shuddered.

If only, thought Adam.

"I'll have to get a ream of tests: extensive blood work, nuclear medicine, examine my creatine levels. Then there's stress tests and ..."

Thor sat like a man, and at nineteen arguably he was one. First of all he really *occupied* the chair. Adam tried for a bit of heavy-duty chair occupying. He raised his right leg and oh-so-casually placed his right ankle over his left knee, finishing off with left hand grasping right ankle loosely. There. Just like Thor. Okay, not comfortable, but *way* more manly. Adam also tried nodding sympathetically at Wolverine, but his heart just wasn't in it. More importantly, Wolverine sounded like he was winding down and it didn't look like anyone else was going to come in.

There was going to be a *lurch*. And he didn't have anything prepared. But mere seconds into said lurch, Robyn shut it down.

"My mother killed herself five years ago today. Exactly. Today." She inhaled just as all the air left the room. She didn't look at anyone, but everyone looked at her. Everyone except Adam. Adam flashed straight back to the black granite headstone.

JENNIFER ROEHAMPTON
MAY 7, 1971–OCTOBER 14, 2008

Today.

Robyn was staring at his shoes—well, *shoe*, given that only his left foot was on the floor. Adam uncrossed his legs. Sitting like a man was going to take some practice.

"So I don't want to talk about it or anything," she said, gaze still fixed firmly on his feet. "Really, I don't. Not today, anyway. I just felt that I should..." Tears threatened to erupt but were sucked back. "I don't know, like, I felt I should note it, somehow. My father doesn't... uh, he wouldn't approve."

Adam exhaled when she exhaled. He *needed* to protect her, and the need was so big and pounding that he thought *he* would break.

So he stared at her shoes in solidarity. He did *not* count the lines on the planked floor.

Admittedly not a big gesture, but maybe she would recognize it.

She wore scuffed Doc Martens. All the girls in his school wore them too, but not quite as scuffed. She was a scuffed goddess.

"We will of course respect your wishes, Robyn," Chuck finally broke in. "And we'll look forward to hearing about your mother when you're ready to share. But right now, how about we close our eyes in a minute of contemplation and celebration of Robyn's mother? If that's comfortable for you."

The air in the room returned as Robyn nodded.

Everyone, including Thor, bowed their heads and shut their eyes. Adam knew this because he tracked the semicircle through his eyelashes. Adam hadn't been able to keep his eyes closed in public since he was seven. So he always kept watch and guarded, keeping everybody safe.

That was his job.

"Okay, people—same time, same place next week." Chuck clasped his hands. "Good work today!"

Damn.

They were finished and Robyn had still not looked at him. And that was tough to do, given that she was seated directly across from him. God, he sucked; nobody sucked as much as he sucked. If only he hadn't sucked so much, he would have sucked less, and she would—

She lifted her eyes from his shoes. "Uh, hey . . . so if, uh, do you . . . ? Are we still going to walk home?"

He probably said, *Sure! Of course, yeah!* But it was hard to hear above his heart hammering in his ears. She smiled—five beats' worth. The smile was like a syringe full of courage. "For sure, fair

Robyn, and if you'd like, how about we stop and get some flowers on the way?"

She would have kissed him if they'd been anywhere but where they were. He didn't know how he knew, but he knew for sure. Maybe. It was as if the Ferris wheel had gone all the way around and Adam was on the very top. That's how Robyn Plummer made him feel. She made him feel stronger than he was, saner than he was. And she needed him. Truth was, Robyn needed him even more than he needed her. But that would stay his secret for now. And God knows, he was good at keeping secrets.

CHAPTER NINE

Instead of daisies or roses, which were pretty much the only flowers that Adam could pick out of a lineup, Robyn chose a pot of purple violets. She squealed when she saw them.

"They were her favourites!" Robyn clutched the little green plastic pot to her. "My mom loved violets!"

"Okay, so let's buy this little hand shovel thingy too and we'll plant it. Look—" Adam pointed to the hand-lettered "60% Off" sign over the gardening equipment. "They'd, like, live there forever, and she'd like that, right?"

She was going to hug him, absolutely for sure. Adam braced himself. He straightened up and sucked in his stomach, although he wasn't sure why. Should he try to kiss her when she threw herself in his arms? Too much, too soon? Maybe he could sneak a little one. No, he'd settle for a hug, a nice long, hard hug. He would count it out. Adam needed to count but didn't. Instead, he focused on the possibility of a hug, of her amazing body embracing his body, which was less amazing but at least getting taller by the day. Yes, a hug would be fine. He would settle for a hug.

But oh, what he wouldn't do for a kiss.

He got neither.

Robyn skipped off to the sales counter with the $2.99 violets and the $3.99 trowel. One kiss and he would have died a happy Batman. His disappointment left him agitated. Adam felt flames lick the edges of his brain as they walked to the cemetery. He so needed to count, but couldn't. There was nowhere to stop and tap, and he had to pay full attention to *her*.

"Isn't it a miracle that we both use the cemetery as a shortcut home?" said Robyn as they rounded into the Bayfield gates.

"Yeah, miracle," Adam muttered. That *miracle* cost him almost an extra hour each time he used the "shortcut." But he didn't mind the time. He was used to blowing all sorts of time on clearing rituals. So it wasn't the time.

It was the lie.

Adam felt like he was lying to her every time they walked together, and he had to do so damn much of that already. The flames in his head flared a bit. So he concentrated on her hair. Better. No braid today. Robyn wore her hair loose and parted down the middle. It looked like black glass. Adam wanted to dive into it, or at least run his hands through it. What would it feel like? He almost got his chance when she stopped suddenly near the weeping willow and he crashed into her.

"Sorry." He reddened.

She ignored him. "Look!" She pointed through the now-yellowing willow leaves. "A purple sky. The sun is shining somewhere while it's raining somewhere else and we're in the middle! It's a good omen. Mom loved purple skies. Purple skies and purple violets—you're a miracle worker, Batman!"

"I aim to please." Adam walked over to her mother's headstone.

Struck again by just how massive and empty it was. All that black with only her mom's name and the birth and death dates. It looked lonelier each time he saw it.

"Uh, here?" Adam pointed with the trowel to the centre front of the stone.

Robyn nodded.

He began to dig. It wasn't as easy as you'd think. The ground was rock hard, and the earth gave way in mean little dirt pebbles. This could take a while. "So back in Group, when you . . ." Adam wiped his forehead with his jacket sleeve. "Well, that was Group, and . . ."

"I was the one that found her," she said simply. "I thought she was sleeping, but I wanted a hot chocolate, so I needed to ask."

Adam scraped harder.

"I didn't want to wait until she got up. She sort of slept a lot, you know?"

Robyn hoisted herself onto Marnie Wetherall, 1935–1939. He knew from their first encounter that Marnie's headstone was surprisingly comfortable. "So I knocked, then I called and called, then yelled, then I went over and shook her hard, then harder and—"

Adam turned. Tears slid down her cheeks, but she wasn't crying.

"I didn't know what to do. Maria, the housekeeper, had gone for the day. I think I sort of ran around the house screaming. I must have called my dad at some point." She wiped her face.

Adam plopped the little purple violet out of its green plastic container and into its new home. He should say something. He brushed back the earth. It needed water. You were supposed to water these things when you planted them, right? Or it would die. It couldn't die. She'd be hurt if it died.

"When Daddy got home, whenever that was . . ." She was looking at the plant as if it were replaying the evening for her.

There was a waterspout by one of the weeping stone angels, the one nearest the path.

"When he finally got home, apparently I was lying beside her, fast asleep. Amazing, eh?"

He had to do something. Comfort her. Kiss her? But the plant needed watering. He felt pulled apart. There were fifteen head-stones within the stone angel perimeter. *Fifteen was a good number, a fine number. Fifteen* . . . Adam stole another glance at the water tap. The plant would die without water *right now*.

Murderer. He tried tapping against her mother's headstone for three quick sets of seven and only in a rectangle sequence. He needed to get up and hug her; she needed him, but . . . "Uh, your mom needs some water."

Robyn started, but he marched off to the tap anyway, plastic pot in hand. When he came back and dumped the water on the unsuspecting violet, Robyn's whole demeanour relaxed, softened. She exhaled.

"Yeah, so I started washing and a few other things a couple of weeks after the funeral." She smiled at the plant, or maybe at him. "I guess it's why I am the way I am."

Adam nodded sympathetically, every nerve ending alive with the need to hold her. Then it dawned on him. It would be nice to have a reason.

But something was still off that he couldn't quite shake. The plant needed more water and Robyn needed holding, but that wasn't it. It was just out of the reach of knowing, like when his mom talked about the letters.

"Still, hey, I'm tons better now, right? I mean, three months residential, I still see my shrink, Group and . . . praying helps." She jumped off Marnie and stepped over to him.

Adam remembered the gift then and patted his pockets frantically. There! "Hey, speaking of praying, I brought you a present." He fished out a blue and white crystal rosary.

"Oh, Adam! It's beautiful! Oh my God, is that a holy necklace? Do Catholics wear it? Is it really for me? I bet it's blessed. It's the most beautiful thing I've ever seen. Thank you!"

Was she, oh no, yes, she was going to . . . yes, yes, yes!

"Oh my God, oh my God!" Robyn leapt right over and actually, absolutely, totally *hugged* him!

Before he could think about it, he put his arms around her, placing one hand at the small of her back. It was full contact. He was in danger of passing out.

"Thank you, Adam-Batman!" she said when she let go. She held the rosary in front of her. "Wow!"

Adam was still reeling from her body being that close to his. He tried to locate his breath. He needed to not move. For one thing, he wanted to linger in the warm liquid memory of what it felt like to hold all of her in his arms, and more critically, if he moved, his body would betray him. Adam visualized Sister Mary-Margaret for quite some time before he dared speak again. Robyn, meanwhile, put the rosary on, took it off, held it up to the sun and counted the beads.

"Here—" He finally exhaled and gently took the rosary back. "It's not a necklace, it's a rosary. Let me show you."

Robyn smiled.

"Catholics *pray* on it. It's like to count your prayers."

"Ooh, I saw Audrey Hepburn with a necklace—"

"Rosary."

"Yeah, like the one that she had in this movie called *A Nun's Story*. I love it! I love it!" she gushed, and then, yes, she hugged him again, awkwardly and around the neck, but close enough that he thought he would explode.

Adam vowed to bring her a present next week and every week until the day they died.

Robyn leaned against Marnie Wetherall. "Okay, so how does it work?"

"Well, first you make the sign of the cross, remember?"

"Hey, I got that one down pat. Don't worry, I'm not going crazy with it. Just a few times a day. That's the God's honest truth." She crossed herself as if to prove it.

"Okay," he repeated. "So this first big bead is the Apostles' Creed."

She looked blank.

"Don't Protestants do the Apostles' Creed?"

Robyn shrugged. "If they do, I wouldn't know. We haven't stepped inside a church since . . ."

"Right. Okay, I'll write that one out for you. The next big bead is the Our Father."

"I know that one!" She beamed.

"Great, then three Hail Marys followed by a Glory To."

Robyn groaned politely.

"Okay, so it's a bit complicated until you get going, you know? Like you're supposed to meditate on the first mystery on that large bead there and then do the Our Father again. And, well, thing is, you're supposed to meditate on different mysteries on different days of the week."

He glanced up, fully expecting her to look dispirited. Instead she nodded eagerly.

"It's perfect! The perfect thing for me, perfect! I'm going to be a Catholic. I swear to God, I'll study my brains out. I can't wait to get at that confession stuff. Do I bring it to confession?"

"Uh, not usually." Adam could tell she was lost—eager but lost. "I'll get you a pamphlet or something on how to do the rosary thing. They have them at school, in religion class."

Robyn cupped the rosary in her hands, brought it to her face and kissed the beads. "It's so, so beautiful, but you really shouldn't have."

"No, it's okay, I got it from home. We have a million of them." Adam winced remembering the drawer full of rosary beads. "Literally."

Robyn turned to him.

"My mom's a collector."

She didn't even blink.

"An intense collector."

"Hey," she said. "I should have gotten *you* a present. Wasn't it your birthday last week? How did it go at the restaurant with your dad and everyone?"

"Good," he lied. "Mainly. Sweetie and me were born, like, not even a week apart. So we always get these combo deals. Last year we were at Warhammer Day at the BattleCraft store in the mall, and this time it was a private room at La Tourangelle. My brother is like this pint-sized gourmand." Robyn smiled while fingering the rosary. "Brenda, that's my stepmom, arranged everything, but it's cool of my dad to get into it the way he does. He makes it a big deal." Adam paused. "He tries—we all try—but we just miss, you know?"

Robyn nodded but didn't interrupt. Adam remembered summoning up the requisite enthusiasm for the Plan B skateboard plus the helmet and pads that his dad had given him at the restaurant. It was the latest and greatest. "Wow, unbelievable, Dad . . . Too much!" His father had almost bought it. And once again, more than anything, Adam wished that he was *that* guy, the guy who would have loved all that fresh stuff. Sweetie, on the other hand, was not quite as polished about faking his enthusiasm over killer hockey skates.

"Poor guy," Adam sighed, thinking of his dad. "All he wants is a kid that will kick around a soccer ball with him, and he's struck out with both his sons."

Robyn nodded. "And then . . . ?"

"And then Brenda got a bit frazzled and my mom got a bit tipsy. I mean, she was fine—you wouldn't know unless you knew, you know?—but I was freaking out for the rest of the night about whether she was going to have another glass of Chardonnay, which may have put her over the limit. But other than that, it was *outstanding!*"

"So Brenda *and* your mom . . ."

"Can both be a little intense, I guess." He said this more to himself than to her. "My mom way, way more than Brenda, to be honest."

"Hmm." Robyn smiled. "You Ross men seem to like your women complicated. Come on, I've got to go. Tonight is a 'Dad dinner night.' He tries for one every week or so and complains about it non-stop while trying. It's soooo *almost*, you know? Tonight he cooks his not-so-famous lasagna. It's like your dad and the birthdays."

"They try," he said.

"Sort of," she said.

It wasn't until he was halfway home and replaying every word, gesture and touch that it hit him. What did she mean back there?

You Ross men seem to like your women complicated. You Ross men! She was including him. Robyn was complicated. Did that mean she knew? She knew, right? She had to know. Girls knew this stuff, so she knew. Absolutely she knew. Not only did she know, but she knew and she wasn't running.

His life was going to be perfect—better than perfect. Adam was on his way straight to *superior*.

CHAPTER TEN

Adam painstakingly drizzled a lemon-and-butter mixture onto the free-range, organic chicken breasts. The chicken was nestled in a special glass microwave container. They had a bazillion glass containers. More, even. Despite the fact that you could barely see the stove or the counter surfaces these days, Mrs. Ross was alive and alert to the dangers of Bisphenol A. She would not allow canned goods into the house and forbade her son to use anything but glass in the microwave lest the BPA mess with his hormone health. You couldn't put your foot down without stepping on a box of something, yet Carmella waged a personal war against a toxic universe. As if to underscore that point, Adam tripped over an industrial-sized box of Greenearth Biodegradable Garbage Bags.

"Ouch!"

He could get rid of some stuff. He could. Adam thought about sneaking stuff out at least a hundred times every day. There was so much, she wouldn't notice. He'd start with a couple of small things in the dining room and if she—

"Honey?" The front door slammed.

"In the kitchen, Mom."

He could hear her picking her way along the hallway and shuffling the mail at the same time. "Damn it to hell." Something was kicked.

When she got to the kitchen, Carmella smiled broadly for her son. "Hey, baby, that smells so good!"

"Thanks, Mom, but I haven't put it in yet. The potatoes are done, though, and the chicken will only be a few minutes."

"Right, well, the potatoes smell awesome. You're a great chef. You and that brother of yours should open up a restaurant someday." Adam glanced at her hand, which was clutching the day's mail. "Except, of course, you're on track for Princeton." She clutched harder. "Right?" Her voice was tight. "I'm raising a Princeton man, right?"

"Right."

His mother crumpled the mail in her left hand. Adam considered telling her about Robyn. He'd sort of wanted to for weeks now. He would tell her about Robyn wanting to be a Catholic. A new friend, a friend who was a girl, and one who was deep into religion. That would have been a Carmella Ross trifecta of happiness, but the time was never right. Her hand held the balled-up mail so tight that it looked like her veins were going to pop.

The time was never right.

"Is Ben's dad still coming to pick you up after dinner?" His mom was in her scrubs and wearing one of Dad's old sweaters. Not that long ago, Carmella always changed and put on a fresh coat of lipstick before coming home, no matter the time, the shift or who was awake.

"Yeah." He didn't take his eyes off the letters. "We're going to video his garage Warhammer set-up for YouTube. It'll be chill!"

Carmella nodded as if she understood what her son had just said. The veins in her hand popped with the strain of clutching. She wasn't paying attention, not really. "He's a good kid, that Ben. Always there for you." The microwave tinged and she jumped. "Oh!" She collected herself. "I've, uh, always liked Ben . . . He's a good boy."

Adam frowned and pulled out the chicken. He tried to direct a plate to her clenched left hand. "Mom?" He had to ask. "Look, what's up with those?"

"Nothing! I'm not even going to read it, honey." She ignored the plate and fished out a cream-coloured envelope amidst the rolled-up junk mail and pleas from environmental groups. It had a typed label, indicating recipient and recipient's address. So innocuous. Adam put her plate down and tapped his forefinger behind him on the counter edge. This would need seven sets of nine taps counter-clockwise. Just as he started, she ripped the envelope apart.

"Mom, don't!" He had to start counting all over again.

"It's garbage, Adam. Ugly, ugly garbage."

Three sets, then. One, three, five, seven . . .

She shut the cupboard door, trembling just a little. "The last one . . . the last one said I had to die, that I was a maggot polluting the world, that I was a—" She did not look at her son. He did not look at her.

Eleven, thirteen, fifteen, seventeen, nineteen . . .

"It said I sucked up too much oxygen and was a greedy, selfish bitch." She turned to Adam, utterly confused. "Who talks like that?"

Twenty-three, twenty-five, twenty-seven, twenty-nine, thirty-one . . .
Wait, wait! The numbers were wrong. It was a nine count. Stupid, stupid!

She caught him tapping out of the corner of her eye and winced.

One, three, five, seven . . .

Carmella threw away the bits of letter along with the junk mail, their telephone bill and what looked like a reminder from Dr. Dave's dental office. He'd have to retrieve those later. Adam finally handed her the plate.

"You're right, Mom. It sounds like some demented kid, or a pissed-off patient."

He heard her exhale. "Yeah, see? It's like I was telling you: it's some kind of prank." She helped herself to potatoes and chicken and a stiff shot of vodka over ice. "I'm going up to eat this in my room, okay? I'm so beat. You have a good time with Ben tonight. Don't get home too late, though. You got enough money for the bus back?"

He nodded.

"Adam, honey?" Her voice slipped like a silk scarf.

He lifted his plate and tapped underneath it as he ladled on the chicken and potatoes. *Twenty-nine, thirty-one. One, three, five* . . .

"You know we can't talk about it, right? Not to anyone."

"Yeah, sure. But what if—" *Eleven, thirteen, fifteen, seventeen* . . .

"No! This is all connected to me, Adam. It's all a part of it. It's like the house." She leaned against the doorway. "*They* will use it as an excuse to . . ."

"Yeah, I know." *Twenty-one, twenty-three* . . .

"Of course you do." She kissed his forehead. "I love you so much." She kissed him again before she turned and left.

Adam was counting with fingers raised and into a thirties set when Ben rang the bell. He hadn't touched his chicken, couldn't eat. Without missing any finger movements, Adam retrieved some letter pieces from the garbage, along with the telephone bill and Dr. Dave's appointment reminder. He shoved them all in his pocket and dumped his untouched chicken in their place. Then he grabbed his jacket and ran for the door.

"Dude!" Ben punched him in the shoulder. "Are you ready for an epic game? It'll be massive, can ya dig it?"

Dig it? Ben must have taken a shuttle back to the 1970s. He did that on occasion. Adam nodded. *Twenty-five, twenty-seven, twenty-nine, thirty-one. One* . . . What *was* epic was just seeing his friend. *Three, five, seven, nine, eleven* . . .

Ben glanced back at Adam as he locked up. Adam knew he'd spied the telltale finger raises.

They both got into the car, and as they did, Mr. Stone turned around to face the boys. "Adam, great to see you, son."

"Thank you, sir." And they were off.

Son. Adam loved that word coming out of Mr. Stone's mouth. *Seventeen, nineteen, twenty-one, twenty-three* . . .

"Dude?" Ben whispered. "You counting?"

"Yeah." Adam nodded. *Twenty-five, twenty-seven, twenty-nine, thirty-one.*

Ben slumped into the back seat. "It's cool, okay? Relax, I can dig it."

"Thanks, man." *One, three, five, seven* . . .

CHAPTER ELEVEN

Adam's cellphone vibrated. He didn't even know it had that feature. But there it was, rattling down his desk like a cockroach caught in a kitchen light. The phone was at least a hundred and seventy-three years old. It used to be Carmella's and it had less than no features. Well, except apparently it vibrated. The stupid thing could barely rouse itself to execute a phone call. Texting made it lethargic and in need of an immediate battery resuscitation. And the phone was a monster, so big it practically needed its own transportation system. And of course, more than anything, it was way, *way* too lame to be seen in public. His mom urged him to consider the thing as his "placeholder" birthday gift, a "training phone." She had promised him a "normal" phone as soon as she got the go-ahead from Chuck, but Adam kept forgetting to ask Chuck about it. He'd bring it up at the next one-on-one for sure.

The trainer vibrated itself right off the desk and onto his slipper.

"Batman?"

"Sweetie?" Adam glanced at his watch. "It's almost eleven-thirty! What's up? I just got home. I'm going to bed."

"I know. I been calling and calling and calling. I've even been calling your new old phone, this phone."

"Don't ever call this phone, Sweetie."

"Okay." Pause. "Why not?"

"Because it will never leave my room."

"Okay," Sweetie said, instantly satisfied with his brother's reasoning. "But you weren't in your room."

"I was at Ben's."

"I know," he said. They were in danger of having one of their circular conversations. "Your mom, Mrs. Carmella Ross, told me that at 9.4.7 p.m. because that's what my clock said. But Mrs. Carmella Ross did not answer the phone before or after that, Batman. Nope."

Adam groaned. He tried to groan quietly. He'd explained a thousand times why his mom didn't answer after the first couple of times when call display announced that it was Sweetie on his private cell. "Who the hell gives a five-year-old a smartphone, for God's sake! I'm telling you, they're bonkers over there." It was just easier not answering, and it was also easier not re-explaining why *not answering* was preferable all around. To further complicate things, Sweetie refused to leave messages. The thought of his voice trapped and disembodied all by itself on a machine made him anxious.

"Why doesn't your mother, Mrs. Carmella Ross—"

His mother. Adam winced remembering the letter. It was still in his pocket. "Look, we gotta cut her some slack, okay? She's kinda more nervous than usual these days." He should fish it out and piece it together.

"Okay," Sweetie agreed. "I thought you were with the girl."

"Robyn?"

"Yeah."

Adam could see his brother's head bobbing up and down in the dark. Well, okay, not the dark; there were four separate plug-in night lights in that room. "No, just Ben," he said.

"I like Ben. I like Ben a lot," Sweetie insisted.

"Good." Adam started undressing.

"I don't like the girl."

"You don't even know her."

"You love her, you said. You said you love her. But she doesn't love you."

"Not *yet*, I said. Remember? I said she doesn't love me *yet*. She will, though. It's like a quest thingy."

"But *you* love her," Sweetie accused.

"Yeah." Adam climbed out of his pants. "But it's totally different from the way I love you, or Mom, or Dad, or—"

"You love me way, way, way better, right?"

Sigh. "Yeah, way better."

"Okay, I like her. You're Batman and Robin, except in all the cartoons—"

"Comics."

"Yeah, in all the comics, Robin is a boy."

"But it's also a girl's name. And, Sweetie, look, we got to keep Robyn to ourselves for now, okay? It's just . . . well, it's in development, you know?"

"So it's just *our* secret?"

"Yeah. Well, us and Ben too. I told him about her tonight."

"So just us boys, right?"

"Right! That's exactly it. Look, it's really late. Why'd you call? You okay?"

Silence. Was he trying to remember?

"I'm scared, Batman."

"There's nothing to be scared of, remember? Nothing. It'll be okay. Is Dad there?"

"Yes, Mr. Sebastian Ross and Mrs. Brenda Ross turned out their lights at 10.4.6 p.m."

Sweetie was a stickler for precision. He hated getting himself into a muddle over which of the two moms they were talking about at any given moment. There were the two Mrs. Rosses, after all, who each had a son, and there were two separate houses, but they shared the one dad. It gave Sweetie a stomach ache trying to sort it all out unless he was very, very specific. "But I'm still scared, Batman."

"Why, Sweetie? *Why* are you scared?"

"I don't know." His little voice got littler with each syllable.

Adam sat down in his underwear and started tapping.

"Can you come over, Batman?"

"No, I can't. It's late and it would piss off Brenda."

"No, it wouldn't, Batman. Mrs. Brenda Ross loves you. She loves you lots. I hear her telling Mr. Sebastian Ross all the time. *He really should be here with us, Sebastian. The boy is not safe in that firetrap.* That's what she says. Are you in a firetrap, Batman? Do you have a big hose? Should we call the—"

"No, Sweetie, no firemen! It's all good, okay? Is that why you're scared?"

Long pause. "I don't think so." Snuffle, snuffle. "I can't sleep. Should I go wash my hands, like you did?"

"No!" Adam's stomach constricted. Sweetie remembered that? He was just—what?—three when Adam was washing. "It doesn't work. I stopped. You know I don't—"

"Should I count?"

"No!" Adam shivered and rooted around looking for his PJs. "That doesn't work either, believe me!"

"But you still—"

"Yeah, and I go to that special group with all the nice people on Mondays to help me stop that too."

"The superheroes! Are they your friends now?"

"Uh, it's not like . . ." He got one leg in. "They're not, uh, well . . ." He shoved his second leg into his pyjama bottoms while balancing the unwieldy phone between his shoulder and his ear. "I mean, I don't know. Kind of, I guess."

It could be true.

"Just a minute." He put the phone down to get his T-shirt off, then picked it up again. "Hey, little guy. We can think about the pretty numbers. How about we think about some nice prime—"

"That doesn't work unless you're here." The voice was tiny now, tears nibbling on the edges. "I'm sooo tired, Batman. And sooo scared."

"Scared of what? You've gotta tell me. I can help, but only if you tell me."

"Of the bad, bad thing that's gonna happen." A beat of silence. "I'm waiting for the bad thing."

Jesus. Adam knew *exactly* what his little brother meant. He couldn't toss off that fear. He knew about the bad thing, about the waiting. Adam had been waiting, preparing, for forever.

"Okay, okay . . . hang on. The bad thing won't happen tonight, I promise." Adam lay down on top of his covers. "Listen, get into bed and pretend I'm tucking you in."

"Smooshing me in?"

"Yeah, yeah, I'm smooshing the covers in all around you exactly like you like."

"Okay," agreed an increasingly tiny voice.

"Are you all tucked in?"

"Uh-hmm."

"Good one. I'll stay right here until you fall asleep. Keep the phone by your ear and I'll talk to you."

"I love you, Batman. You are the best, most perfect Batman in the world!" The words broke through cascading yawns.

"Yeah, okay. So I'm right here, right? I won't go away, I promise. You're safe, okay?"

Soft, shallow breathing.

"Sweetie?"

Adam shut his eyes, but he still held the cumbersome phone tight against his ear. He'd look at the letter tomorrow. Yeah. He could only do so much.

"Sweetie?" Adam turned off his lamp.

Nothing.

"I love you too."

CHAPTER TWELVE

"**S**o." Robyn crossed her legs and uncrossed them, hypnotizing Adam. "So when I think a shame thought, or if I snag on a trigger like being such a pig, or dying babies in Somalia, or the ambulance coming for my mom, or . . ." The superheroes shuddered, except for Snooki. Snooki was not a shudderer. "Well, then I either just make a quick sign of the cross or, if it still won't let go, grab the rosary beads. *Not* all OCD-like. Just the one round, you know?"

Most of them nodded but didn't say anything. They wouldn't know a rosary from a gear shaft.

Adam was at the ready, as he always was when Robyn spoke up. He was keyed to jump in and, and . . . what exactly?

"But it's different than before, you know?" It was like she was on sharing steroids. Robyn was talking more in this one session than she had in all the other weeks combined. And it was killing Adam. He had to hold up the plane for the whole time she had the floor. "For one thing we're cycling me down from the meds quite a bit."

They, including Snooki, and even Thor, turned as one to Chuck for confirmation. Chuck didn't move, gave nothing away. He was not her attending, after all. Dissatisfied, they turned back to Robyn looking for signs of . . . something.

"Believe me, the God stuff isn't like the other things were for me. And it's so not at all like the cutting."

Wait.

She was a cutter?

Was a cutter, Adam reminded himself. *Was a cutter. Was a puker. Was.*

"So I'm going to learn lots more about religion and . . . well, about being Catholic actually."

At that, Robyn smiled right at Adam and again the superheroes turned as one, this time to consider him anew. What did Batman have to do with anything?

Hmm.

Are she and he . . . ?

Thor stopped scowling long enough to snort, which Adam took as a sign of approval.

"See, it's not like a crutch or a compulsion, not really. The religious thing just helps with the hyper-anxious bits. It's like behaviour therapy, sort of. I know it doesn't *stop* the bad thing, or *change* the consequences, see? So it's different from the OCD. It just helps a little." She seemed surprised, as if she hadn't really noticed that singular fact before.

Adam could tell she was taking an instant inventory of her compulsions, checking some off, erasing others completely.

"Like I said, I know I won't stop resident evil if I say the rosary—it just makes me feel better, you know?"

"Come on!" Snooki wasn't having it. "It's called scrupulosity and it's a bona fide OCD thing," she accused. "In fact it's probably one of the top ten—right, Chuck?"

"Well, it can be, if indeed—"

"Yeah, maybe even top five. It's in the damn manual."

"Still, she's not cutting or any of the other crap," offered Wonder Woman.

"That's it!" Robyn crossed her legs again. "That's it exactly. It's different. *I'm* different. Look, I haven't cut since I got here. That was bad—I was bad. I was sick. Between the cutting, the washing and the food sorting . . . well, that's how I ended up in residence."

Everyone, including Adam, looked to Chuck for confirmation. This time he nodded.

"But *this* is *not* that. It's not any of that. I swear to God, I don't even think it's scrupulosity, really. Praying is just helping me, like maybe yoga or meditation or . . ."

"I sort of get it," said Green Lantern, mainly to himself. "I'm thinking that praying to the big guy might help when I'm freaking out about harming people I love. It helped my mom with the drinking for sure. AA is big into the higher-power stuff."

"Whoa, people, religion is not a panacea." Chuck was writing things down at a furious pace. "In fact, religion is not even a recognized tool in most OCD recovery kits."

"Well, I don't see why not," Wonder Woman stopped twitching long enough to huff. "It works for drunks, right? I think I might even be Jewish. Well, my mom is, so that means I am, but no one practises, so I don't know where that leaves me."

"That's just like me!" Robyn brightened. "I think we're Presbyterian or proletarian or some kind of Protestant, but neither Dad nor Mom believed in anything much. And since Mom . . . well, my father *really* doesn't believe in anything. But the praying and the Catholic stuff—did I say it was Catholic stuff? Yeah, Catholics have so much good stuff." She turned back to Wonder Woman. "But I'm sure that Jewishness would be packed full of great stuff too! The thing is, in the hospital they kept telling me to keep up 'my practice.' So this is going to be 'my practice.'" Robyn smiled at Green Lantern. "Batman is helping me with all the Catholic details. Look, I know they're unhinged on a bunch of issues, including the gay thing, but Batman says that Holy Rosary is way loose with all that. We're going to sit in his church and contemplate the big cross right after this session."

"No shit?"

It was Thor.

No one moved.

Was it Thor?

Two separate and distinct words?

No one had heard Thor speak before. Chuck stopped taking notes.

Thor looked right at Adam. "I think all that praying is making the kid taller." His voice was granular and dark, as if he'd been gargling with gravel. A man's voice. And as quickly as it came, it disappeared. Thor climbed back into his silent cave.

"Wow. Uh, you know, I think that's right," said Iron Man, examining Adam. "And I sort of get the religious thing. I suck at meditation, even though my mom's bought me a shelf full of CDs and music that sounds like cats being tortured. Maybe lighting a Jesus candle would help me when I think I've just destroyed or am about to destroy someone with my poisoned thoughts. Toxins R Us."

"So can we come too?" asked Wonder Woman.

"Where?" asked Robyn.

"To the church, with you and Batman."

"Whoa, people," said Chuck, leaning into the semicircle. "Remember the word *panacea*? Religion generally, and Catholicism specifically, is so not—"

"Yeah, yeah, *whatever*. We know that the church won't fix us. Don't sweat it, Chuck. We're crazy, not stupid," said Snooki, who was absolutely neither. "Thing is, Robyn here has hardly said squat since she came three months ago, but it's super clear she's making some kind of progress, and Batman's Catholic gear is in on it. It can't hurt to have a look-see, right? Field trip, guys?"

"Damn straight!" said Captain America. "Can Jews go? Unlike Snooki's, my family does practise, at least on all the High Holidays. So can Jews go?"

"Sure . . ." said Adam, unsure of what was happening here. "My best friend, Ben, came to all my big things—you know, Holy Communion, Confirmation . . ." They all nodded at him encouragingly, not having a clue what he was talking about. "And I still go to Holy Blossom for some of the High Holidays and his bar mitzvah, of course, and—"

"I'm in," said Green Lantern and Wonder Woman at the same time.

Adam's heart jackhammered. How did this happen? What exactly *did* happen? Wait, was he taking his heavily medicated OCD support group to *church*? Sweet Jesus. Adam was sort of with Chuck on this one. He wasn't even sure of the "appropriateness" of doing that. And to tell the truth, even with Robyn, he thought of it in terms of *sneaking* her in, especially since he himself had not gone in years.

"Okay, I know when I'm whipped." Chuck was smiling.

Why was he smiling? Surely he should put a stop to this,

because of . . . because of some excellent reason that Adam couldn't put his finger on.

"Well, you're in good hands with Batman. But don't get all carried away with this."

In good hands with Batman? What was the matter with this man?

"It'll do you guys good to bond a bit, and accessing spirituality as one of the tenets towards healing is valid enough, I guess." He glanced at his watch. "Which church, Batman? The one that's affiliated with St. Mary's?"

Adam gulped and shook his head. "No, Holy Rosary." He nodded again. "It's only five blocks away."

"Okay, I'll look forward to hearing about it next week."

Then, horror of horrors, everyone got up and turned expectantly to Adam.

"Uh, I think we should all take the stairs down, because"—he tried not to look at Wonder Woman—"it's another, uh, 'get our asses in gear' opportunity."

Wolverine rolled his eyes but headed straight for the door and over to the stairwell.

"You're such a doll!" Wonder Woman gave Batman's arm a little squeeze.

And off they went. Eight superheroes down thirteen flights of stairs.

Wait a minute, *eight*?

Thor was right behind him.

CHAPTER THIRTEEN

"**C**rap," Wolverine muttered as soon as they reconvened outside the building. "I gotta say, we're the most sorry-ass-looking group of superheroes I have ever seen."

Snooki put her arm through Robyn's. "Robyn and me aren't even superheroes."

"I am too," Robyn corrected gently. "*R-o-b-i-n.*" She turned back and smiled at Adam. "Batman and Robyn, get it?"

His heart stopped beating.

She was teasing, right? He would have picked it apart except he was too consumed by abject terror.

"Hell." Wolverine sidled up to Robyn. "I'm just saying that as a group of superheroes, we blow."

"Shouldn't we be there already?" Wonder Woman asked after one block.

"Relax, WW, and enjoy the moment," said Iron Man, who was home-schooled and just happy to be on the street with some friends, even if they looked like the escape scene from *One Flew Over the Cuckoo's Nest.*

Adam, who was caught between Thor and Green Lantern, didn't pay attention to any of them. There was no room in his head. Every crevice was filled to the brim with worry. He worried about being called out by one of the nuns—or worse, by Father Rick. How would he explain *them* or, more importantly, *him* being there? Adam hadn't been to church in almost three years, ever since Carmella put a stop to it. "They're all way too damn nosy over there for their own good. They all think I'm ruined 'cause of the divorce. I bet I've been excommunicated already. We don't need them looking at us that way. You're nobody's pity party, kid."

So Adam worried about that right up until there was a worse thing to worry about.

The church doors.

How nuts was that? He felt it clear across the street. It was a bad threshold. Jesus. How could *church doors* be evil? Now what?

Should he tell them? He had to tell them.

He couldn't tell them.

The shame would shut him down for good. The look on Wolverine's face alone . . .

Unlike the tapping, the threshold stuff at this level was visible. There was no way they wouldn't notice. The humiliation of knowing that he had done the thing—*his* thing—in public, in view of God. Church doors, those beautiful, blessed bronze doors . . .

"What's up, Caped Crusader?" It was Snooki.

Robyn stopped, turned and looked at him questioningly. Then they all did, even as they kept walking.

"Uh, across the street, halfway up the block."

They stopped, the eight of them huddled together, and looked at Holy Rosary.

"Cool," said Iron Man, trying to be cool.

"Guys?" Adam said.

Everyone turned to him. Captain America was perspiring in response to God knows what, and Wonder Woman was twitching in fear of the potentially small confined spaces lurking inside. It was a testament to her courage and curiosity that she had come this far. The girl was definitely escalating. Still, no one looked more outwardly nervous than Green Lantern, who carried a considerable and not completely irrational fear about entering a Roman Catholic church. Adam had to acknowledge that any way you sliced or diced it, they were indeed one messed-up cadre of superheroes. Especially since they were looking to *him*, of all people, for leadership. On the other hand, the sheer breadth of their combined messed-upness gave him a wonky kind of courage. Turning back was not an option. Adam shoved down the shame.

"So, guys, thing is . . ."

Robyn nodded, urging him to say whatever it was he had to say. He fell into her smoky eyes.

"The thing is, I, uh, apparently have a threshold issue with those doors."

"No shit, Sherlock!" Wolverine shook his head. "Threshold crap? With church doors? You gotta clear *church* doors? That's rich. Does the Pope know?"

"Go to hell, mutt." It was Thor. "Kid's got to clear what the kid's got to clear. What's it to you? Batman, do your thing. We'll look away until you call us."

Wow, so Thor *had* been paying attention all this time.

Once again, the superheroes were shocked into a stupefied silence. But they all turned around and stared intently into the Korean grocery store window. The kimchi was on sale, $7.49 a jar.

"Right." Adam ran across the street, trying not to think and just do what had to be done. He walked up and down the stairs three times, leading with his left leg. When he was ready to address the threshold, he raised both arms at his sides as if in embrace and held that for nine counts. Next he circled his right finger into his left hand three times and then tapped the door exactly one hundred and eleven times. Finally, he placed both hands flat against the bronze carved door and applied exactly equal pressure for seventeen seconds. *One steamboat, two steamboat, three steamboat* . . . He swallowed a gallon of shame. Good thing he couldn't cry.

"Okay!" He turned to catch Robyn beaming at him from across the street and he got that liquidy feeling that only she made him get. Adam would take on the gates of St. Peter's for her.

"Come on!" He waved from across the street and saw them as Father Rick would see them. Thor, at six foot three, wore a black T-shirt and black ripped jeans accessorized with multiple piercings and sleeve tattoos. Captain America, Robyn and Adam wore their various school uniforms. His looked the least superhero-like, since both the jacket and pants were now so pathetically short that he was solidly into dork territory. So was Robyn's skirt, but that just looked supremely outstanding. Iron Man looked like page 23 of the boys' section in the Sears catalogue, and Wonder Woman wore a too-tight pink hoodie, which was nicely balanced by a too-short blue jean miniskirt. Snooki wore those legging things and a massive floaty top that was kind of see-through. Okay, not just kind of. Green Lantern was the most regular-looking guy in the whole group, but then it was a pretty low bar.

"It's okay." Adam waved them closer. "I'm clear now."

He held the door open. He'd done it. Adam had done a ritual in public and the world hadn't ended. Good to know. It seemed that he had crossed more than one threshold. Big breath in, big breath out.

"Let's go, guys!"

CHAPTER FOURTEEN

"**H**oly shit!" said Captain America as soon as they got into the vestibule.

Snooki smacked him in the arm. "You can't say *shit* in a church, right, Batman? Especially the Catholic kind." Snooki spoke with unassailable authority because the entire *Jersey Shore* cast was of good Italian-Catholic stock.

Adam nodded. His stomach constricted to the size of an acorn, giving the fear more room to roam around.

"Okay, sorry, *Jesus*," said Captain America, rubbing his arm.

She smacked him again.

"Wow!" said Robyn and Iron Man at the same time.

Even the vestibule was designed to inspire awe, hinting at the Gothic arches to be found inside. Adam took it in as if for the first time.

"What are those?" asked Wolverine pointing to the two receptacles on either side of the entrance to the nave.

"The fonts for the holy water," explained Adam.

"Holy water? Now that *is* righteous. How much can we take?" asked Wolverine.

"Uh, you don't, uh, *take* the . . . I'll show you in a sec."

"When do we kneel? Do we kneel here before we go in?" asked Iron Man. "I know Catholics are big on kneeling. That's what my mom always says."

"No. You don't have to kneel everywhere." What *had* he got himself into? Adam was now deep into free-form sweating. "You just kneel before the Eucharist."

"Ohhh," they all said, still completely clueless.

"Batman." Thor leaned over to him and growled, "Kid, you gotta get new pants; those are going to be shorts by next week."

What was it with this guy? No one knew he had a voice for months and now he was a fashion maven?

"Okay, so quick one before we go in, guys? Guys?" Much to his surprise, they stopped pointing and asking and touching long enough to turn and face him. "Right. So, Robyn, those receptacles with the holy water?" She nodded. "It's the same deal as for the sign of the cross, except you dip your forefinger and middle finger first." Everyone turned to Robyn. "Uh, maybe do it out loud so the rest of the, uh, of us can hear you."

"Okay." Robyn floated over to the font and followed his instructions.

"Like this guys, watch."

In the name of the Father,
and of the Son,
and of the Holy Spirit,
Amen.

Everyone rushed to the receptacle, eager to give it a try. They followed her movements exactly, but crashed around on

the actual words, which came out more like one long mumble:
Nameyourfatherhasasonandhisholyspiritsamen.

"Close enough," said Adam. "Let's go in."

They formed a double line of three behind him.

"Wow!"

"Holy shit! OW! Sorry already!"

"Man, catch those windows!"

Their tight double line disintegrated about halfway up the
nave as everyone fanned out taking in different wonders.

The church, praise the Lord, was empty. A miracle in itself,
since there was usually a smattering of little old ladies in the pews
doing the rosary or waiting for a glimpse of Father Rick.

"Wow, look at that, will ya!" Adam walked right into Snooki's
pointed finger. Everybody stopped. Everybody looked.

High above the marble altar and well in front of the hundred-
year-old stained-glass window was a massive suspended bronze
Christ nailed to a wooden cross.

"Christ!" said Iron Man.

"Exactly," said Wonder Woman.

They were riveted. The scarred and protruding ribs, every
perforated wound, the nails fixed through his hands and feet, the
crown of thorns, and the excruciating, silent pain rose off the warm
bronze to greet them.

"Come on, guys, this way. I was going to take Robyn to the
candles. They're on the far side of the sanctuary." No one moved.
He might as well have been speaking in Latin. "Guys? You can
drop some coins into the slot, but it's not a requirement. And you
can light a candle for someone you loved and cared about who is
no longer here." They nodded but didn't move, still hypnotized by
the suspended Christ on the cross.

"Awesome," said Green Lantern. "I swear he's breathing."

"I feel like I'm going to cry. Am I having a religious experience? Is this what that's like?" asked Wonder Woman.

"Naw," said Wolverine. "You just cry a lot."

That broke the spell. They tore themselves away from the Christ to take in the sweeping Gothic arches, the marble and the majesty of all those stained-glass windows.

"Are we going to need a lighter?" asked Captain America. "I got a lighter for my doobies. I got a lighter. Do we need a lighter? In fact, I hate to break it to you, man, but there is a distinct aroma of doobieness in here."

"That's incense," said Adam, and he was reminded that a thousand things could go wrong here. Actually, he was pretty much counting on it, but trying not to *count* on it.

"I'm just going to run back to the water thingy for a sec," said Wonder Woman.

"No! I mean, no, you don't need a lighter, and no, sorry, but you can't go back and use the holy water to wash up."

"I so was not—"

"Yeah, you *so* were," said Snooki.

"Let's just go over to those candles, okay?" Adam did a quick three-sixty—still safe: no priests, no nuns.

The stand of candles was under an incandescent statue of the Blessed Virgin Mary. The stand itself was about four feet by two feet—four votive candles deep and twenty-four long, for a total of ninety-six candles. This was unbearable, of course, so he immediately removed a votive and placed it under the stand. The superheroes said nothing. They assumed that he had just performed some Catholic ritual that was necessary before non-Catholics could start lighting stuff.

"It's so, so pretty!" said Robyn somewhere behind him.

Adam nodded. He was lost in counting out the lit candles. Thirty-three. That was okay, and whatever the number was after they were through, he would come in and correct the outcome. Yes. And that calmed him: thirty-three flickering lights. Thirty-three was good.

Robyn was still gushing. "Proletarians don't have this stuff, I'm sure of it. I'm definitely signing up."

Adam turned in time to see Wolverine smile at her. Wolverine made a big show of reaching into his pocket and pulling out a ten. "I've got this covered for all of us, so long as Robyn goes first and has her pick."

Adam felt like hurling.

"Thanks, Wolverine. That's so sweet."

Sweet my ass. Who does he think he is?

Each superhero lit at least one candle, Snooki lit seven, and they each executed the sign of the cross with varying degrees of success. Adam's head buzzed as he tried to track the number of candles lit as well as where Wolverine was in relationship to Robyn at any given moment.

He had no early-warning system. The voice came out of nowhere and everywhere, all at once.

"Can I help you?"

Father Rick. Damn.

"Adam Ross, is that you? Adam, how great to see you!"

Led by Thor, the superheroes instantly and as one knelt on the granite floor and executed the world's messiest signs of the cross.

"Well!" Father Rick stopped cold. "Well?" He looked to Adam and back to the seven kneeling superheroes. "What are you guys doing?"

"Batman said Catholics kneel when they see the Eucharist," said Iron Man helpfully. Except for Adam they were all still kneeling.

Father Rick turned back to Adam, who threw up his hands because he honest to God didn't know what else to do.

"How's it going, Father?"

You could tell that the priest was sucking back a smile. He waited, seeming to gather himself. "Please get up, guys. I'm flattered, but I am not the Eucharist. I'm just a normal man who happens to be a priest."

Yeah, right, thought Adam. He watched his crew rise, confused but eager for the next test.

"Adam?"

Okay, how to explain? "These are my . . ." Adam was so nervous he couldn't remember anyone's Christian name and he couldn't very well introduce everyone by their superhero handles. "They're my friends." And in the saying, it was true. "So this is uh . . . um—"

"Hi, Father. I'm Robyn!" Robyn leapt up and curtsied. "Adam's helping me to be a Catholic!"

"Is he, now?" said Father Rick, who to his credit did not look the least bit surprised.

"Yup, and I'm loving it so far—love, love, love!" she gushed. "The holy water was great, by the way, and I'm big into the rosary thing and the sign of the cross, of course. I've also got one of your pamphlets with, like, the top ten Catholic prayers on it. So I'm pretty much there, right?" Father Rick looked faintly alarmed. "Oh look, I know I'm going to have to take classes or go to Rome or something, but I'm getting ready to sign up for the whole deal."

The priest nodded encouragingly at his potential new congregant.

"Real nice place you got here, Father."

"Thank you, Mr. . . . ?"

"Wolverine," said Wolverine, extending his hand.

"Wolverine," Father Rick repeated. "Mr. Wolverine. If I may, for just a moment . . ." He extended his arm towards Adam and led him away from the still semi-kneeling superheroes.

"I'm happy to see you branching out in your friendships, son." He glanced back at the group. "Do you still see the Jewish boy? I liked him. When you were little, you two were joined at the hip."

"Ben? Yeah, sure. Stones and me, we're still tight. He's just moved and he's definitely not so little anymore. You wouldn't recognize him. I'm, like you said, just branching out a bit."

The priest smiled and frowned at the same time. It was a signature Father Rick expression.

"They're my *Group*. Capital G, you know? We, uh, help each other. Weekly."

"Oh, got it! Sure. That's good, fine. Excellent." The priest glanced back at them. "And how's your mother doing?"

Okay, welcome to my landmine. He *could not, would not* betray his mom. But this was Father Rick! Adam was a pretty fair liar, maybe even a gifted one, but he would lie to nuns only when there was no other choice, to priests only in extreme emergencies and to Father Rick never. To lie to a priest, especially to the priest who you made your First Communion with *and* your Confirmation *and* who used to hear your confessions even as they started to go whack . . . well, that could land you some awesomely serious time in Purgatory.

Adam looked at his feet. "So yeah, Dad's real good, Father, and . . . Look, we paid for the candles. Wolverine, the guy you talked to? Well, he stuck a tenner in the slot. You can check."

"I see. I think." Father Rick blew out of his lips in a way that made his cheeks flutter. It was one of his best tricks. It used to break Adam up at mass. "Well, I like your new friends, Adam. They're . . . eager. My door will be open whenever *any* of you need it to be. You're welcome here is all I'm trying to say. Whenever and always. Welcome back." He nodded at Adam before heading back to the sacristy.

Adam felt lonelier as soon as the priest turned around. He missed this: the candles, Father Rick's weirdo way of knowing stuff without being told.

Didn't matter. Not important. He started for the candles.

"Okay, guys, have you had a chance to say a prayer for who-ever? There's an evening mass, so folks will start coming in soon." Most of them seemed to be reluctant to leave.

"He was real sweet, your padre," said Snooki. "I thought Catholic priests were . . . I don't know, way scarier. Have you ever seen *The Devil Inside* or the far superior cult classic *The Exorcist*?"

"Uh, no on the movies and, yeah, he can be major decent." They were almost at the doors by the time Adam's body realized that they were near the doors. And there it was. No! That hardly ever happened. *Not going* out *too? Not here, not with them. No!* Adam stopped short.

Why?!

Snooki caught it. Confused at first, she crooked her head this way and that. Her earrings swatted her shoulders. "Okay," she said brightly. "So we'll meet you outside, right?"

Before Adam could even nod, Wolverine, with a greasy flourish, opened the damn door for Robyn. "After you." He smiled.

Robyn looked at her feet. "Thank you, Wolverine."

Adam watched them file out. Shame and raw anger competed for dominance.

Thor was the last one out. "New pants, kid." And with that the massive bronze doors shut, taking away most of the light.

"You bet, Thor," he whispered. His eyes burned as he began what was now an unbearable exit ritual.

Even though nobody saw.

Adam moved backwards thirty-three precise paces, then forward thirty-one, then back twenty-nine . . . hating himself more with every single humiliating step.

CHAPTER FIFTEEN

Adam didn't look at Chuck, couldn't. Eye contact made him twitchy. He knew he was messing up. He hated knowing it. He didn't mean to, didn't want to, but there he was in the passive-aggressive hall of fame.

He kept his eyes trained on the bookshelf right behind the therapist. None of the titles, he realized with a mixture of interest and alarm, were learned volumes from the psychiatric field. They were works of fiction. And they appeared to be ordered but not in a pattern he could discern, certainly not alphabetically by either author or title. There was Mark Helprin's *Winter's Tale* and David Mitchell's *Cloud Atlas*. It looked like he had everything by Don DeLillo, Richard Ford and William Makepeace Thackeray. Chuck had *Animal Dreams* by Barbara Kingsolver, *The Secret History* by Donna Tartt, *Bel Canto* by someone whose name was obscured, two copies of *The Curious Incident of the Dog in the Night-Time*, three books by Philip Roth and lots and lots of skinny poetry collections. And that was just the top shelf. Adam had never heard of any of them. There was no Dickens or Steinbeck or Melville or anybody that he was forced to read at school. And there was no non-fiction.

Chuck lowered his aviators and turned around to face his bookshelf. "Don't worry, I get all I need professionally from the online sites the hospital subscribes to. Can we continue?"

Adam must have nodded, because they did.

They talked about how it went at church with Group, a bit about the door thing, about maybe trying out for track in the spring, about how amazing Robyn was and about how he hadn't been able to get to any of the lessons in the OCD manual. "No, none, sorry."

"Have you been keeping up with your breathing exercises?"

"Yes," he lied, while eyeing Jerzy Kosinski's *The Painted Bird*. Maybe he could borrow that one.

They did not talk about what a dick he was. Adam knew he was being a dick. But he didn't know why and he didn't care to find out. He still hadn't touched the manual and he'd had it for months. He also knew he was supposed to ask Chuck about something but he couldn't remember what. It was okay, didn't matter. Forty-seven minutes in. He was squirming on the inside.

"You okay?" Chuck almost frowned. "You look a bit fidgety, my man."

Maybe on the outside too.

"No, sir, I'm cool," he lied. Again.

"Is there anything that's ramped up the stress or anxiety, Adam? Your mom? Anything at all?"

The letters, the letters, the letters. Adam still hadn't pieced together the one in his jeans pocket. That's how much of a dick he was.

And she had received another one on Friday.

Carmella had taken a bottle of Chardonnay to her room that night. She had never done that before.

"No, sir," Adam said. There were also books by Ian McEwan. He'd heard of Ian McEwan. Maybe. "No, there's nothing."

Chuck nodded and glanced at his watch. "Okay, so the List?"

"Uh, yeah." Adam pulled a sheet out of his jacket pocket. "I didn't have time to finish it, sorry." That was because he had just started it in the waiting room. "Look, I'm . . . I'll do better next month, I promise, sir." *Dick.*

"I know you will, and don't call me sir." Chuck said it in such a way that they both believed it was possible. "Hey, you didn't even *do* one last month, so this is a step up." He unfolded the paper.

Not much of one, thought Adam.

"How about I read it out loud this time?"

Adam flinched.

"But we don't have to discuss it. Fair?"

"I guess." *One, three, five, seven . . .* At least he didn't have to tap in order to count anymore.

Chuck cleared his throat.

November 17   **THE LIST**   Adam Spencer Ross

Meds: Anafranil 25 mg 2 x per day
Ativan as needed 5–7 per week

Primary presenting compulsions: Counting, Clearing, Threshold issues

Chuck looked back up. "Are the meds okay, the levels? Should we raise the Anafranil? Maybe it's time to switch over from Ativan to clonazepam?

"No!" Adam was hit with a physical flashback of all the nightmare side effects, the roller-coaster nausea, the itching, the thick-tongued numbness he'd felt with all the drugs before they'd finally settled in on the Anafranil/Ativan combo. "It's cool, really. I'm good." He edged forward to the end of his chair, ready to leap. *Five more minutes.*

Chuck returned to the crumpled piece of paper.

1. I believe that Robyn is starting to see me different and that she's the best thing that has happened to me since all this crap started.
2. I believe, no, I KNOW that I am 5 feet 7½ inches tall and I'm growing even as I write this. Almost three inches so far!! I believe that this is a superior example of the power of love.
3. I believe that maybe the threshold thing is ratcheting up a bit and maybe the counting too, but I'm getting way better at doing that in my head.
4. I believe I have to work on the I have to stop lying so much. It's kind of making me sick.
5. I believe that my mom is

Chuck looked up again.

"I ran out of time." *Thirty-three, thirty-five . . . One, three, five . . .*

"Do you want to—"

"No. I don't, if it's okay." Adam had screwed up by mentioning the letter the last time. That was a mistake. He would have scribbled out number five but Chuck had opened the door to call him in, so he couldn't fix it.

Chuck turned the paper over as if the rest of the List would magically appear on the other side. "Adam, when we get into exposure response and prevention therapy we're going to need your mother's support. She'll have to come in and at least—"

"Not gonna happen, Chuck. You know it and I know it. We're on our own here. Hey, look: five-thirty! Time's up. I know there's some other wing nut out there that's desperate to get in here."

"Adam."

"I'll do better, sir."

They both stood up.

"Look. I *know*." He finally met Chuck's eyes. *"Okay?"*

"Okay." Chuck nodded. "See you Monday."

"Yeah, you bet." He made a beeline for the door. "That was awesome, thanks! See you at Group."

He had to get out, couldn't breathe. *Seventeen, nineteen, twenty-one, twenty-three . . .*

CHAPTER SIXTEEN

"**D**ad?" What the hell?

Adam, Robyn *and* Wolverine were exiting the clinic's ground floor together when Adam saw him.

"Dad?" he repeated. He would have bet his Warhammer collection on the fact that his father didn't know he even went to a support group, let alone where it was. No, that was a lie. His old man paid the bills.

Mr. Sebastian Jeffrey Ross was leaning against his blood-red Jaguar, arms crossed, one leg in front of the other. He straightened as soon as he caught sight of Adam. "Son."

"Everything okay? It's not Mom, is it? Sweetie? Brenda?"

Mr. Ross threw his hands in the air. "Hold up! Everything's good. Well, you know, mainly. Going to introduce me to your friends?"

"Uh, yeah, sure."

"Hi, how ya doing!" He extended his hand towards Robyn. "I'm Adam's father."

Robyn blushed and shook his hand. "Robyn Plummer, sir."

"This the girl Wendell's been talking about?" he asked Adam.

Impale me on a rusty sword and feed my entrails to buzzards! "Dunno, maybe." He was going to kill Sweetie, immediately and often.

"Hi, Mr. Ross," said Wolverine. "I'm Peter Kolchak, Wolverine."

Wow, his Christian name, thought Adam. Not even Father Rick had got that out of him. Adam's dad nodded at Wolverine but kept smiling at Robyn. "It's a real pleasure to meet you, young lady. Is that a Chapel High blazer? Good school."

Robyn answered while Adam agonized.

What was this about? He *needed* to go to the cemetery with Robyn. He needed to be with her, to see if . . . In the week since the church field trip, Adam had been replaying Wolverine smarming her, opening the door, brandishing his ten-dollar bill, being all smooth and tall. So he needed time alone with Robyn at their spot to see if she . . . well, to see if they still were . . . What *were* they exactly? What if she'd already gone out with Wolverine? There'd been a whole weekend in there. He was developing an ulcer as they stood there.

But then again.

Wolverine didn't have that smug, I've-been-with-her-already look. Not that Adam was airtight sure that he'd recognize that look, but he was pretty sure that Wolverine wasn't sporting it. Did she like Wolverine? Of course she did. Even Adam liked Wolverine. The guy was older, cooler and, as of late, slightly less crazy. Speaking of which, Adam's anxiety was erupting like silent farts all around him. His father snapped him back to the crisis at hand.

"Sorry, kid, you're needed at home. Uh, I mean my home."

Well, *that* was awkward.

"Which is *your* home too, *of course.*" His father cleared his throat. "Wendell"—his father would chew tinfoil before he called his younger son Sweetie—"Wendell's a bit sick with strep and is inconsolable and that means no one will do but you, champ."

Robyn stepped over to Adam. "It's okay, we can walk over next week."

Yes! This meant that she had intended to walk with him in the first place. They were good, they were tight, they were a *they*. Practically. Relief bubbled over him. "Yeah, next week for sure! Yeah. You bet, Robyn!" He'd tripped back into SpongeBob mode.

"Well, then, Robyn, how about the two of us walk together as far as the subway station?" Wolverine asked, all casual-like.

Before she could answer, Adam's dad threw his arm around his son. "Yup, you would not believe how much this guy's baby brother adores him. Worships him, in fact. And Adam steps up every single time, no matter what the inconvenience." He slapped his son on the back. "Helluva thing!"

"That is so, so sweet, Batman!"

"Hey, that's what Wendell calls him too! It's a thing you guys do, right? Cool."

This was crazy. It was as if his father knew exactly what to say and how to say it. *His* father. "Yup, as soon as I come in with old Batman here, Wendell will be right as rain! Happens every time!"

Robyn looked at Adam like he was a piece of chocolate.

"Well, it's been a pleasure, Wolfman." Adam's dad turned back to Robyn. "Robyn, a *real* pleasure. But now we gotta go. A super-hero's gotta do what he's gotta do, right?"

"Later, man." Wolverine punched Adam in the arm.

Adam did *not* wince. "Yeah, man."

"Bye, Adam," said Robyn.

"Bye, Robyn. Catch you next week, okay?"

She turned. Wolverine turned. Adam and his dad got in the car. The blisters in his stomach came back.

"I'm sure she nodded," said his dad.

"Huh?"

His father turned the ignition key. "When you said that about catching her later. I'm sure she nodded. You'll definitely have to watch that wolf guy, though. Hey, she's older, eh? Real cute too. Quite a find, I have to say—yes, sir! Now that's my boy!"

"*Daaad,* you're, like, creeping me out here."

"Oh. Sorry, kid." His father stared straight ahead as he drove. Adam felt shorter.

"But . . . well, thanks for back there, for what you said about Sweetie needing me."

"Hell, it's true."

"Yeah, but the way you said it, you made me look real good, I think. Don't you think? *I* think you did."

His father contemplated the stop sign. "She likes you."

Adam thought of the prayers and the rosary and the holy water and all the Catholic trappings. "No, she *needs* me."

"That, you will soon come to realize, is pretty much the same thing, my son."

Sweetie needed him *and* loved him. Adam was knocked flat as soon as he got in the door.

"Batman, you came! I knew you'd come, they promised you'd come! I'm sick, Batman. My troat is stripped. Do you want some of my banana medicine? It's delicious. I'll give you some. We can have it with dinner. Our mom, Mrs. Brenda Ross, is making us lamb stew. Thank you, thank you for coming home, Batman!" Adam was slobber-hugged some more.

The kid still felt hot. Adam forgot about killing him.

"Mrs. Carmella Ross called and wants you to call her back."

"Let the poor boy breathe, Sweetie!" Brenda came into the

hall, took Adam's backpack and kissed his head at the same time. "You're growing like crazy! You are! Speaking of growing, I got you two new pairs of grey flannels. They're on your bed, in your *real* bedroom. You'll be taller than your father by next week!" She smiled at him like she was proud of every inch.

"Let's go, Batman!" Sweetie put his hot plump hand into Adam's.

"No, Sweetie, give Adam a minute to wash up and call his mom, okay?"

"Okay." Sweetie sighed, and then sighed once more just in case they had missed the first one.

Adam took the stairs three at a time. No anxiety blisters at all, not here, not now. He had a major mojo going for him. He should do his List right now. Robyn *needed* him. He was growing. Dad tried real hard to do a cool thing for him. He had new pants and there was lamb stew for dinner! He punched in his phone number.

She finally picked up after six rings.

"Mom? Hi, it's me."

Nothing. The temperature in the room changed.

"Mom, are you there? I can hear you breathing."

Still nothing.

"Are you okay, Mom?"

"Adam? Adam, I can't stand it. There's been another one. Another letter. Adam, who could hate me that much? Who, Adam? Who?"

CHAPTER SEVENTEEN

"I'll come right home. I think I should come home."

"No." Her voice was strangled. "I shouldn't have called. No, Adam."

"I'm going to come home now."

"No, baby, don't. I'm fine."

"Mom, I'm coming," he said. He said it many times and his mom refused each of those times.

"No, it'll make them all suspicious . . . make it worse."

They argued.

She won. And she was calmer, stronger in the winning.

Adam stayed with a feverish Sweetie and worried just as feverishly. He should have gone home.

No wonder he was nuts.

After he had "smooshed" Sweetie in good and tight, Adam went in search of his jeans to retrieve those bits of paper from his pocket. He had conveniently forgotten all about the letter when he'd gone off with Ben that night and then he'd kept on forgetting. The letter fragments were shoved into the overflowing junk drawer of his mind. Adam had many such drawers. Unfortunately, neat freak that Brenda was, she had washed the jeans. The papers had rolled themselves into tight little worms.

It took him over an hour using Brenda's tweezers. There was some photocopy-type paper, but there were magazine and newsprint worms as well. He unrolled them on his bed one at a time.

It was like on TV. The guy was cutting up magazines and newspapers and pasting his crap onto the most common paper there was. So they were dealing with your garden-variety psychopath who had watched too many *CSI* reruns.

The words were bone-marrow ugly. Adam retrieved *bitch, die, slut, cow, diseased,* two *whores* and three *shoulds,* and a word that was so disgusting he re-balled it as he read it. The rest of the worms were unreadable. Thank God. He couldn't stop shaking. Adam shut the junk drawer again.

Douchebag.

He tried a few breathing exercises, but since he didn't really know what he was doing, they didn't work. He thought about Robyn. He thought about how her hair smelled like ginger but she somehow smelled like peaches. He stopped shaking. He thought about how she crossed her legs at the ankles and had that one deep dimple on her left cheek, about how her freckles moved around when she laughed and about how all that made him dizzy. And yet even with all that Robyn immersion, the letter with all its filth would sneak in like a sprinter and take off again. And his fear would bloom all over again.

When he got back home the next day, his mom pretended that everything was okay. It was as if she had never even called him.

There was no call, no letters. And Adam, because he was such a gutless douchebag, pretended right along with her.

Chuck was on him at next Group. Adam could feel the therapist tracking him during the session.

"Batman?" Chuck leaned in. "Do you have any further thoughts on Iron Man's condition or on Wolverine's suggestions?"

Wolverine had offered suggestions? When? Damn. Adam crossed his legs, the manly right-foot-over-left-knee way. "No." He shrugged. "No, I'm with the Wolf on this one." He shrugged again for good measure.

"Okay, superheroes, that's about it." Chuck shut his file folder. "Good session." He took off his glasses and smiled. "Class dismissed, go out and play. Adam, a quick word?"

Noooo! She'd leave without him.

The others evaporated. Chuck turned to him.

"So it's just you and me. You're clear that Group is your safe place, right? You still down with that?"

He had to tap. He hadn't needed to tap in so long. "Yeah, sure." Just counting wouldn't do. But Chuck would see, would know where to look. *Thirteen, fifteen, seventeen . . .* He tapped his tongue on the roof of his mouth.

"I've noticed the past couple of weeks that you're not really here. That's not like you. You cycling up again?"

Thirty-one, thirty-three . . .

"Adam, you were doing so well."

"I'm on it," Adam said. "No worries. It's nothing I can't get a grip on. Same old, same old, you know?" *Except for the new stuff.* "Group has been amazing for me." As he said it, Adam realized that it was sort of true. When did it become true? "If it ratchets up any more, I'll reach out. For sure."

They nodded at each other.

"Cool. Just try to remember I'm here and they're here for you. Talk, Adam. Got it? Talk."

"Got it."

If he ran he could catch up to her. If nothing else, Adam was getting to be a fair runner. He'd taken to running back to his house once he parted with Robyn at the cemetery gates. Then, for no good reason, Adam had started running another couple of times a week. In the middle of all that buzzing anxiety, running made him feel . . . well, if not like a Batman at least a bit more normal. He was definitely toying with the idea of trying out for the St. Mary's track team in the spring. Yeah, he could catch her. He raced down the stairwell at lightning speed and into the lobby.

"Hey! Where's the fire?"

Robyn.

"Hey, wow! You're . . . you waited."

"Of course I did." She smiled, looking like a goddess in a red puffy ski jacket. Adam got liquidy again, except for the part that didn't. Thank God he had on a big coat.

He should kiss her now. She'd waited. She had *waited* for him. He moved towards her.

"Wolverine would've waited too," Robyn said brightly, "but he had another specialist appointment right after Group."

Talk about your mood killer.

They set off.

But he *should* have kissed her.

"Oh, and before I forget." She gave him a folded piece of paper. "I know you don't have a cell, at least one that you'd be seen with, but that's my cell *and* my home phone number. Like, you could call me from home and we could talk, you know? So call, okay?"

"Okay."

She wanted him to call her! He had her number. They might as well be engaged! Maybe he should kiss her now.

No, they were walking too fast.

The cemetery was like a different country in early December. The headstones, grass and trees had all slipped into comfy grey and brown pyjamas. When they got to the old willow they stopped without a word.

Robyn turned to her mother's grave and made the sign of the cross with a careless grace that would have made Father Rick proud. She pulled out the rosary. When she prayed, so did Adam. He prayed for God and the stone angels surrounding them to keep her safe and sane even if he couldn't.

"I told you I was the one who found her, right?"

Adam nodded. The hairs on the back of his arms bristled. He was alert, sensing if not danger exactly, something—some dark thing. But he did not tap or even count. He stayed with her. She shivered. He shivered.

"A plastic bag." Robyn frowned as if still surprised by the choice. "Chuck knows, and my shrink, of course. Yeah"—she looked up at the willow—"Mummy put a plastic bag over her head. Like, how do you not yank it off, you know? How? I tried it once."

"Jesus, Robyn!" Adam swallowed a sick panic but did not count or tap. He held his ground.

"It's okay." She squeezed his arm. "It was for less than a second, honest, just to see." She pulled him back onto the path. "Hey, brighten up. I have great news. It's official, I'm off meds!" She squeezed harder. "As of last Friday. My shrink feels I'm making unbelievable progress. I just have the clonazepam for emergencies."

Unbelievable. "Hey, unbelievable! Congratulations!"

"Well, I may have to go on a little something for some other thing, but we're monitoring that. But yeah, I *am* getting better, Adam."

And he wanted that for her. It was everything. For sure.

His mouth felt like it was full of dirt.

He'd be better too, maybe. If it weren't for the letters . . .

He should kiss her. A congratulatory kiss would be entirely in order. It would be righteous! Yes! Instead Adam threw his arms around her. Coat on coat, mittens on mittens, wool scarf against wool scarf. Lame. How *much* did he suck? He was king of the sucks. But he hugged hard.

And she hugged back, nestling right into him.

Adam buried his face in her neck, her hair, inhaling peaches and ginger and Robyn.

When he finally let go, Adam was taller and older, basking in her smile.

It would all be brilliant—*he'd* be brilliant—if it weren't for the letters. The letters were torpedoing everything. Who the hell was doing it? It could be anyone, from anywhere, even someone they *knew*. *He* knew. Like Wolverine. Yeah, to get at him? No, that was too whack, even for him. But the timing sort of fit.

No, Wolverine wasn't that sick.

But someone was.

"What's up, Dark Knight?" She put her arm through his. Proof positive that they were a *they*.

"Nothing."

She stopped, turned to him.

"No, really. I am so righteously stoked right now."

And she laughed. *He* had made her laugh.

But even with all that superior excellence, two singular thoughts snaked their way into his brain and nested.

The first was about the letters, always the letters. He couldn't shake the memory of his mom's anguish when she'd got the last one.

And the second was that Robyn was getting better while he was getting worse. His mom was losing it and Adam would lose it right along with her if he wasn't careful. He needed to be more vigilant.

When they got to the gates, he risked all and hugged Robyn again. "Congratulations on the meds thing. You are amazing, I mean it!" He risked even more by grazing her cheek with his lips, an *almost* kiss.

"*You* make me feel amazing, Adam. You do every single time." She hugged him right back even after the kiss, even with people walking by and seeing and everything. "Call me, Adam—I mean it!"

He watched her walk away with his protection, his armour. And then he was left without any, alone with his racing thoughts. The damn letters. Whoever wrote them was possessed by a sickness so putrid that it felt like a hot, smothering wind. And still he was cold. *Seven sets. One, three, five, seven, nine . . .*

CHAPTER EIGHTEEN

"Hello."

"Hello, may I please speak to—"

"Batman? Adam? It's me, Robyn! It comes up as 'private caller.' Hey, you called! And only four days after I thought you would, but hey!"

Was she mad? No, she was teasing. Wasn't she? Should he tell her that he had picked up the phone exactly one thousand and thirty-five times in the intervening four days?

Probably not. But maybe. No. *Stop!* He had to stop his mind from jumping hurdles that weren't there.

"Hey, yeah, I've been real busy practising my casual but cool phone conversation."

Robyn laughed.

She thought he was kidding.

God he loved the sound of her voice. "So yeah, how are you?"

Her pillowy lips were on the other end, right near his. In some alternate-world way it was almost like kissing. Okay it wasn't, but Adam was getting desperate, so yeah, it was.

She would taste like peaches, for sure.

"I'm good. Just about to start in on chem, but I'm glad you called. Really glad."

They both breathed into the receiver for seconds that seemed to grind on for hours.

"So, uh, is there . . . *why* did you call?"

Yes. Why?

"Just wanted to hear your friendly voice, I guess and . . ."

"And?"

"Well, we sort of didn't finish our conversation back at the cemetery the other day. Not really, or at least I didn't. Okay, I didn't even start it and, like, you were so open talking about your mom and how you're getting so much better and everything."

"Yeah, I don't know why I blabber so much to you. Maybe because at Group, with the others, you're so solid, you know."

Solid? Him?

"Definitely not just another *pretty boy.*"

"Wait, are you saying I'm *not* pretty?"

"Stop fishing, Adam."

He could hear the smile in her voice.

"And hey, maybe I'm kind of hoping that you'll talk too. Talk to me, Adam. It helps. Whenever I tell you something, you're just so . . . well, it helps. *You* help."

His face warmed. It was her lip-gloss that smelled like peaches. He remembered now from when he'd hugged her in the cemetery. That didn't mean that *she* would taste like peaches.

"Adam?"

"I'm here, sorry."

"Look, maybe I trust you, and maybe you could trust me too?"

Did he? Was it about trust? He got lost in the *wanting* again.

It was just always so right there with her. He had wanted to kiss her *so much*. Maybe she would still taste like peaches, even if it was only lip-gloss that made her *smell* like peaches. "There *is* something—something I haven't even told Chuck."

"Not even Chuck?"

"No, not even Chuck. Well, I started, but I stopped. It's complicated because it's not about me, not directly. Sort of like with your mom."

"I'm here. I *get* complicated. I promise."

"So yeah, she, my mom, is getting these, like, anonymous letters and they're sicko and they freak her out. And I, I've got to say they're sort of freaking me out too. It's . . . they're that bad."

The relief was faster than instant.

And relief trumped shame. Relief even trumped his fear of her reaction. So much relief from letting go of one dirty little secret? Or were all secrets dirty? Maybe even the clean ones were like magnets inevitably attracting slithery things.

He was stunned.

Adam *told* and the world didn't wobble. Robyn did not mock him, or threaten unwanted action. The secret lost its power, *poof*.

"Okay, that's sick, Adam. Way harsh. How many so far?"

"Three or four or five or more. I don't know. She used to try to hide them. I just saw a bit of one. It was like in the old serial-killer movies, you know." Adam made an executive decision *not* to go into how he fished out shreds from the garbage and then forgot about them in his pocket. "Like when the deranged guy cuts out words from newspapers and magazines and glues them onto the paper."

"Wow, that's extra creepy. Do they threaten her? Like, really technically threaten?"

"Yeah, well, maybe no," he said. "They're nasty, but not directly, I don't think. I haven't seen them really, but it mainly sounds like they call her terrible things and tell her to die, but not like he is going to kill her."

"Or she," corrected Robyn. "Did you google 'threatening letters' or whatever?"

"No, see, I can't. Only at school. And I—"

"Sorry, sorry, I forgot. Hang on. Let's just see, shall we? I'm going online now. I have a new iPad! Daddy got it for me the day I got off meds. Cool, eh?"

"Yeah, for sure." Again, the scraping inside his stomach. "You deserve it."

There was a pause. "Adam, I started off way worse. I was in residence, remember? For months." Another pause. "But you're going to do great too and I swear you're, like, ten feet taller. Hell of a Group, all in all, eh? Here it is, I'm looking up 'receiving anonymous letters.'"

"What?!"

"On the iPad. I'm looking up—"

"No, the other thing. The taller thing."

"Come on, don't tell me you haven't noticed. It's *your* body. Snooki's noticed."

"She has? I mean, that doesn't matter. But you can actually tell?"

"Geez Louise, you're taller than me. You're heading into Thor and Wolverine territory. Didn't you notice when you hugged me?"

"Uh." *When he hugged her and her lips smelled of peaches.* "Uh . . ."

"Got it! www.ehow.com. *How to cope with receiving anonymous letters.*"

"That sounds good. What's it say?"

"Okay, sooo there are five tips. One . . . *mutter-mumble . . . Remain* calm and form a plan to cope with the person and any future letters."

"I've been telling her. Thing is, she just rips up the letters. What next?"

"Okay, two . . . *mutter-mumble* . . . *Only cowards write anonymous letters, and most of them will tire if they receive no response from you.*"

"Yeah, I sort of thought or hoped that, but it's so many letters now. When does it stop?"

"So number three is . . . Never mind, that's on e-mails. Number four says, *Check with local authorities. They can help you track down—*"

"Yeah, that's not going to happen."

"Okay, the last tip is to, uh, basically call a lawyer or a private investigator, to seek professional help because this can threaten your physical or mental health and—"

"Not gonna happen either. But thanks, I'll keep it all in mind. Promise."

"You're the kid, Batman."

"Huh?"

"Look, I know you're a guy and you're fifteen and everything, but your mom, she's the parent, right? And she is, like, a big deal at a hospital. I overheard Chuck say. She would know about this stuff."

"No. Well, maybe, yeah. She's like a supervisor and she heads committees, so yeah. I guess."

"You're not the one in charge."

Wanna bet?

"Adam?"

"I'm here."

"Okay, so why not the cops?"

"She has other issues that could be a problem if anyone . . . She's not . . . She has issues, and it's complicated." Adam felt more disloyal with each word. He was shaking by the second "issues."

Silence again. Not so awkward this time. He could hear her breathing at the other end. If only he could see her, see her lips.

"The *collecting*?"

He nodded, even though she couldn't see him.

"Adam?"

"Yeah." He kept nodding. "Yeah, the collecting. It's a no-go."

"Okay, how about good friends—of your mom's, I mean?"

"Yeah, not so much. Not anymore. There is no one else, Robyn. *I'm* the one she tell things to. I'm everybody."

Silence.

"I get it, and your dad's out with the divorce situation and everything." Adam could almost hear her thinking. "I know this is nuts, but how about your stepmom?"

"Brenda?"

"Yeah, you talked about how her and your mom are bordering on being friendly."

"Yeah, that's true, but no. You see, Brenda's cool and all, but she kind of has her hands full with my little brother. He gets a bit anxious and that makes her anxious and off they go. But you gave me some real good ideas off the Net. That whole 'plan for the next letter' thing and that it's a coward, et cetera. Good to know. I mean it, thanks. I'm glad I called."

"Are you?"

"For sure. I get to hear your voice, and yeah, like, it was good just to get it out of my head and say it out loud." And the funny thing was, it was.

"You know what *I* know for sure?"

You don't have to *see* a smile, you can *hear* one. Her beautiful mouth turned up, one dimple at play. It was contagious. Adam smiled too. "No, what?"

"That it's all good for me. Like, maybe *you're* good for me. See you Monday, Batman!"

Robyn hung up while Adam was constructing what he should say and how he should say it. He held the phone in his hand long after he heard the dial tone, still smiling.

He did not count.

CHAPTER NINETEEN

Adam's heart ran laps around his chest, threatening to break a land speed record. He could conquer the universe.

He had *told*. He had told *her*. And Robyn had not run off; she'd stayed and they'd talked just like two *normal* people out there in world who cared. Normal. This was what *normal* felt like?

Su-weeet.

Adam bolted up the stairs three at a time. He needed to measure himself against his door jamb right away. But once there, he froze. It wasn't a threshold thing. It was a confusion thing. What if she was just messing with him? He leaned hard into the door, waiting for the nausea to pass.

From the time he could stand upright, Adam's height had been dutifully measured and recorded by his father's pencil markings, and then his mother's, and now his own. He grabbed a ruler and laid it flat on top of his head. The temptation to angle it upwards and make himself taller had to be resisted each time. Five foot seven and three-quarters! Yes! He'd be six feet by Christmas. Anything was possible!

He was good for her! She'd said it. Out loud. Maybe she didn't mean it, though. Maybe she just felt sorry for him. His stomach lurched. No! She wasn't like that, wouldn't do that. He *was* good for her. And she liked him. He picked that option and tried to stay with it, but couldn't.

Adam's feelings stumbled and tripped around like out-of-control drunks; he was jubilant one minute, drowning in anxiety the next. This was love? It was like being held hostage by a terrorist. The feelings from hope to horror were crazy intense and changed on a dime. If only he knew what she thought. Why couldn't girls tell you exactly what they were thinking the moment they were thinking it? The world would be a better place, yes, sir. But at the same time, he couldn't stop grinning. Adam felt like he was starring in an Italian film. If only he smoked. He should smoke. Maybe smoking would calm him down some, focus his mind without the tapping. He would *not* tap. He should go for a run. No, his mom would be home soon.

Adam paced around his room but stopped as soon as he realized he was doing so in precise concentric patterns. He reached for the figurines but did not touch them. He could do the List. Yes! He felt instantly awful for not keeping up with the List. He'd promised Chuck, promised himself. This time he'd have it all ready to go for his next one-on-one. It would blow Chuck away.

Adam ripped a sheet out of a notebook. He was perspiring, but began writing before he lost his nerve. He wrote it all while standing.

December 11 **THE LIST** Adam Spencer Ross

Meds: Anafranil 25 mg 2 x per day
Ativan as needed 4–6 per week

Primary presenting compulsions: Ordering, Tapping, Counting in Head, Magical Thinking re: Thresholds

Damn. He remembered now why he hated doing these. Full-frontal reality. Reality sucked. He sucked. What massive suckage to see just how much he sucked on paper. And he was getting worse— no use denying it—which was suckier still. The Ativan dose was a lie, but he did not correct it.

"Adam? I'm home, finally!"

He heard his mom shoving things away and knew that she did so without really seeing the mess. "I'm just finishing up some English homework," he called. "Dinner's in the blue CorningWare thingy. Stick it in the microwave."

"Thanks, baby!"

He heard rattling, shuffling, ice clinking. Vodka on ice. Adam shut his door. Robyn. He could do it if he thought of Robyn.

1. I believe that Robyn Isobel Plummer is my one true love and that love CAN conquer all.
2. I believe that if I am good and strong and courageous and above all NORMAL, Robyn Isobel Plummer will love me back. I can wait. I am patient. It will be worth it.

3. I believe that it is possible to be fixed. Most of the time. And I believe that my mom will get helped, somehow, but I don't know how.

4. I believe that Stones is still my best friend and that maybe the guys in Group are kind of like friends.

5. I believe that my mom loves me, and that my father loves me as best he can, that Brenda loves me, that Sweetie loves me and that they all worry about me, and it makes me feel bad. Well, Sweetie worries about everything except me. He thinks I'm invincible.

6. I believe that even numbers wreak havoc in the world and I am trying not to believe that Wolverine has a similar kind of effect.

7. I believe that lying is sick and makes everything sicker, and that liars can never be trusted. But then again, everybody lies.

8. I believe that thresholds are becoming a bigger problem for me. They now include, in various degrees of toxicity: the gym doors, biology lab doors, vice-principal's office, English class and south entrance at school; the front bronze doors to Holy Rosary (in and out); the side doors to Brenda's place; the John Street subway entrance; the 7-Eleven near the cemetery; and as of today, just a bare hint, so maybe not, but . . . okay, maybe as of today, the front door to 97 Chatsworth. This scares me.

9. I believe that I am a coward but I'm working on that. I mean I WILL work on that. Really.

10. I believe that there are times that my molecules are nuclear and that they'll explode, raining radiation on all those I love unless I execute certain cleansing and clearing rituals, but I'm going to work on that too.

There. Adam touched the paper eleven times as he reread his List. It was bad, no doubt. But not nearly as bad as he thought it would be. Chuck was right. Lists were good. Staring at it straight on was like taking himself straight on. That's what Chuck said. Big long exhale. Okay.

He'd kind of been scaring himself lately.

"Honey? Adam, come down, baby, and keep your old mom company. I brought apple fritters from Sweet Jenny's just for you."

He nodded to himself. "Okay," he called.

He read the List one more time, congratulating himself on his honesty and progress, before he ripped it to shreds. One more inhale, one more big exhale. Adam got up, dry-swallowed two Ativans and went downstairs.

"Coming, Mom!"

CHAPTER TWENTY

Group had just started and already Adam had trouble hearing through the blood rushing in his ears. That happened sometimes—okay, a lot. He'd have to cut down on the Ativan. It could be a new goal, a good goal. He strained to listen, which only elevated the sound of his own breathing. Chill. This was a *safe* place.

"So what do you say?" asked Chuck. "Shall we adjourn to more festive surroundings for our last session of the year. Field trip?"

"Like, you want to go back to the church? I'm up for it." Green Lantern nodded with alarming enthusiasm.

What!?

"Yeah, the church was cool," agreed Iron Man. "And I'd like to see Batman's pope again."

"Priest," Adam managed. "Father Rick is a priest."

Chuck shook his head. "No, not the church."

"Well, I'm not doing that politically correct shuffle," huffed Snooki. "I for one am not going to drag my ample ass to a mosque and then to a, a . . . what is it that you Jewish people go to?" She turned to Wonder Woman. "A temple or a synagogue?"

"Don't look at me. I've been to a church now more than I've been to temple," said Wonder Woman. "Anyway, I wouldn't mind lighting more candles. I got a real buzz out of that."

"Yeah! Yeah, for sure!" snorted Captain America, and this was followed by vigorous head-nodding from Iron Man. Wolverine looked bored.

"Whoa, guys!" Chuck put up his hand. "Not today, okay? You can go back to Batman's church whenever you want, but for today I was proposing we go over to a coffee house. I called up Jeff at Slave to the Grind around the corner and he's keeping that whole back area open for us. What do you say? Coffee, anyone?"

"I'm in!" Wolverine was up and ready.

Snooki yanked up Wonder Woman. "Us too. May we assume they do a non-fat latte?"

"Skim milk has calories too, you know!" sniffed Wonder Woman.

"I could do with a double espresso!" said Captain America. "A double espresso would be good. Double espresso. Ass up, Batman."

Adam and Thor rose as one. Thor looked as baffled as Adam felt. He growled in Batman's general direction and off they went, slipping into coats and scarves and mitts on the way down. No one suggested it, or made excuses—they all just took the stairs.

At the café, Adam got separated from Robyn while they were lining up. Chuck was at the head, followed by Wolverine, then Robyn, then Green Lantern, then Adam with the rest of them in a fidgety formation behind Thor.

"Hey, Robyn, let me get this." Wolverine waved a twenty. "My treat."

Adam bit down and gritted his teeth. Wolverine had offered just as Adam was trying to figure out if he had enough money to pay for two coffees. This whole thing SUCKED! He needed an Ativan. Adam had never been in a coffee shop before. He was *so* not part of St. Mary's after-school Starbucks club. How much would it be? What should he order? How should he order? They could charge him anything—fifty cents or fifty bucks—for all he knew.

Chuck stepped out of line and waved his arms. "Yo, super-heroes, I've got this, okay? It's on the house—"Then he stopped, realizing that everyone in the place was looking at him. He lowered his voice. "It's on me. Enjoy, okay?"

The other customers were still staring. Again Adam wondered what they all looked like to regular people. It had gotten so that he could barely see them without imagining some aspect of their superhero costume magically appended. Except for Snooki, of course. Adam still had no idea what a Snooki was or what her costume would be, except that it would be formidable.

Without warning it was his turn. The girl behind the cash asked him for his order. Robyn, Wolverine and Chuck were ahead of him, waiting by the "barista" for their orders.

Adam started to sweat energetically. Maybe they had tea, but he only liked Earl Grey and he couldn't see Earl Grey on the chalkboard. What the hell was a green chai latte?

Thor leaned into him. "Americano black, double shot, and don't put any shit in it. Milk and sugar are for pussies. They're all watching."

Jesus, the guy had turned into a motormouth.

"An Americano, double shot, please?"

"Small or large?"

"Oh, um, well, sma—"

Thor cleared his throat.

"Large, please," he squeaked.

"And drink the whole damn thing, or they'll know you're a faker."

Adam nodded. "Sure. Thanks, Thor." Okay, how bad could it be?

Nine chairs were already arranged around three small tables. Since Thor and Adam didn't need any embellishments for their manly Americanos, they caught up to Chuck, Robyn and Wolverine. Thor not so delicately blocked just enough space to allow Adam to wedge in and sit right across from Robyn. This way he could look at her *and* touch her. She pulled her braid around and forward. God she was beautiful. It shocked him every time he saw her. Her lips were all shiny and peachy again. *How do girls do that?* He'd swear he hadn't taken his eyes off her since Group.

After a seemingly interminable wait for coffee ordering, sorting, running back for waters and a round of biscotti for the table, Chuck raised his large cappuccino, extra-dry. "To us. Good work this semester, lots of—" He did a quick scan of the room to make sure that no one else was paying attention. "Lots of good progress. I wish you all great holidays, and I want you to know that you're a terrific group of . . . well, you guys are awesome, and I mean that."

"Aw hell, he likes us better than his other nutjobs." Snooki raised her cup.

"To us!" offered Green Lantern. This was followed by clumsy cup-tapping, cheering and coffee spilling.

Even though he was unsure of the protocol, Adam also raised his cup and cleared his throat. "And I propose a toast to our teacher, healer and shrink, Dr. Chuck Mutinda, who's responsible for making us the superheroes we are today."

Thor came in with a "Hear, hear" so deep and rumbling that it sounded like a subway was running underneath them.

None of them quite knew what to do with the new Thor. His

mouth was set in less of a grimace—if not a smile, then some neutral expression, which on Thor exuded goodwill. Robyn mouthed "That was so sweet" at Adam from across the table. He did not think his world could get any better.

Then he took a swig of his Americano.

That he did not projectile-spit it out was a testament to his love for Robyn. That he did not cough violently was a testament to his fear of Thor. Instead Adam gulped. It was like black tar thinned with diesel fuel and flavoured with essence of dirty socks.

"How's your coffee, Batboy?" asked Wolverine.

"Rich," he said, taking another gulp. "Good."

"The superhero stuff *was* inspired, Chuck." Wonder Woman said this so softly that everyone leaned in. "And it's kind of a hoot when you think about how the identities either line up to us or are, like, the exact opposite of us."

"What do you mean, WW?" asked Wolverine.

"Well." She took a sip from her black coffee, and Adam noticed that she was jiggling her left leg. She did that a lot in Group too. "Well, you're a bit of a hypochondriac, right? And Wolverine has this magical healing factor."

"Hmm . . ." Wolverine folded his arms. "I grudgingly concede your point."

"And, like, Iron Man's alter ego is a billionaire super-cool playboy," said Iron Man. "And I . . . well, let's face it, me not so much."

"Yeah, and Green Lantern's alter ego is always facing down his fears," said Tyrone about his namesake, "while I just wish I could. And, and Captain America was like a frail little kid who was super-enhanced to the point of human perfection, and old Jacob here, he could do with a bit of enhancing."

Captain America threw a wad of napkins at him.

"And Thor . . ." continued Wolverine unwisely.

Sharp intake of breath all around.

Adam took another gulp of goo before declaring, "Mighty Thor is forever exiled from his homeland and therefore slips in and out of Warrior's Madness. Nuff said, right, Thor?"

Thor growled.

"We're definitely a sketchy mash-up of the Justice League and the Avengers." Adam took another deep swig of liquid dirt and willed his eyes not to water. "We should franchise. Am I right, or am I right?" Was he talking too loud?

"Damn straight, our ever-so-dark-and-handsome Dark Knight!" Snooki leaned over to high-five him, her breasts not quite delivering on the promise of tumbling out of her tube top.

Once the male superheroes got over that particular disappointment, the two Leagues settled back into little groups to dissect holiday plans, potential Christmas gifts and medication variations. Adam was buzzing with his newfound . . . well, he was just buzzing.

When it was time to leave, Robyn took Adam by the arm and drew him aside. "I'm not walking today."

She was mad? Was it the Snooki thing? He shouldn't have looked; she must have caught him looking. No, she was smiling at him. Why was she smiling at him? Thank God she had such a supremo smile, because if she didn't, he wouldn't have been able to take his eyes off her chest. Snooki's seriously ample tube top had re-alerted him to the potential wonders of that real estate and now he couldn't un-alert himself.

"I'm meeting my dad at his office and then I'm going to help him buy the four presents he has to buy each year, including mine."

"Oh yeah, sure. Well, yeah, yeah, yeah, but see . . . thing is." Thing is, Adam wanted to give her his present. He had bought a small crystal bottle. It reminded him of her as soon as he saw it in the antiques store window on Greene Street. The antiques guy said it was for perfume, but Adam had filled it with holy water from the church. Well, Father Rick had filled it for him. And Adam thought it was such a fine present that it might be deserving of a kiss. Never mind *might*—for *sure* it would be deserving of a kiss. Kisses, even. Multiple *kisses*. Yes! *Kisses, kisses, kisses.* Adam's heart galloped at a speed unknown to him, even in mid-anxiety. "So I was actually thinking that, before you said you couldn't . . . I mean, I was thinking that I wanted to, but then you said, and I understand, but . . ." Adam had that sinking feeling that he was making less than no sense.

"But"—Robyn touched his arm again, interrupting his high-speed bumbling—"but I hoped you'd come over one day. To my house, I mean. Over the holidays?"

He was stupefied into stone. Then he erupted again because he heard Thor's *grrrarruh* somewhere in the distance. "Sure! Absolutely great. Yeah sure, you bet! Are you kidding!" Adam nodded so forcefully it felt like his head was going to fall off and roll under a table. What was the matter with him? "Great, great, great!" He was shivering but only on the inside. And he wanted to dance. He wanted to hold her close and dance. Where did one go to learn how to dance?

Wolverine, who had been bantering with the superheroes, socked Adam in the shoulder. Why *did* guys do that? "So Merry Christmas, Batboy, and see you in the new year, kid."

Kid? Kid! Who is he calling a kid?

Adam wanted to slug him, was going to slug him, and would have slugged him for sure, except that he had to pee real bad.

Wolverine turned to Robyn. "Heard you're going downtown. Me too. Let's catch the subway together."

That's it! Just as he was winding up to hit him, Robyn put her hand on Adam's again. "So call me, Batman." She said that loud. The whole coffee shop heard. More importantly, Wolverine heard.

Adam wanted to jump up and down, really needed to jump up and down.

Then she leaned into him. "It's the coffee. Don't worry, it'll pass." And she winked.

He'd never seen that before. Well, not in real life. He winked back and then couldn't stop.

Still winking, Adam looked up and over to Thor, hoping to catch him as he left. Thor looked disgusted.

People hugged him and punched him and shook his hand while wishing him the best holidays ever. And even though he felt like he was going to bust a kidney, couldn't stop twitching and his heart kept revving, Adam couldn't remember ever feeling this good. Coffee. Why had no one ever told him about coffee? Like, damn! He could conquer the world on coffee. Maybe Robyn would make him some at her house. He was going to call her and they would arrange a time for him to come over!

It had to be a date, for sure it was a date—calling and time-arranging sounded definitely date-like. It was official: they were dating.

God he loved coffee.

CHAPTER TWENTY-ONE

"It doesn't last, honey," his mom said. "I hate to burst your bubble, but your body gets used to the caffeine and the buzz goes bye-bye." Carmella stood on her tiptoes and kissed Adam's head. "Hey, cut that out! I can't reach the top anymore." She ruffled his hair. "Come here, let your old lady show you how to make a cup of filtered coffee. Use lots of milk and sugar or you won't get it down." She plugged in the kettle. "You can practise drinking it non-stop over the holidays so you'll never get caught short with your friends again."

"But at the coffee shop—"

"Yeah, I know you said you got down an Americano—straight." Carmella smiled big, but only with her mouth, not her eyes. "I suspect that had more to do with the object of your affection being there than any real ability to drink that stuff."

She knew. Somehow, his mom suspected that there was a girl. It was all the showering—he'd bet on it. He should have told her. When had he stopped telling her things? He should tell her now. They could have a "moment."

The moment passed.

"Now, do you need any help with your Christmas gifts?"

"I got it under control, Mom."

And he did, at least the present part. Despite his Ativan increase, the escalation of the threshold issues and even an ever-so-slight increase in interior counting, Adam felt certain this would be the best Christmas ever. Maybe other "divorced" kids wrapped themselves in longing for Christmases when they were little and had an "intact" family. But Adam had had enough sessions with Chuck to be clear-eyed about how those *family* holidays actually went down. Year after year, Christmas was poisoned by arguments and long dirt-dry spells of his parents not talking to each other unless it was through him. There were entire holidays when the three of them were held hostage in the same house, wanting to be anywhere else. His mom would say things like, "Adam, tell your father that if he wants to have dinner waiting on Christmas Eve, he has to give me a clue as to when he might deign to come home." And his dad would say, "Adam, you can tell your mother that my work doesn't revolve around a punch-clock. I come home when I'm done, get it?"

He didn't. Adam never "got it." To this day, despite all his sessions, he didn't know what, if any of it, was his fault. Should he have "told," gotten more traction in the middle? Should he have warned her about the "collecting"? If he knew, why didn't she? Brenda's house was all gleaming surfaces, right angles, glass, steel and marble—a cup on a coaster looked wildly out of place—and his father loved that. Even as a little boy, Adam knew that his dad did not like counters cluttered with six kinds of cow-shaped butter dishes. Why didn't his mom?

He should have warned her. Did he even try?

Chuck used to say that wasn't his job, that he was just a child. And Adam believed him eventually, and most of the time. So he had no illusions about the magic of a childhood Christmas. But he *knew* that this would be the best Christmas ever. It would be the Christmas when he got superior, stellar Christmas gifts and gave everyone gifts that were even more amazing.

Yeah, it shouldn't matter so much.

But it did.

This year's circuit was Christmas Eve at his mom's and Christmas Day at Dad's. The first miracle was that there was no drama or bitching about why and with who and for how long. It just worked.

Both parents had long come to terms with the week-to-week custody stuff, but they usually reverted badly at Christmas—until this Christmas. On December 24 Adam and his mom exchanged gifts when they got back from midnight mass, their first in years. Still, giving his mom anything was always fraught for him. The thought of adding any item to her smothering swamp of stuff bathed him in anxiety. But he gave her a little lacquered black box with a red satin interior. He had unearthed two of them in the antiques shop on Greene Street.

As much as she cooed and oohed over her gift, it couldn't match how blown away Adam was with his. The big-ticket item was his very own Kindle preloaded with a superior stock of graphic and dystopian novels. "I know the computer stuff is still verbo-ten"—Carmella grabbed his face and kissed him—"but no one said anything about a Kindle, and soon, baby, soon, you'll be back on smartphones and computers driving me crazy."

The even *bigger*-ticket item was garbage bags.

"Wait here, Adam, this is the *real* present." His mom disappeared into a section of the dining room that was long past habit-able and, with some effort, lugged out two big bags full of garbage.

"See, honey, I'm bringing them to the curb right now! And there's two more. Merry Christmas!"

"Wow, Mom! Let me help." Adam jumped to his feet.

"No, baby. I need to do this on my own."

And out Carmella went into the bitter cold night with her shredded slippers. Then she scurried back in and hauled out two more green bags. When his mother returned she promised on her life that she would fill at least two bags a week until the clutter was all gone. "Merry Christmas, Adam Spencer Ross!"

Yet Carmella's biggest gift was one she didn't even know she gave. Adam knew his mother had received another letter and kept it from him. She didn't let on, didn't react, didn't freak out. She held it together the whole day. It must have arrived on Christmas Eve with the afternoon mail. Adam only found out when he spotted the torn strips of paper in the garbage. For weeks now he had taken to carefully examining the kitchen trash on a daily basis.

His mom had wanted to give him a great Christmas. She did.

Adam did not fish out the scraps.

On Christmas Day, Adam's dad presented his son with a very elaborate yet poorly wrapped big box that contained increasingly smaller awkwardly wrapped boxes until he got to a single envelope, which contained a $300 gift certificate for the BattleCraft store in the mall. His dad looked like he was going to burst when Adam immediately called Ben with the news.

Brenda bought him clothes, which sounds lame, except they were clothes that she'd picked up at the TNT store. Adam had grown out of just about every dork non-school outfit he had, and the new T's and jeans and hoodies were beyond superior. He knew this because his four-year-old, deeply unusual brother always looked way cooler than anyone else on the monkey bars.

Sweetie could not be contained. He flew at Adam with a perfectly wrapped box that he then helpfully proceeded to unwrap for him. It was a Batman Dark Knight beach towel.

"It said 'Our price $14.99' and Mrs. Brenda Ross said that I had that much, so she bought it for me online, but I picked it by myself. And I paid, because she took my money. When the doctor lets you, you can go to www.ultimateshirt.com, the Batman Collectibles section." He galloped around the living room. "I love it. Do you love it? You *must* love it."

"I love it to pieces!" Adam tackled him. "It's totally badass!"

"And if you really want"—Sweetie sighed with all the gravitas of a tenured professor—"I mean, really, *really* want, you can even take it to your other house with Mrs. Carmella Ross."

"That's very generous of you," said Adam.

"Yes," he agreed.

Sweetie was pumped about the new dragon night light that Adam had bought him from Pottery Barn. Sweetie *loved* Pottery Barn.

"It's *our* Puff the Magic Dragon, right, Batman?"

"None other," said Adam.

Adam's dad had bought Brenda a double strand of pearls that even Adam recognized as beautiful. Usually, his father told Brenda her gift was from both of them, but this year Adam had bought her a present of his own for the first time. His gift was the twin of the black lacquered box that he'd bought for his mom. Brenda acted like he was the one who had given her pearls.

"Oh, Adam!"

"Batman," corrected Sweetie.

He had done good.

"I'll treasure it forever. It's gorgeous and I'm so touched and . . . well, thank you. Thank you so much."

On Friday afternoon, December 27, Adam's dad drove him to Robyn's house. It was hard to tell who was more wrecked.

"So you got her a gift?" asked his father.

"Yeah, of course I got her a gift."

"You gift-wrapped it? Girls like gift-wrapping."

"Yeah, of course I gift-wrapped it. See?" Adam retrieved the little red wrapped box with gold ribbon from his backpack.

"Hmm, good wrapping." He nodded approvingly. "You know you can invite her to our house, right? Brenda would be cool, I promise. I mean, you know you can't invite her to—"

"Chatsworth, yeah. Believe me, I know." Adam winced. Aside from the condition of the house, there was a small issue of Robyn still thinking that he lived nearby. *Everybody lies.*

"And don't babble. You tend to babble when you're nervous."

"*Dad!* I won't babble. I know enough not to babble. *Geez.*"

"But don't go mute either; it pisses them off. I should know."

Adam groaned.

"And compliment her on her shoes."

"Her *shoes?*"

"Yeah, it's like a thing with girls that apparently everybody knows. If you notice their shoes, it shows, uh . . ." Adam started tapping the car armrest and his dad fiddled with the windshield wipers. "Shit, it shows artistic integrity, for all I know. I dunno. I *do* know that women like their goddamn shoes."

"Okay."

"And the most important thing, whatever you do, don't stare at her breasts."

"What? Dad! You are, like, so grossing me out!" Adam squirmed, thinking back to the coffee shop.

"Be that as it may, I was your age once, and I'm saying do as I say, not as I did. It's like the opposite of the artistic thing. She's 'into you,' Adam, or whatever the kids say these days—don't screw it up with breast hypnotism."

"Really, *really* grossing me out here!"

And then they arrived. The house was a big old Victorian. A home built for a family.

"Nice." His father nodded. "Take a cab home, it'll impress her. Remember, only eye-to-eye or eye-to-shoe contact, and I'm proud of you, big guy, 'kay? Now, go get her, tiger."

Adam got out of the car. It felt like he was being frog-marched to a firing squad. This kind of thing was not for him. What was he thinking? He wasn't thinking. His height had gone to his head. *This* was for other guys, *normal* guys, not freaks who obsessed about whether they were going to have some schizoid threshold issue in front of their beloved's doorway. *Snap out of it!* He made the sign of the cross. Couldn't hurt, right? He did not backtrack or tap. Instead, Adam kept putting one foot in front of the other on the never-ending path to her door, rehearsing his laid-back cool pose with every step.

When he finally knocked and realized that he had had no threshold vibrations whatsoever, Adam almost keeled over with relief.

Robyn opened the door, exuding peachiness and shiny lips and breasts, amazing perfect . . .

"Hi," he said. "I like your shoes."

CHAPTER TWENTY-TWO

"Hey! Oh! Yeah, uh." Robyn looked a little confused but kept smiling. "They're UGG slippers, got them for Christmas—but thanks!"

"No problemo!" Adam had never noticed Robyn's teeth before. Given that he was so kiss-obsessed, this surprised him. Robyn had beautiful, pearly, almost-perfect teeth behind those peachy, pillowy lips. Almost perfect. She had this one rogue eye-tooth on the left side. It turned outward and was slightly askew. It was adorable. He wanted to touch it.

"Let's go into the kitchen. Maria's prepared real hot choco-late—I mean, really real, with melted chocolate and milk."

He'd been hoping for coffee but said "Cool" and followed her like a puppy. Adam wondered if all housekeepers were named Maria. Brenda's housekeeper was named Maria, as was his mom's when she had one, all those years ago. He had adored his mom's Maria, and his mom's Maria had adored him.

Within seconds it was clear that Robyn's Maria did not.

The introductions were excruciating. Maria seemed to know

that he was from Robyn's Group. She therefore knew that he was *not* normal.

Robyn took them both in and got it. She directed Adam towards a big old harvest table that was pushed against a wall in their big old kitchen. Maria did not take her eyes off Adam as she poured the chocolaty liquid into a mug that proudly declared he was *The Best Dad in the Universe*.

"Maria, Adam is the one who has been teaching me about becoming Catholic."

Maria's dark, coal eyes warmed, but only by half a degree. Clearly, Catholic did not trump crazy for her.

"He goes to St. Mary's and he introduced me to Father Rick at Holy Rosary. But remember not to tell Daddy."

Robyn beamed. Maria snorted.

Adam took a careful sip of the best thing he had ever tasted and said, "This is the best thing I have ever tasted!"

Maria snorted again, finished pouring and reluctantly left the room.

"She likes you," said Robyn.

"Yeah, she has that Thor-like warmth."

"Exactly!" Robyn laughed. "You're the only one who registers with him. I swear he hates the rest of us. You, Adam Spencer Ross, are like the horse whisperer of Group."

"It must be my trusty armour of honour."

Robyn blushed. Why?

Still in mid-blush, she jumped up like a Pop-Tart. "Ooh! My friend Jody and I made triple-threat brownies this morning. Wanna try?"

Adam slurped his hot chocolate. "Hey, in for a penny . . ."

"In for a pound," Robyn finished. "My mom used to say that."

"My stepmom says that all the time."

While she was cutting up the brownies, he had a perfectly reasonable reason to stare at her. "I love brownies. Cut lots!" Actually, Adam wasn't all that fond of chocolate, but it was the first time he had seen Robyn out of her school uniform. His ears got hot—like, *who else* does that happen to? Robyn wore skinny jeans and a nice bluish top that hugged in a way that made him hurt. *Think of Sister Mary-Margaret! Whatever you do, don't look at* . . . but there they were, right there under that top, her amazing, brilliant brea—

Look at her eyes, look at her eyes, look at her eyes. "That top makes your eyes look awesome, you know?"

Robyn stopped mid-stride with the plate of brownies in hand. It looked like she was struggling to say something. Instead she smiled.

"Why, thank you, Adam. I didn't think you even knew what colour they were." She shut them tight.

"Grey," he said. "Shades of grey most of the time, except days like today, when they're blue."

"Touché, Adam." She placed the brownies on the table and immediately began rearranging them. "Did you have any trouble with my door?" Robyn asked it casually, like she was asking whether it was still raining.

His heart whooshed. Casual or not, it was *so* not a normal thing to ask a normal boy. He had to count. He would *not* count. But now his skin felt too tight, like he should get up immediately and jump right out of it.

He shook his head. "No, not your door."

"I'm glad."

Twenty-one, twenty-three, twenty-five, . . .

But then it was good again. They gossiped a bit—well, quite a bit—about Group mainly. Robyn tried and failed to explain the premise of *Jersey Shore* to him. She also tried to look blasé when she revealed that her dad was taking them to Bermuda for the rest of the holidays. "It's that 'they try' thing again." But she was beaming, so he bit down on his disappointment and tried to beam right back at her. They also talked about the idiosyncrasies of their "normal" friends. Adam just had butterball Ben, but she looked genuinely interested as he laid out the intricacies and pure pleasure of marathon Warhammer games. Robyn, of course, had a pile of friends and went on to list the food disorders and pill-popping antics of three of them, including Jody of the brownie baking. "The girl is a walking bakery, but she does not touch anything she bakes," said Robyn in wonder. "No licking of fingers, no crumb nibbling, nothing, nada."

"How is that possible?" He shook his head. "The whole not-eating thing . . . Hey, I know I have my thing—okay, things—but *not eating*? I so don't get how you can not eat."

"Exactly! I purged for, like, a minute but I *ate*, you know!" Robyn reached for a third brownie. "She looks like hell too, a real lollipop."

He must have looked blank.

"You know, all head, stick body. I tell her all the time but she can't see."

They chewed happily for a few seconds, each revelling in a tiny thrill of righteousness. *At least we aren't crazy like that.*

"People can't listen until they're ready," Robyn said. "I sure couldn't. I was, like, deaf to everyone except the thoughts. They were the boss of me." She stopped, looked at her feet. "You know, I never talk like this to anyone, not even the shrinks." She finished her hot chocolate. "You're good with everybody, and you were right from the beginning. Wonder Woman, Thor, even Wolverine."

Adam's head shot up.

"Okay, maybe not Wolverine," she allowed. "But what is it about you?"

You, he thought. *The thing about me is you. When I'm not crazy, all I think about is you.* "Nothing." He shook his head. "Absolutely nothing."

"Ah, but it is something, Dark Knight." She seemed to be searching. "You make me feel ... I don't know, kinda good, I guess."

Safe, Robyn. I make you feel safe. It's all I want. He wanted to say that. To tell her. He should tell her.

He didn't tell her.

"Thanks," he said. "So how are you doing?"

"I took a couple of clonazepams over Christmas, but just a couple," she confessed. "Christmas is weird."

"I'll say," agreed Adam.

"But I'm still off the big guns, and I'm good most of the time. The praying helps. How are you doing with ... well, how are *you* doing?"

"Not as good." Adam shut down. He shouldn't have shut down; he knew better. Robyn liked it when he talked. *Just two sets: one, three, five, seven, nine ...*

He would have sworn she was going to reach for his hand but instead she glanced up at the wall clock. "Oh!" Robyn covered her mouth. "Sorry, Adam, but my dad will be home in a minute, and although he knows I'm having a friend over, it's just better that for now, uh ... Next time for sure. I'll manage him properly and you can meet, but Dad does take some prep."

"More than Maria?"

"Maria is like being stoned on happy pills and getting a massage at a spa compared to my father."

"So you're saying I should go?" He smiled. "I should be insulted."

"Sorry, but . . ." She walked over to him. Close. He could feel her breath, could smell her brownie-infused hair. "I'll make it up to you."

"No, if I should go, I should go," he said, trying not to look relieved. Adam would also need some serious prep before meeting the father of the girl he was going to spend the rest of his life with. "I'll take you up on the make-it-up-to-me promise, though." Who said that? What was happening to him? He felt thirty. He wasn't counting, didn't even finish the second set. He felt great. Keeping up with himself was exhausting.

"But wait, wait!" Robyn dashed over to a cupboard and came back bearing a small box. "Your Christmas present!"

"Right! I am a total douchebag," Adam said, rummaging through his backpack. "I've been thinking about this moment for, like, two weeks—since the coffee shop, even. Here's *your* Christmas present."

"You shouldn't have!"

"But I did," he said, growing at least another inch.

"On three," she said. "One, two, three!" They tore open their gifts.

Adam cut through first. "Wow! What's in this?" Robyn had given him a big black ceramic coffee mug embossed with a gold Batman logo. It was filled with a bunch of oddly shaped things wrapped in cellophane.

"Chocolate-covered coffee beans, to break out only when necessary. As I recall you're seriously in touch with your inner superhero when you're high on coffee."

His ears got so hot, he was sure she would be compelled to say something about it. She didn't.

"It's my favourite gift, Robyn."

She swatted him.

"No really, and it's been a banner year for once. Thank you." He had a moment where he knew he could—should—kiss her. That it would be okay, appropriate even. The moment passed. "Now you," he said.

Robyn reddened to burgundy as she opened the box from the antiques store.

"Careful," he warned as she lifted the little bottle.

"Wow! It's so precious! I've never seen anything like it. What's in it? Is that perfume?" *The way the curve of her beautiful neck dipped . . .*

"No." Adam shook his head. "Holy water from Holy Rosary."

"Oh, Batman . . . er, Adam . . . It's so incredibly thoughtful. I love it."

"I would give you everything in the world if I could."

"Damn it, Adam!"

What!?

She looked pained or something. Oh, what he wouldn't give to be able to read girls' facial expressions!

"That's it . . . I just can't anymore."

His heart, which was now firmly in his throat, stopped beating altogether. *Can't anymore?* "What did I do! What? I'm sorry!" *Shoulda kissed her when you had the chance, douchebag.*

"No." She shook her head. Tears puddled in her eyes. "I can't stand it, not with you, not *to* you. Look, I have to tell you something and then you have to go right away. Please, please, please. I talk and then you go? Not a word or I'll disintegrate, okay?"

Adam nodded. It was the best he could manage.

"You'll hate me, and I'll hate that you'll hate me, but now I hate me more and it's making me slide."

"Robyn, Jesus." He reached for her. Took her arms into his hands.

"Shh! Don't say anything, promise? We'll talk about it later, at the cemetery. I'll answer your questions, or try, but not now, not now."

He nodded again.

"My mother did not kill herself."

Whoa. He loosened his grip and she wriggled away. He started to say it didn't matter, nothing mattered but her. She put her hand against his chest to ward off words.

"Don't even look at me right now. I'm a monster but I have to just say it. She's dead and everything—that's her real grave we go to—but she died of breast cancer. My . . . my mom died way too young, but sort of ordinary. It wasn't enough, see? Or so I thought. When it all started, when the thoughts and the compulsions, the cutting, when I became its prisoner, I think I needed a big-ass reason as to *why*."

He reached for her again, and again her hand shot out. She wouldn't be touched.

"How screwed is that, eh? I know, I know, dead is bad, but it wasn't bad enough, get it? I thought I needed *more*, a *bigger* reason for why I was so crazy. So I told some kids at school in 'secret,' and then . . ." She looked up at the ceiling. "Then I couldn't untell it. But killing herself, me finding the body . . . well, I thought that would be a way better reason to explain the way I am, *was*. See, everyone would say, like they still say, 'Well, of course, what do you expect? The poor kid found her mother. How could she not be a train wreck?'" Robyn shook her head. "You should have seen me then—the past few years, I mean. I was one hot mess, and *that's* the truth."

And still, I would have loved you. He tried to tell her. He shouted it silently.

She didn't hear. How could she? His pounding heart obliterated all sound.

"How warped and, and . . . never mind. I'm going to tell Chuck. The shrinks at the hospital know, but I am a shockingly good liar, so the kids at school, my friends, don't know. And I would totally understand if you never . . . You're the first person . . . I am so sorry that I lied to you, Adam. Especially you." She put her hand through his arm and led him to the door. "I'm disgusting." All the blood had drained from her face. She was whiter than a cloud. "I would absolutely, totally understand if—"

Adam lifted her chin and caressed her face. "Everybody lies, Robyn. Everybody."

"See," she said, leaning into him. His lips grazed her hair. "See, there you go again." And she kissed his cheek before she shut the door.

CHAPTER TWENTY-THREE

Adam took the bus home. He had money for a cab, but since Robyn thought he lived just a few blocks away, that would have been mental. *His* lie. Okay, there were a few others, but that was one of the big ones. Adam also needed time to sort himself out before he got home. He took the bus and then he walked.

Her lie was massive no matter how you dressed it up. Monster, really. It would be brutal living with that big a lie. It got complex. He knew from experience.

And he loved her more today than yesterday.

The truth was that Adam loved her *way* more today than he did yesterday, and how was that even possible? Maybe because Robyn *needed* him. Okay, maybe not right away, this minute, since she and her dad were leaving tomorrow for Bermuda. But as soon as she came back, Robyn *would* need him. He *had* to get better. Fast. He had to take care of her. *Time's a-wasting! Chop, chop! Let's go! Smarten up! Hurry up!* And then he was there, home, 97 Chatsworth. He cratered, but just a bit.

Before he did anything, Adam checked to see if the coast was clear. A middle-aged man was dragging his golden retriever down the street. The dog had on those bizarro shoes to protect its paws from salt. He looked embarrassed—the dog, not the man. The wind picked up and bit into Adam's face, but he didn't move. He waited until they passed. It grew dark in the waiting. Adam checked again: clear. He inhaled and walked up to his door.

Step one at this point comprised putting his forefinger and index finger together in a mock blessing. Fingers just so, Adam began outlining the entire door precisely two feet away from it. He had to do this five times to the right and seven times to the left. He heard it on the third time to the left. The crying.

Inside.

His heart sped up. But he couldn't break through. What was it? Christmas? Another letter? Some fresh new hell? Adam muffed the last trace and had to start again. Now he was sweating despite the cold. First, trace out the door starting on the right side. *Focus, Adam! Concentrate!* The first round completed, he backed up for fifteen perfect steps and forward in the exact same steps as if they were marked. If he missed one, he had to start again. Not just to the backing up but all the way to the initial tracing. At his second full confrontation of the threshold, he had to extend his right arm as high as it could go and tap out the evil one hundred and eleven times. Again, if the position was incorrect or he got distracted in any way, shape or form, he had to begin all over. The final steps were palming the door handle thirty-three times in one direction and eleven times in the other, then turning it and pushing with both palms flat on the door with precisely equal pressure. The equal-pressure thing was tricky.

On average that week, it took Adam approximately eleven minutes to enter 97 Chatsworth, and it was rising. He knew it was bullshit, just his stupid thoughts; it meant nothing, didn't do a damn thing. Yet he felt the need to layer on ever-newer rituals in order to keep his mother safe, in order for it to feel "just right." This time, despite the corrosiveness of his mother's crying, Adam was almost flawless in his execution, with only the one repeat needed. He entered within nine minutes of starting.

"Mom? Mom, I'm home."

The crying stopped. The kitchen faucet went on. Pots clanged.

"In here, baby! I'm making your favourite—beef stew! I thought you'd had enough of turkey, huh?"

Adam's favourite was actually lamb stew, but what the hell. He could smell it now, as the panic in him subsided and he made his way into the kitchen. "Great. Hey, Mom, you okay?" He examined her as she dried utensils and stirred the pot at the same time. Eyes red, but dry. She gave him a big shaky smile.

"Sure, baby!" Carmella nodded at the pot. "Onions, garlic, you know. But it's going to be delicious! I confess to a fair bit of sampling. Can't wait to hear about your Christmas and your visit with *Robyn*!" She sang out her name. "Sorry, kid, your father ratted you out."

"Yeah, no, I'm sorry." He struggled to get an even breath. "I've been meaning to tell you." Adam scanned the counters. Clear. Well, at least free of letters or paper of any kind. It had to be in the garbage.

"That's okay, baby. It's a guy thing—I get that." She stirred the pot so hard, the stew was going to be churned into soup at this rate. "I know you'll love it. Lots of potatoes and no peas, just for you! Happy day after the day after Christmas! Hey, take off your coat, stay a while."

"Okay." He continued scanning. She could have tossed the letter into the next room and there would be no way of telling.

"I'll just get rid of the trash while my coat's still on."

"That's my boy."

Was she relieved?

Adam opened the cupboard door and struggled to free the full-to-bursting Greenearth garbage bag. She only ever bought on sale but she also only ever bought that brand. Carmella was loyal in a thousand ways. He picked up the bag and pretended to tie it up while his mother rustled for plates and cutlery. When he got to the curb Adam rummaged through the potato and carrot peelings, the onion and garlic skins and a layer of beef fat. There it was: a crumpled white ball. It wasn't torn up this time. She didn't have time. So soon after the last one. Why? Who? Who could hate her that much? Adam shoved it into his coat pocket. Shivered.

The garbage hadn't been picked up yet because of the holidays and the big green bin was full, so Adam just laid down the kitchen trash beside the four green plastic bags of hoarding trash that his mom had thrown away as part of his "present." He turned towards the house and then turned back again. Adam picked up one of her garbage bags.

It was so light.

Too light.

Adam untied one as razors scraped his stomach. Then another and another and . . . they were all the same. There was nothing in any of the bags except crumpled-up bits of newspaper. None of her stuff, none of the hoarded garbage, none of what she'd promised. Just newspapers. He could tell under the streetlamps that it was *The Sentinel*—they didn't even get *The Sentinel*. She'd gone out and bought it!

Jesus.

Adam carefully retied the twist bands.

Oh, Mom.

He was tired and the cold snow and the garbage of 97 Chatsworth seeped into him. But then he thought of Robyn and warmed up all over again.

"I told you," he whispered to her through the night. "*Everybody lies.*"

CHAPTER TWENTY-FOUR

They got stoned on Red Bull and chocolate-covered coffee beans. Pathetic but true. More precisely, after five and a half Red Bulls and a bowl of Robyn's beans, Benjamin Stone and Adam Spencer Ross were flying higher than out-of-control kites.

The boys had spent New Year's Eve day at the BattleCraft store in the mall burning through most of Adam's Christmas gift certificate and Ben's Hanukkah money. It was a superior day and the evening was better. Ben's parents were staying overnight at his uncle's place in Springhill, so the house was theirs. Not that it mattered. In the face of all that freedom the boys stuck to the garage, maintaining a steady caffeine buzz while trying to break their Warhammer marathon record. Mr. and Mrs. Stone had long ago given up on the dream of ever parking their car in that garage again. Ben and Adam made a break for the house only to pee and replenish. A Warhammer game, Cheezies, Sun Chips, Maltesers and said Red Bull was their idea of heaven. Even though Adam may have talked about Robyn too much, it remained a fiercely righteous way to ring in the new year.

"Geez we suck, Stones," Adam burped at precisely 2:17 a.m.

"IknowIknowIknow," agreed Ben, who was vibrating from the caffeine. "The place is ours, the liquor cabinet is totally open, I *know* the 'rents wouldn't even notice if we helped ourselves, and here we are mainlining Cheezies. We suck. We are the very definition of 'suck.' In the dictionary beside said word will be a picture of you and me, dude."

"Hope it's a good picture."

This flung Ben into a fit of giggles.

"Damn, Stones!" Adam opened a fresh Red Bull. "We are even beyond sucking, man." He took a swig and passed it to his pal. "Thing is, *I* didn't want to drink because I was freaking about what booze might do to the Ativans I took after we left the mall."

"Holy rat-crap," said Ben.

"Yup," said Adam. "You know, you're the only guy on the planet who would put up with my wing-nut stuff."

"Right back at ya!"

"Serious suckage," they said at the same time, clinking their Red Bulls.

"Happy New Year, Stones!"

"We may suck," said Ben, examining the game table intently, "but we suck righteously. Thanks for being here, dork!"

"Geek!" said Adam.

"Nerd!" said Ben.

"Suuucker!" they said in a hopped-up unison.

The boys didn't return to the house until 5:15 a.m., after which they fell into a coma on the living room couch and floor, not waking until Ben's parents came home late that afternoon.

It *was* righteous, as were his two days at Brenda's with Sweetie and his dad, but not righteous enough to claw back on the Ativan. Adam was burning through his prescription too fast.

There would be some explaining to do to Chuck. The List—he should do the List.

Later.

Adam called Robyn twice the weekend she got back. The first time, Sweetie followed him everywhere repeating each word while mimicking Adam's every facial expression and gesture.

"What the hell were you doing?" Adam asked when he hung up.

"Practising," said Sweetie.

"What, driving me crazy?" asked Adam, trying to stay mad.

"Practising what to say to *my* most beautiful best girl when *I* fall in love," explained Sweetie. "Does your girl have a big chests?"

"Sweetie! That's so . . . no, she doesn't."

"Mine will," he insisted.

Adam had to promise to bake with Sweetie, in order to get fifteen *private* minutes for a phone call with Robyn the next day. It was worth it. It was a bad day. No reason, just was. His stomach clenched and unclenched so much that he fully expected to develop washboard abs by dinner. But he unclenched as soon as she said hello and he stayed that way right up until the start of their new ritual, the timeless argument about who should hang up first.

"You hang up, now," she said.

"No, you. I'll hold on."

"No, you."

"You."

"No, it's okay, you."

"No, really, you. I'll wait."

And on and on they went, teasing and testing. *Thank God* Sweetie wasn't around for that one.

Baking was a small price to pay. Sweetie became enthralled

with a lemon cheesecake photograph from *The New York Times Magazine* and he marshalled his forces accordingly. Brenda prepared the ingredients, read the instructions. She also operated the cobalt blue KitchenAid mixer that Adam's dad had given her two Christmases ago and Sweetie coveted. He was marking the days until he would be allowed to operate it by himself. Sweetie poured, combined, stirred and supervised. Adam was in charge of the lemon zest, making super-skinny worms of candied lemon peel, which would decorate the finished cheesecake. He took his duties, which included peeling, boiling the lemon in sugar water, drying and decorating, seriously. The cheesecake was genius.

"Adam made the lemon peels!" Sweetie said to his father in an uncharacteristic show of generosity. "But I bossed."

It was all so great, until it wasn't.

When it was time for Adam to leave, Sweetie was inconsolable in a way he had not been for months. Bribes, threats and general cajoling proved useless.

"But *why? Why* do you have to go?" he wailed. "We love you more than Mrs. Carmella Ross loves you. I heard Mrs. Brenda Ross say that to our dad! You'll be safe here, she said! You need to be here with us, she said."

"That's enough, Wendell Jefferson Ross!" His father dragged a stunned Sweetie, kicking and screaming, all the way to his room.

It was a largely silent car trip home.

"Sorry about that, son," his father finally said, wiping his face with his hand.

Son. It had a nice ring to it. His dad had been calling him that more and more these past few months.

"S'okay." Adam nodded. "No biggie."

"It's just that he—"

"I know he loves me. I know that, Dad."

His father exhaled.

"I had a good time, though."

"Good." His dad seemed to be absorbed with something in the middle distance. "Look, I don't want to pry into another man's . . . but, well, the girl?"

Adam smiled at the dashboard, remembering the sound of her voice. "It's good, Dad. I'm, like, *simply irresistible.*"

His father reached over and messed up his hair. "Yeah, you are, kid. You remember that even if I don't tell you often enough."

They returned to a companionable silence until they got to 97 Chatsworth.

"Don't wait, okay? Don't wait for me to get in."

His father's arms stiffened on the wheel. "Look, son—"

"Okay, Dad?"

"Yeah, yeah, okay."

After he heard the car drive off, Adam reached into his right-hand pocket, felt it and shuddered.

The letter.

It took him seventeen minutes to get into his house.

"That you, baby? I'm in the kitchen. Hungry?"

"Hi, Mom. No, I'm good. I'll be down in a minute, okay?"

"Okay, can't wait to hear all about it!"

Adam picked his way up the stairs carefully. He shoved a man's slipper to the right. Where had that come from? By the time he got to his room his heart was hiccupping. He felt a gnawing need to walk in concentric circles. No, he needed a labyrinth! He needed a labyrinth like the one set into the granite floor of Holy Rosary. He longed for it. Adam hadn't walked it since he was an altar boy, but he remembered with a crystal clarity how walking the labyrinth had calmed him in the days before the drugs, before therapy, before Group, before, before. Hell, *that* boy was practically normal.

He reached in for the letter and carefully unfurled it onto his bed. A few colourful pieces floated onto the floor, magazine word-bits that had come unglued. Judging by the empty spaces, Adam placed the bits into the spots he figured they belonged.

His head exploded.

DIE YOU STUPID BITCH DIE. WHY ARE YOU STILL BREATHING, YOU SLOVENLY COW, YOU PIECE OF SHIT? YOU ARE NOT A MOTHER. YOU ARE A SELFISH, PATHETIC, PSYCHOTIC. EVERYBODY HATES YOUR FESTERING GUTS. YOU ARE A DISEASE-RIDDEN MAGGOT AND SHOULD BE PUT OUT OF YOUR MISERY. YOU ARE RUINING YOUR SON'S LIFE AND THREATENING HIS WORLD. KILL YOURSELF BEFORE IT'S TOO LATE. DO ONE DECENT THING YOU WHORE. GIVE HIM A CHANCE AT HAPPINESS. YOU ARE AN ABORTION. DIE GREEDY BITCH DIE.

"Oh, Mom." He slumped to the floor. "I'm so sorry, Mom." Adam knelt in front of his bed. "Sorry."

"Adam, honey? I baked you a peach–rhubarb pie with the last of the frozen rhubarb we picked. Remember?"

Adam exhaled slowly, washing his face with his hands. *Aaargh, snap out of it!* "Great, I'll just clean up, okay?"

He rooted around in his desk until he found the lighter that he used for his models. Holding the letter over his wastepaper basket, Adam set it on fire. The burning paper made his throat feel as dry as burnt toast. *Oh, Mom. What the hell are we going to do?*

"Adam?"

"Coming," he said.

CHAPTER TWENTY-FIVE

The next time they talked, Robyn was on fire. "Okay, this is way past disgusting. You've got to tell Chuck. Next week, after Group. You should have told him last week. I'll stay with you. It will be okay, I promise."

This was wrong. She was taking care of *him*. He was supposed to take care of *her*. That was the plan, and the plan was everything. Adam would get fixed for her, be *normal* for her, save *her*.

"You know why I can't," he said. "The risks are too . . . Chuck is a professional and there are, like, rules about reporting and he might have to . . . My mom knows this stuff, you know."

"Yeah, yeah, I got that, but this has gone way off the road here, Batman. You have to talk."

"I *am* talking. I'm talking to you."

"And that's brilliant, really, but you still have to—"

"I can't, Robyn. I just can't. Look, it's complicated. You have to trust me on that. It's not going to happen."

"Okay, okay. For now. I'm just so worried for you, and her of course, but mainly for you."

So wrong.

"Hey, no one's threatening me, right? It's got nothing to do with me."

And on they went, hashing it out until it was time for their ritual of *who should hang up first.*

Adam spent the rest of the night agonizing. It was a massive mistake telling Robyn in the first place. What a turd he was. It was a load, a big one, too much for her fragile shoulders. How could he? What was he thinking?

He had to fix it.

But how?

The first ten minutes of Group had a reunion-party vibe. Not that he'd ever been to one. Everyone seemed stoked to see each other again, and that included Adam. While they were still milling about, he noticed that his motley mates were transforming into their alter egos, literally.

He noticed it first with Snooki, who got more tanned with each snowfall. "What's that on your head?" he asked. It looked like she was sporting a small hat made of hair.

"Oh!" Snooki patted her head. "I almost forgot! It's my poof."

Adam must have looked sufficiently unenlightened because she continued to explain.

"It's like a fake bump thing that you put under your hair to lift it right up so it looks like a poof."

"But why?" asked Adam.

"Men!" Snooki rolled her eyes. "So you'll look taller and thinner and like you have more hair."

While she was explaining, Adam realized that he had probably stepped in it. Had he hurt her feelings? "Well, it looks real nice on you. Not that you need to look taller, or thinner, or need more hair, or, or anything. I mean, you look great with or without hair."

"Why, thank you, Batman. I think." She batted her false eyelashes at him. "And Wonder Woman has her golden cuffs, see? Hey, WW!" she screamed across the room. "Show Batman your cuffs!" Wonder Woman raised two gold wrist cuffs with a red star in the centre of each.

"Righteous!" Adam gave her a thumbs-up.

"They were $31.50 on eBay and worth every cent!"

"Hey, whaddya know?" Iron Man came over to Snooki and Adam. "Look!" He pointed to his chest, where a round disc glowed impressively.

"Wow, man," said Adam. "That's the Iron Man light-up thingy!"

Iron Man snorted. "Please! It's my Arc Reactor. My mom actually gave it to me, if you can believe it."

It was like they'd all phoned each other. Captain America was flipping a red, white and blue shield. Tyrone was toying with a Green Lantern mask, and even Pete, who had already cornered Robyn, was growing in some manly Wolverine sideburns. Of course. Adam was going to start shaving with more vigour and twice a day from then on. He'd heard that the more you shave, the faster—

"Amazing, huh?" said Wonder Woman, who had bounced out of her chair to join them. "Did you get any superhero sompin' sompin'?" She winked at Snooki. Wonder Woman smiled but her eyes still had the same haunted look that had been chasing her since before the holidays.

Adam grinned. "Yeah, but it was like a Batman beach towel and a coffee mug with the insignia, you know?" Robyn looked over. "Which was my for-sure favourite gift, actually!" he said loudly. "I'll bring it in next week."

"No, you goof." Snooki gave him a playful push. "What are you going to do, threaten Gotham's diabolical criminal element with a cup of coffee? A mug is so not a part of the Batman brand. Here!" She passed him an oddly shaped ring.

"Put it on!" insisted Wonder Woman. "It's a Dark Knight ring and it glows in the dark with the Batman signal. Très cool, huh? Snooki and me bought it online when we got our stuff!"

"Wow, I don't know what to . . ." After a few tries it fit on his index finger. "Guys, I can't . . . Geez, this is—"

"Aw, save it, Batpants," said Snooki. "It was only $6.99, but you rock it!"

"Yeah!" agreed Wonder Woman while she checked out the room. "Now there's only Thor."

Even though he was clear across the room, Thor heard his name and frowned. Their Thor seemed to have superhero hearing.

"Who is so clearly Thor without a need for any kind of prop or anything," said Adam. "I mean, he has the long dark blond hair, rippling muscles . . . well, he's just the complete package as is, right?"

Their little group nodded vigorously. "Absolutely! Right! Perfect!"

Thor grunted.

"That leaves our little Robyn, or is she above all this?" asked Snooki.

"Oh, don't be such a bitch." Wonder Woman nudged her while Chuck called them to order.

Still, Wonder Woman tried to get Robyn's attention over the din of moving chairs and Wolverine's death grip.

"Robyn. Robyn. Pssst, Robyn."

Robyn finally turned in her direction.

"Want us to get you some of those green Robin gloves that come to here?" Wonder Woman tapped the crook of her arm.

Robyn looked around the room, taking it all in at once.

"Well?"

"Okay, Justice League and Avengers, welcome back and happy new year," said Chuck.

"Green gloves, $15.64?"

"No thanks, I won't be—"

"So who would like to start us off?"

Wonder Woman, Snooki and Adam all stared at Robyn, who reddened at record pace. *I'll get them myself, thanks*, she mouthed.

As usual, Wolverine led off and chewed up an endless amount of self-reverential airtime, which was almost okay because it left Adam free to count and wonder. *Thirteen, fifteen, seventeen, nineteen, twenty-one, twenty-three . . .* He was sure that Snooki had caught him even though he was strictly interior. It didn't matter.

I won't be what, Robyn?

Wonder Woman spoke in an increasingly smaller voice. Adam wanted to jump in and say something supportive or decent, but it was the food thing, not the small space thing, and Adam sucked at the food thing. Chuck wrote copious notes.

Just as they were winding down, Captain America took the floor and proposed that the superheroes go back to Batman's church for some candle-lighting to start the new year off with good karma.

"Yeah!" said Snooki and Wonder Woman in unison. The rest, except for Thor, agreed instantly.

"Batman?" Chuck asked.

"Yeah, cool. I mean it," said Adam as he got into his coat. "And there's, like, this labyrinth in the granite floor, right after the holy water receptacles but before the pews."

That had their immediate attention.

"Outstanding!" said Captain America.

"That place has this deep *Game of Thrones* feel to it," said Snooki.

"Yeah," Adam agreed, even though he didn't agree. "And, like, I've been thinking it would be kind of excellent to walk it again."

"Walk it?" asked Green Lantern.

"Yeah, you walk the pattern on the floor. Labyrinths are ancient holy things. You walk them and it's, like, instant chill."

"I'm in!" said Snooki, standing up.

"Me too!" Robyn snapped to attention and stepped smartly over to Adam.

The rest of Group fell in behind them, with Thor once again protecting or dragging the flank, depending on your perspective.

"Well, okay, then. I'll look forward to hearing about it." Chuck gathered his files and papers, smiling. "See you next week."

Adam was pumped about going back to Holy Rosary with his people, with Robyn. He felt clear, free of the sticky cobwebs and the ceaseless hammering in his head. It was like someone had hit a reset button on him. Adam didn't count once the whole way over, which was a miracle in itself since he hadn't been able to go a few minutes without counting the past few days. It was righteous—no, it was a sign from God. That had to be it.

God was pleased with him.

CHAPTER TWENTY-SIX

The church, thank the Lord and all his angels, was empty again. And again it was like a coming home, only better. It was like walking into a hug. It had happened that first time too, but it was then obliterated by the dread he'd felt about bringing his crazy-ass Group to a church he hadn't set foot in for years.

This time, Adam sent them on ahead while he stayed to perform his cleansing ritual, which was a good thing because it took him twice as long as the last time. *No matter, doesn't matter.* And it didn't matter. The superheroes waited semi-patiently for him at the base of the labyrinth. They all swore that they had faithfully executed "damn good" signs of the cross after liberally dipping into the holy water.

"Except Thor," Green Lantern whispered. "He just shoved his whole hand in, pulled it out and then nada, nothing." Green Lantern glanced over at Thor, who was pacing in the vestibule. "Not sure he has the hang of it yet."

"Okay!" Adam reached over to a table that held various pamphlets and lifted one. "So we start at the start. See that opening?

Stay on the pink path and it will squiggle you in the right way. It's not a test or anything, but try to stay off the dark grey granite part."

"Okay, Batboy, it's your show," Wolverine said, putting his hand to his chest and leaving it there. "If I suffer a myocardial infarction from the exertion, I'm assuming that this is a quasi-decent place to be, right? Your pope guy knows CPR, right?"

No one laughed or rolled their eyes. If none of them quite "got" his thing, they now recognized it as a *real* thing and left it alone.

"It's a good place, Wolverine. You'll be cool," said Adam as he squinted at the instructions. "All right, so the first part is walking to the centre medallion in the, uh, centre." He pointed to the bloom of pink in the middle of the squiggles. "That's called Purgation, which is a 'releasing and shedding' as we walk. Then we rest at the centre to 'receive inspiration,' and finally we make our way back, which is called Union and brings a 'new awareness and calm' to our lives."

"All that from walking a circle?" Green Lantern was astounded. "That is sick!"

"Okay." Adam motioned with his hand. "Follow me." Just as he stepped in, he noticed Father Rick coming towards them. The priest stopped and sat in a pew, but turned to face them.

Jesus. They'd looked weird enough before, but now they were sporting masks and gloves and glowing discs, while stepping gingerly into an invisible labyrinth. All eight of them entered, even Thor.

"Don't push!"

"I'm not pushing!"

"Are so!"

"You're not giving me enough room!"

"You're walking too slow. Hop to it!"

"Guys, enough!" Adam raised his hand. "Everybody out!" *Mutter, mutter, mutter,* but out they went, even Thor. "Look, guys, you're supposed to enter this in the spirit of contemplation and with an open heart kind of thing." Wolverine sighed, his hand still firmly on his chest. "So let's start again, but give the person in front of you lots of room before you step in. Ready?"

They nodded somewhat sheepishly.

"Okay, then. Let's commence."

This time there was a concentrated silence.

"Holy crap!" said Captain America as soon as he exited. "Sorry, man, but that was superior! Absolutely superior. It was superior, wasn't it?"

The rest of them mumbled in agreement before they turned towards the cross and then raced over to the candles. For them, Holy Rosary was better than a theme park.

"Adam?"

It was Father Rick.

He moved towards the priest and was surprised to feel Robyn's hand slip into his.

"Hey, Father, how are you doing?"

Father Rick wore his clerical clothing, black pants and shirt with the white-collar tab. It made him look so official, all Roman Catholic Church–like.

"I'm sorry if—"

"Your friends are welcome here anytime, Adam." He smiled at Robyn. "I hope Holy Rosary is a refuge for them, and for you especially."

Adam stood mute, whiplashed by memories of compulsively counting the stained-glass windowpanes, the gold granite specks on the floor, the candles, the carvings in the pews . . .

"You taught them the labyrinth?"

"Yeah, Father. I forgot how much I used to like it."

"Did you know, Miss . . ."

"Plummer," said Robyn.

"Forgive me, I should have remembered. Miss Plummer, did you know our Adam was my very finest altar server?"

Robyn looked confused.

"Altar boy," Adam explained. "Thanks, Father."

"It's true."

"Oh, I'm not surprised at all." They were distracted by the unmistakable sound of coins hitting the stone floor. "Hey, I'd better—" Robyn let go of Adam's hand, taking away all her warmth. "I'll go over with the guys and monitor the signs-of-the-cross part. See you later, Father."

"I hope so, Miss Plummer."

They watched Robyn thread her way through the pews.

"Adam?" Father Rick stepped closer as soon as she was outside of earshot. "You did—do—have a spiritual gift. We'd welcome you back in any way, whenever you're ready. Whenever it becomes okay with your mom to . . ." The priest glanced over at the candle stands and back at Adam, then glanced away again. "Uh, forgive me, but your friends are fine, mainly, aren't they?"

"Oh yeah. OCD is the major presenting and we're all medi-cated and not violent. Not even Thor." They both locked onto the behemoth, who was immobile and transfixed before the candles. It looked like he was going to eat them. "At least not that we know."

Adam would have to count and adjust the candles before they left; at the moment there were thirty-four lit ones.

"And your mother? Are things okay for you at home?"

Home. Adam sat down in the pew behind Father Rick and started. *Five sets.* Just like that. It was back. *One, three, five, seven, nine, eleven . . .*

"Adam." Father Rick spoke so softly that Adam had to lean in to hear him. "I'm here. I know you need more. I can sense it, like before. But sometimes God can help a little too."

Adam must have nodded. But not very convincingly. The priest looked pained as he got up and walked towards the altar. He turned back for a moment. "Anytime, Adam, *anytime.*"

He could sense it? Just how crazy was he? Father Rick could sense *what? Seventeen, nineteen, twenty-one, twenty-three . . .*

Could people see?

Jesus, they could see!

And there was no reset button after all. *Twenty-five, twenty-seven, twenty-nine . . .* Not for him. Wisps of smoke formed into strands and then knitted themselves into the familiar spider's web that had trapped his mind for so long, Adam could only note its absence not its presence. Jesus, not again. Adam raised his eyes to the crucifix that had so mesmerized them on their first visit. Christ looked back.

Are you with me or not?

Suspended and sad.

Well?

Silence.

Answer me for once, goddamn it!

There was a kerfuffle by the candles. His friends were scrounging for quarters, blowing out tapers and making inept signs of the cross. Half of them were kneeling. *Three, five, seven . . .*

Adam returned his gaze to the cross. The Jesus was hurting. Guilt simmered and then boiled in him. Jesus had a whole world of suffering and horror to worry about and here Adam was in all his punk puniness. He didn't want to add to Jesus's burdens, but . . .

Sorry about that. Look, I know you're busy and I don't want to get greedy with your time, but still, if you could just help me . . . If you could find a minute, please, please, please, dear sweet Jesus, fix me.

It took Adam twenty-three minutes to get into his house that night. It would have gone much faster but he was interrupted. He was racing through the rituals when Mrs. Polanski from across the street came trotting over in her Sunday grey wool coat with the fake fur collar and slippers.

"Adam, dear? Adam?"

He turned to her.

"Are you okay, dear? Locked out? I sometimes see you, see that it takes so long to—"

"I'm fine, Mrs. Polanski, really. Thank you very much. I'm not locked out and I think Mom's home. It's just . . . I have to . . . well, see, I have to do things in a certain way before . . . I'm fine, ma'am. Really, I am." Shame shot through every syllable and strangled the words. "Sorry if I worried you, but honest to God, I'm fine."

Mrs. Polanski wrapped the coat around her a little tighter, nodded and began to walk away, but then she turned around again. Clearly, she was not happy about leaving him at the door. "You know I'm right across the street, if ever . . . well, I'm home is all." And off she went.

The universe was dialling down and Jesus, as it turned out, *was* busy. So later that night, Adam called Chuck.

He thought he was going to leave a message. But Chuck picked up, even though it was 8:37 p.m.

"I need help," he said.

"Adam?" Chuck's warm voice stilled the tremors.

"I need help."

"Are you okay for tonight?"

"Yes, sir. I think so."

Chuck sighed. And Adam remembered just how much the therapist hated being called "sir."

"Tomorrow? Can you make it for three-thirty?"

"Yeah, I can skip biology."

"Good. I'll write you a note if need be. And, Adam?"

"Yes, sir?"

"Breathe."

"Yes, sir. I'll start right now." *Seven sets. One, three, five, seven . . .*

CHAPTER TWENTY-SEVEN

The next day Adam felt better, so he felt like a punk for calling Chuck. Not better-better, but better. True, he couldn't stop counting and there was that annoying low-level vibration that seemed to be buried somewhere in his bone marrow. Still, it was douchebag-ish to call Chuck at home, and to get Eric Yashinsky to cover him in biology, and to lie to his mom about why he'd be late and . . . well, so many things. This was a mistake.

"This is a mistake," he said to Chuck while hovering at the door. "I feel better. Sorry, this is nuts."

"Sure, but come in anyway, Adam. Take a load off." Chuck moved from around his desk to the plush beige armchair he sat in for sessions. Adam didn't budge. "If you're not having a threshold issue, come in and relax. Look, we can do this rather than next week's one-on-one if it makes you feel any better."

Adam sat in the big overstuffed wing chair he liked best. Chuck let his people choose from four different chairs. The wing chair had a mushy pillow that Adam always hugged into himself even though he felt like a wuss every single time he did it.

"So how did it go at the church?"

"Good."

"The Group?"

"Good. They were good. It was good." *What the hell was he doing? Why was he here?*

"So what triggered last night, do you think? Any thoughts? Are things, the rituals, escalating?"

"Trigger? What was the *trigger*? You're kidding, right? My life is the trigger, sir." Adam became aware of his breathing. It was like he was breathing into a microphone. The sound filled up the room.

"Fair enough. The threshold rituals, are they escalating in response?"

"Don't know." He shrugged. Now he could hear his heart. *Thump, thump, thump, pa-thump, thump.* Wait, was that right? That didn't sound right. *Thump, thump, thump, pa-thump.* He was per-spiring. Was this how it was for Wolverine? He was going to have to cut the guy more slack—this sucked. But what if it *was* Wolverine who was sending the sick crap to Mom? No. That just didn't make any sense. He wasn't *that* crazy. He was just like him. Poor guy. *Pa-thump.*

"Adam? Is it the tapping?"

"No." He sighed in relief because that, at least, was the truth.

"All right, then. Uh, dare I ask if you completed a List?"

The List! He did! He remembered doing it in the library last week after he'd finished his homework and trying to hide it from Eric Yashinsky, who was keeping him company.

"Yeah, I did one!" Adam fished around in his backpack. "By the way, don't you think it's time we stop punishing me about the Internet access? I am so over—"

"It wasn't a punishment, Adam. But I agree the rituals don't seem to centre around the Internet compulsions, and so very soon we can—"

"Here it is!" He handed his List to Chuck.

The therapist unfolded the paper.

January 24	**THE LIST**	Batman

Meds: Anafranil 25 mg 2 x per day
Ativan as needed

Primary presenting compulsions: Counting, Thresholds

1. I believe

"Adam?" Chuck took off his aviators. "There's nothing here."

Adam got up and retrieved the paper. *Thump, thump, thump, pa-thump, pa-thump.* "Oh. Oh yeah. No more Ativan; I need another prescription. I forgot to tell you after Group. I lost a bunch down the school drain the other day." He hadn't written *anything*. He could have sworn . . .

"I'll call the pharmacy as soon as you leave, and maybe we should increase the Anafranil to 75 milligrams—25 milligrams three times per day."

Adam was already doing that. It didn't help. He'd crank it up some more.

"But, Adam, the List is—"

"I did, like, a million of them, I swear to God. It's just that I rip them up after. I don't know why, honest. I thought that was a finished one." He had to fight the instinct to jump up and run out of the room.

Chuck leaned forward. "Try it straight. This is important. Has the counting moved exclusively into your head, no physical or visual ritual attached?"

Adam shoved the pillow into his gut. "Pretty much." *One, three, five, seven . . .*

Chuck nodded. "That's significant. Even or odd numbers?"

"Both," he admitted. "Different situations call for, uh, different scratchings."

"Scratchings?"

"It's like my brain gets itchy, uh, hot sometimes." Adam barely said it out loud. Chuck had to sit at the end of his chair to catch it.

"How are things at home? Is your mother's hoarding escalating?"

Adam shouldn't have told about that. That was disloyal. That was wrong. It would hurt her. It would come back on him—it *was* coming back on him. Betraying her, making everything worse. He remembered the garbage bags, winced.

"She's, like, taking out two green garbage bags a week." And it was true. She still was. She made a big show of it every single week.

"Excellent." Chuck nodded. "So something else with your mom. Do you want to talk about her a bit?"

"No, sir." *You are an abortion. Die bitch die. You are ruining your son's life.* A dread hiding a guilty truth pounded harder and harder. Jesus. Was there some disgusting part of him that agreed? Adam shook his head. Jesus, *thump, pa-thump.* Jesus. He was a monster. "No. I'm good."

Chuck frowned. "Okay, we'll leave that for the moment. How about at your dad's? How is it going with your stepmother?"

"Brenda?" *Brenda? Mrs. Brenda Ross loves you more, she said.* "Brenda's good." *Thump, pa-thump, pa-thump, pa-thump, thump, thump.*

"Adam, I feel it's time for us to seriously consider commencing with the exposure response and prevention therapy. Now, I can't make you talk and I certainly can't *make* you undertake this stage, but the interior quality of the counting has moved it into what some in the profession call pure OCD and . . ." *Words, words, words.*

"Yeah, sure, Doc. Absolutely. But not now. I've got a lot on my plate right now. I think that I had a panic attack is all and I didn't have any Ativan left, like I said. Yeah, for sure that was it! So . . ." He stood up. "If you'd just call the pharmacy. Thanks for helping me sort that out in my own head." *Three, five, seven, nine, eleven . . .* "Sorry for freaking you out." He headed for the door.

"Adam, you didn't. Adam, wait! Our time—"

What are you going to do? Stop talking and fix me! Just fix me. I need to be fixed.

Fixed!

"It's good. I'm better. Plain old panic attack, sorry. Thanks, Doc. I'm way better, seriously clear and everything."

He was reeling when he got into the elevator. He was alone, at least in the beginning. It felt like he had walked into a vacuum tube. Adam rode the elevator up and down, as he sometimes did after a session with Chuck. The compression was soothing, as was the soft *ding* of the floor indicator. As Adam rode, he reviewed every word and gesture. Seventeen minutes later, he walked out into the cold towards the pharmacy.

CHAPTER TWENTY-EIGHT

He took an Ativan before he called her. He thought she'd be pleased about the whole impromptu Chuck session. She wasn't.

"Did you tell him about the letters?"

"Not in so many words," he admitted. He walked over to his fish tank. The boys swam over to him and then swam away in a huff when they realized he wasn't going to feed them. All except Steven, who stayed and looked at him pityingly.

"In *any* words, Adam? I mean words that actually left your head and came out loud into the world?"

"Not so much."

She eventually wore him down. It was a war of attrition and Robyn was better armed. In every conversation, every evening that week, she hinted not so subtly that he had to get more support, more ammo, more help—in other words, tell Group about the letters.

"Uncle!" he groaned on Sunday night.

"Good decision," she said sweetly. "I've been praying on it."

———

The superheroes all checked in with their accessories that Monday. Batman wore his ring. He wore it all the time now, and Robyn brought in a new pair of long green leather gloves. She smiled encouragingly at him as soon as he sat down. Adam found that irresistible and had to concentrate on not throwing himself across the room and kissing her. Instead, he spoke up right after check-in.

"Adam, you'd like to start us off?" The therapist looked pleased.

"Yes, sir. I think. So, guys, well, you all know I have the counting and, uh, the threshold thing, right?"

Everybody but Wolverine nodded. Wolverine just looked bored—or was he checking his target heart rate? Thor offered Adam his signature death-stare. At least it meant that he was paying attention.

"Yeah, so it's expanding. Maybe."

Snooki turned in her seat to face him.

"A lot. New ones. I don't why. There's more places at school, and you know about the church. There's the side door at my dad's now, and the worst"—Adam's mouth dried up—"the worst is the front door of my house."

"Your own place, man?" Iron Man shook his head. "That is so the bitch." You could tell by the way he said it that he'd been practising that phrase, working it hard and waiting for the perfect moment to roll it out.

"Yeah, yeah, it is. I'm, like, scaring the neighbours."

Adam elaborated and could quite legitimately have taken up all his time on that rather salient and considerable problem, but he noticed that Robyn had given up on being *encouraging* and had careened straight into being *anguished*.

"But that's not the real problem."

"No shit, Sherlock!" said Wolverine. "You've gone from tapping your brains out every session to not being able to get into your own house and that's *not* the problem? What about that pretty speech you made in September? The one about getting clearer every week until you could blow this place?" He leaned forward shaking his head, radiating concern. "Man, you're circling the drain."

Chuck cleared his throat.

Thor glowered.

Wolverine shut up.

Adam noted all this while exhaling, slowly. He did not count or choke on Wolverine's passive-aggressiveness. He also did not get up and fling himself at Wolverine as he moved his chair closer to Robyn's. "Maybe I am, but no, that's not the real problem." He took a couple of raggedy breaths but still did not count. He'd be damned if he would count in front of that mutant. "So, and like this *so* has got to stay here . . ."

What was he doing? Sweat beaded on his forehead and then on the sides of his face until all the beads found each other and decided to form clammy streams that raced down his neck.

Danger. This was a betrayal. Danger.

He didn't know how to begin. He should have practised, like Iron Man. Adam fumbled around in his head searching for a path, until he remembered how Robyn had talked about her mother.

"Okay, so . . ." He looked at his feet, which were on the floor. He crossed his legs the wrong way, undid them and crossed them the right way. "Uh, I think I got to lay some ground rules?" He looked to Chuck, so they all looked to Chuck. Chuck nodded and everyone returned to Adam. "Right, so like I said, except I didn't say anything. So I'll say it, but I don't actually want at this point, right now, any solutions or comments, okay? It's crazy complicated and I can't go to the cops or tell any authorities. *Any*. You just have to believe that. I feel like I'm taking a big risk and . . . like I'm going to make it worse."

Wolverine groaned, but Thor emitted a low soft rumble. Again Wolverine shut down.

"Sorry. Okay, thing is my mom . . . my mother has been getting these deranged, threatening letters that call her disgusting names and keep pushing her to kill herself." Adam noted a soft gasp, and he stumbled. He looked to Robyn. He could *feel* her across from him, pleading with him, urging, nodding, cheering for him. The girl was burning up a lot of energy.

"The letters, they're like toxic vomit." Fear spiked down his spine and then spread. He did not take his eyes off Robyn. "They're deranged, but in case you're wondering, they don't threaten *her* directly, which means something legally, and they're like those old-school cut-and-paste jobs, like in the movies. It's like somebody wants to drive her crazy, get her locked up." Adam's heart erupted in uneven *pa-thumps*. He had said out loud and to *them* what he had refused to say to himself.

No one breathed.

No one said anything.

"Big step, Batman. Maybe you need a minute, and maybe everyone else does too," Chuck said gently. "So I'll ask a couple of questions just on facts, nothing loaded. I agree that the situation is loaded enough. If you don't want to answer, just shake your head, okay?"

"Yeah, I'm okay with that."

"How many letters?"

Adam thought for a moment. "Five? No, six that I know of for sure, but I'm guessing seven or eight when I think about how she acts after."

"Do you have any idea who?"

Did he look at Wolverine? He didn't mean to.

Adam dropped his head. "Could be work, or someone we know. No, I have no idea, and we don't—*she* won't—talk about it."

"And how *is* your mom? Is she coping?"

"She has her issues—other ones, you know? But she puts on a good front. Thing is, I know she's strung out; the house vibrates with it, or she's vibrating. I don't know. I just don't know."

"Okay." Chuck took off his glasses and rubbed his eyes. "That's enough for now. You know to call." Chuck and Adam surveyed the room together; most everyone in it looked uncomfortable. "We won't comment, but good one, Batman. Splendid break-through. I'm very pleased that you could share what you did. Big step, young man. Big, big step."

And he was right. It was like a high-pressure front blew in and swallowed up everything that was thick and heavy.

Snooki leaned over to him and patted his thigh.

Robyn lasered Snooki.

And Adam felt fine. Shockingly, brilliantly fine. Once again, he had *told*. Once again, a relief so pure and powerful rocked him to the core.

He tried staying in tune for the rest of the checks and even managed to comment on Green Lantern's latest running-over-someone-in-the-car drama. Adam was still feeling lighter and brighter when they stacked chairs forty minutes later. He couldn't wait to get to the cemetery with Robyn, to be alone with her. She would be pleased, proud. He would hold her. She would make it even better.

He was still smiling when Thor loomed up behind him, cast-ing a shadow over the stairwell. His footfalls reverberated like gathering thunder until he had just passed Adam on the stairs, and then he turned. Even though Thor was one step down, he still towered over Adam.

"I'll find him, kid."

"What? Uh, Thor, no. You don't have to . . . you shouldn't . . ."

"I'll find him." Thor's voice was so low that the actual words were barely audible. "I'll find him and I'll kill the prick," he said, or Adam thought he said. He definitely said something close enough to that to shred Adam's stomach before he took off.

You tell and all hell will break loose, Adam. Promise me you'll never tell. Promise!

Adam leaned against the rail trying to steady himself.

What have I done?

CHAPTER TWENTY-NINE

"**I** don't know why you're tripping out so much. I thought it went good. They've got your back, you know. All of them."

Was Robyn annoyed?

Annoyed would not be good.

Angry?

Angry would be bad.

Scared?

Scared would be badder.

But then Robyn put her arm through his as they walked through the cemetery gates. And they were close enough for Adam to get lost in the promise of her.

"I mean it, Adam—all of them! They are *so* for you!"

"Yeah," he said. "Especially Wolverine."

"No . . ." Robyn withdrew her arm. "*Especially* Snooki."

Wow. Were they having a fight? Was this their first fight?

This had to mean that they were definitely a *they* in order for them to have *their* first fight.

Once the novelty wore off, a full two seconds later, Adam felt nauseated. He tucked her arm through his again. "I'm sorry, Robyn." He didn't have a clue what he was apologizing for.

"No." Robyn shook her head. "*I'm* sorry. I forced you and now you feel worse. And I'm such an idiot, and I'm really, really sorry."

"No, I don't feel worse, really," he lied. Adam felt worse by the hour, it seemed. There were moments when it felt like he was disintegrating. The time and attention that the compulsions demanded, the humiliating aftermath of the rituals, all pierced through and left puncture marks in their wake. He was exhausted.

Each ritual, each time, required more and gave less.

But Adam had to be strong for her. Robyn needed a strong defender, protector, warrior . . . something much more than he was. Yet he would and could be that for her, and also for his mom and for Sweetie. There was no time to be *tired*.

Last week's ice storm had left its mark on the cemetery. Though the path was cleared, snow and ice draped every available surface, glittering even in the dusk.

"Wow, eh?" Robyn squeezed Adam's arm. "It's like how I imagined Narnia to be when the White Witch turned it into the Hundred Years Winter."

Adam traced the icicle-decorated branches scratching against the gathering darkness. And then they were there, at her mother's headstone. The big black granite an aggressive scar erupting from all that white.

Adam reluctantly let go of Robyn so that she could make the sign of the cross and say her rosary.

It was while she prayed that he knew.

It was no longer an act, a compulsive tic or a driving necessity. Robyn was not obsessing. He reviewed the last few weeks, at church, at her house, in Group and here with him. There was no sense of desperation.

She was better.

Adam could hear himself exhaling in that way you can when you're at the bottom of a swimming pool or running in the woods by yourself. This was wrong. Who was saving who here?

No, it was even wronger than that somehow. He knew it at the core of his being, but couldn't put his finger on what or how. He shivered.

Robyn turned back to him. It was almost dark. They would close the gates. The rules were loose, but usually they shut the gates when night fell, not at any set hour. He'd gotten caught a couple of times in the autumn when he'd doubled back rather than returning home along the main streets. Adam now knew all the perimeter fences and which ones were scalable. Robyn had to know the rules; she'd been coming far longer than he had. Yet the darkening sky didn't seem to concern her.

"You know, I don't remember her ever *not* fighting."

"Fighting?"

It was as if Robyn were addressing an audience, not just Adam. "Even when she was unconscious, I swear she fought. She, he, they fought when she was drugged, radiated, hair falling out and throwing up. They flew her everywhere, for every possible trial or quack treatment. The fight took up everything, you see, for years. It was . . . exclusive." She hugged herself. "There was no room in that kind of battle for a little girl. There was no air left for me, and . . ." She turned back to the stone. "I—I hated her for it."

Then Robyn tried to smile.

"So, my superfine superhero, I guess I was praying right now that you could maybe understand why I went with the suicide story as opposed to this disgusting selfish-brat story. Do you think you can, even a little?"

Even in the sooty dark, Adam could tell that there were tears struggling down Robyn's face. He bounded up to her.

"Why the hell do I tell you these things? They are so, so ugly . . . and still I tell you. I don't get it. Why?"

"Because you know that I will love you no matter what. It doesn't matter what you think you did. I will always love you, Robyn."

"You love me?"

He went to her and thought he would implode with want.

Instead of devouring her whole, Adam wiped her cheek as gently as he would Sweetie's. "I love you. I love you so much that I tell you all my . . . and I—"

"You're talking too much," she whispered. "Stop talking, Adam, and just—"

Adam cupped her face in his hands and kissed her. He kissed her forever and then longer than that. His body was shot through with shards of hot and cold at the exact same time. Her lips were softer and, yes, peachier than he could ever have imagined, and still they kissed. Adam moved one hand to the back of her head and the other circled her body as if he did this every day, and still they kissed. Robyn threw her arms around him and pulled him into her, and still they kissed. They kissed that one long, hungry, uninterrupted first kiss that went beyond the now and would last as only first kisses can, in time and memory, until they breathed no more.

Until they were caught by harsh intrusive high-beams.

"Oh."

"Oh."

They blinked like startled owls at the security car in front of them.

A car door opened. "You kids want to get a room? The gates have been closed for half an hour!" The security guard heaved himself out and, to add insult to injury, beamed his flashlight on them. "Hell, I take it back. You *are* kids. Go home right now before I haul you in and call your folks! I'll drive over and open the Main Street gates. You all think the cemetery is some kind of make-out mansion. Now, get home! Go!"

Robyn kissed him one more time and then once more again. Everything in him ignited. Adam grabbed her hand and they ran to the Main Street gates, laughing the whole way. Even with all his long-distance training, he had trouble catching his breath. And that was okay. He held on to the heat of the kiss, of her. He was not tired. He did not count.

"Robyn—"

"Shh." Robyn smiled, touching his lips with her gloved finger. "Shh . . . I love you too, Adam, really I do. I have almost from the beginning, and I will love you"—she turned, looking back to the cemetery—"I will love you *until* . . ." She reached for him and kissed his cheek and then his eyes and then his lips one last time before disappearing down Main Street. He heard the gates clank shut behind him.

Guess it was going to be the long way home tonight.

Who cared?

Not him.

Robyn Plummer tasted like peaches.

And Robyn Plummer *loved* him.

CHAPTER THIRTY

Adam ran home without his feet touching the ground. Wow. He got it, he really got it. So *this* was what *that* was like! This was better than anything! This was worth anything! Love, man. Love was amazing. Miracles sparked in the night air, bloomed and burst open before him.

Until he got home.

And he got to his door.

And nothing had changed. So everything did.

It was a bad reset. And it was one that happened *that* fast. It took Adam twenty-three minutes to get in. And in that time everything turned upside down. He had to retrace and start again seven times.

It must have been a pity kiss.

Because he was that pitiful.

He felt like an open wound by the time he turned the key. Thank God his mom was on late shift all week.

When he got to his room, Adam just sat there in his coat in the dark and counted until the phone rang.

"Robyn?"

"No, doofus. Don't you have call display? It's Ben."

"Stones?"

Adam unzipped his jacket and started wiggling out of it.

"What's up, man?"

"Nothing much."

The guys had never developed much of a telephone relationship over the years. They relied more on monosyllabic and heavily coded texting. But that had not been available to Adam for almost a year now. So, on the phone, each out-wrestled the other in tortured conversation. Their "conversations" rarely lasted longer than a few seconds and usually involved little more than setting the date and time of their next meeting. But sometimes, Ben Stone called for no reason whatsoever.

Like this time.

As always they began with their standard awkward pause, and then . . .

"Yeah, so I thought I'd just call, you know?"

Adam nodded, but of course Ben couldn't see him.

"So I called . . . And so, dude, how are ya? You still nuts?"

"Pretty much," said Adam.

"Thought so."

"You still fat?" Adam wanted to take the words back as soon as they were out of his mouth. "Sorry, man, that was pissy."

"Oh, stuff it, dude. I am *fatter*! Can ya dig it?"

"That's, uh, righteous. I think."

"Yeah, bro, it *is* righteous!" said Ben.

"Yeah?" said Adam, perking up. "Why?"

Ben laughed. "Dude, I'm gonna gain at least seven more serious pounds!"

"No way!"

"Way! Spring training for the junior football team wannabes, man. What I gotta get me is some firm fat. I'm going to definitely try out for the football team next year. So I'm going to work on getting into big-man shape."

"Sounds like a helluva plan, Stan. I'm with you. I'm thinking about trying out for track this spring."

"No way!"

"Way!"

"Why the hell not, eh? Who says a whack-job can't be the marathon man and a Jew can't be an epic nose-tackle?"

"Not me!"

"Perfection! I'm gonna do it, Adam. I'm gonna be a football star. I decided this week."

"With a side order of cheerleaders to go!" Adam turned on his light, shaking his head and smiling.

"You bet your bony ass. They'll all be after me. Let us pause for a moment and hold that photo."

Adam grinned. He couldn't help it. "I got it!"

"Are you smiling at your stupid fish?"

"You got it in one, Stones."

"Primo. Well, my work here is done. See you Sunday."

How did he know? "Sunday, yeah. Stones?"

"Yeah?"

"You have no . . . Just thanks, man."

"Hey, glad do my bit for the Batman."

They both hung up at the same time, and Adam just knew that Stones was wearing the same smile he was. It was a three-minute phone call and not even half an hour since Adam had reached his door. But he felt good. And that's when he knew.

The changes were cutting too deep and quick. He had to find himself a better safety harness or this roller-coaster ride was going to kill him.

CHAPTER THIRTY-ONE

At 8:59 a.m. on Thursday, February 23, Adam threw his hands up. *I give up.* He walked away from his first class, which was biology in the big lab. The little lab was still okay, but the big lab had been trouble for months, and that morning, he couldn't break through with all the distractions.

Signing up for spring track tryouts, Ross?

Did you see that ass-kicking Warhammer YouTube link?

Can I borrow your notes from last week's experiment?

Et cetera, et cetera, et cetera.

Adam had arrived at the door at 8:40, as he always did when it was first-class big lab. This gave him plenty of time to perform the necessary cleansing rituals, get in and pretend he was trying to catch up on the experiments by the time everyone else straggled in. It always worked. Everybody bought it. Never underestimate the cunning of the damaged. But not today. Adam wasted precious alone time at the threshold obsessing about Robyn. The look and feel and taste of her. The sadness and need in her kisses. Need? Whose need?

Either way, Adam was definitely on the wrong side of the threshold by the time the first few kids started down the hall towards class. It was a double period. At 8:43, while Adam was orchestrating the very first of the cleansing moves, he was hijacked by panic. He would lose her. Of course, that assumed that he *had her* to lose. But considering and reconsidering the kiss, as he had done exactly one hundred and thirty-three million times since it happened—that kiss, no, *kisses* plural, and the feel of her hand in his and her body against his body—well, maybe he *did* have her to lose. But now, today, in front of the large lab, it was clear that Adam would lose her, would *have* to lose her. This was inevitable because it was inarguable that Robyn was getting better. Maybe she was even fixed.

Why was she still in Group?

Adam's heart had been hiccupping ever since and he kept screwing up the clearing. So at 8:59 he threw up his hands and headed for the library, doing his level best to impersonate a normal boy.

And that's where they eventually found him. Sister Mary-Margaret and his dad entered together, and Adam's hiccups stopped cold.

"Son, we've got to go."

Adam shot up like a sprung coil.

"No, Adam, it's okay. It's just that Wendell—"

"Sweetie? What happened to Sweetie?"

"He's okay and it's all going to be completely fine, but he's in the hospital." His father raised his hand to stop the torrent of questions before they started. "He broke his arm rather badly on the monkey bars and they're going to check for a concussion. They want to keep him in overnight for observation and to continue with tests." His dad sank into the library chair beside him. "Thank you, Sister."

She made a face. Sister Mary-Margaret did not care for being dismissed.

"Adam will not be returning to class today."

Sister pursed her lips. "As you like, Mr. Ross. I'll inform the office."

As soon as she was out of earshot, Adam's dad leaned into him. "Well, there's a face that only the Church could love."

"Dad! Harsh . . . if accurate."

"Yeah, I'll fry for that, but that old brick has been making everybody miserable since I was here."

Adam blushed, remembering how he used thoughts of the poor sister's person to douse his hysterical hormones.

"Look, son, don't worry. Wendell's going to be fine. But right now he's having a major fit because he needs his Batman."

Adam gathered up his stuff in seconds and off they went.

"Do I want to know why you weren't in class?" asked his father.

"No, sir."

"Okay, then."

"Dad?" Adam pulled his father's arm. "Not the south doors, okay?"

"But the car is—" Then he caught his son's expression. "Front door?"

"Front door." Adam almost tripped over his guilt. His dad already looked wiped.

They went straight to Glen Oaks Hospital, his mom's hospital. Sweetie lit up as soon as he saw Adam, but he still looked as white as a Kleenex.

"Batman! Batman, I knew you'd come. Don't go, okay?"

Adam gave his little brother a big squeeze, which was tricky given the bizarre contraption they had his arm in. "Well, this a superior mess you got yourself into."

"Yeah, a mess! And they're going to screw me up! I don't want to get screwed!"

"Oh, sure, you say that now," said Adam, patting Sweetie's good arm.

"Adam!" His father tried to keep a straight face. Even Brenda smiled, or tried to.

"So?" Adam turned to his dad and stepmom. "What the hell?"

"They just came in and the resident said that he may need surgery to put in stainless steel screws." Brenda's lip quivered but she continued gamely. "They'll do more x-rays and, uh, different kinds of x-rays." Even from a distance he could tell that her eye makeup had dried into tire tracks down her face. "We just couldn't wait until you got here, but Sweetie has been very brave."

"They want to put me in a cat tunnel. I'm not going to a cat tunnel, Batman. No sir, no. Not unless you come in it with me." He clung to Adam with his good arm. Adam returned to Brenda for a translation.

She sighed softly. "Sweetie was so incredibly brave during his x-rays, but they hurt a bit, didn't they, dear brave boy? But they feel they want to do a CAT scan to be sure about the concussion."

"And they take my blood, and this is a horrible, horrible place!" Sweetie's chubby little arm finally released its viselike grip on his brother. "And they poke me and pinch me! Let's go home now." Sweetie tried to swing his legs off the bed.

"Whoa! Hey, little guy, I think they need you to stay here for tonight. You can go home after the CAT tunnel and maybe a couple of other little things."

Sweetie's lower lip trembled.

"But I'll stay for all of the tests, okay? Even the tunnel one, I promise. It'll be righteous."

"I don't want to have screws in my body."

"Hey, they didn't say that you need them for sure, right? Maybe you'll just get to have a really cool cast."

"Really?" Sweetie's eyes widened. You could tell he was mulling over the concept of "cast as fashion accessory."

"Absolutely!" Adam ruffled Sweetie's hair. "All the best people have the best casts. I had one."

"For real? I don't remember."

Adam picked through his memory banks. "You weren't born yet, goof. I was, like, three or four and I broke my wrist."

Sweetie looked to his father for confirmation.

Mr. Ross nodded. "You were just about to turn four, and you broke it *and* the bed frame when you and Ben miscalculated on your mattress turbo-torpedo routine. It was a navy blue one, as I recall."

"I can have colours!"

The crisis had passed.

"Thank you, Adam." Brenda scrubbed her face with her hands. "No one loves you more than Sweetie—or than us, really. When this is over, you . . . well, your father and I have been talking about this a great deal, and it's time. We both want you to—"

"You keep your goddamned claws out of my son, you bitch!"

It was Adam's mother. She loomed in the doorway.

"Carmella, stop!" His father stood up.

She was still in her scrubs and was glaring at Brenda. "Haven't you taken enough?"

"Carmella, enough!"

She waved him off. "I've read all the reports; the kid will be fine." She turned on her heel. "Adam, get up. We're leaving!"

"Nooo!" Sweetie threw off his covers.

Adam felt blood surging in his ears. He needed to count and clear, but there was no time. He turned to Sweetie and put his finger on his lips. "Shh, it's okay. Stay still, I'll be right back!" He jumped off the bed and was out of the room before anyone could say anything.

Adam caught up to his mother halfway down the hall. She looked broken. He could tell from watching her from behind, from her walk, her shoulders. He had failed.

"Mom, wait!"

His mother slowed her pace.

"Mom, holy hell! What? Did you get another letter?"

She stopped.

"Look, Mom, I'll come home tonight after all his tests, but I can't come now." They could both hear Sweetie crying for him. "Dad will drive me back after I do the CAT scan thing and whatever else."

His mother just stood there, immobilized in the hospital's fluorescent light.

"Mom, come on! This is big for Sweetie and it's freaking him out. Brenda too. She didn't mean what—"

"Don't you *dare* tell me what *she* did or did not mean. I know what she's up to." She crossed her arms but it was too late. She had lost. Again. They both knew it.

"So I'll see you later." He gave her a quick, hard hug. "I love you, Mom."

It didn't make the betrayal any easier for either of them to swallow, and she didn't hug back.

CHAPTER THIRTY-TWO

Adam helped Sweetie into the Kung Fu Panda pyjamas that Brenda had rejigged so they now had no left sleeve. "See, I told you that you wouldn't get screwed."

Sweetie beamed at him. "I love my cast!" Sweetie, of course, had chosen a glow-in-the-dark neon-orange colour. Between the cast and the night lights, the bedroom looked like it was tricked out for Halloween.

"So what the hell happened? You are *the man* on the monkey bars. I've seen you—you're Cirque du Soleil material."

Sweetie considered that for a while, stumped by the Cirque reference. "I fell down, and then I don't remember none of it until Mrs. Brenda Ross was crying and crying and driving the car and then I was crying and crying. Was I bad?"

"No, goof!" Adam finished buttoning. "You were doing regular, real tough-boy stuff. I bet Dad was secretly relieved."

"Relieved," repeated Sweetie, memorizing and storing the word in his Sweetie Filofax.

"*And* you were unbelievably brave, even in the cat tunnel."

"Yes, I was." Sweetie nodded. "I was very, very brave." Then he got up from his bed and helped himself into Adam's.

"Hey, cut it out! You're hogging all the covers."

"I have a secret," said Sweetie, tucking the covers into himself with his one good arm. "I'm not really a brave boy," he whispered. "I'm a little bit scared a lot."

Adam kissed the back of his brother's head. "Look, that's no biggie. Most people are. Don't you worry about it. You're the bravest scared five-year-old I know."

"Will I be for sure brave by the time I go to the senior kindergarten school?" Sweetie yawned.

Adam knew that this was more a question about when fear would stop than when bravery would start. "Yeah, maybe. But if not, soonishly thereafter."

"How about when I'm fifteen?" The voice got smaller and smaller.

"When you are fifteen, little guy, you will be a bona fide superhero, I promise. Now go to sleep, it's almost midnight."

"I can't, Batman, can't . . ."

Adam threw his arm over his brother. "Shh, think of the number one hundred and eleven. Remember the one, one, one?"

"Okay . . ."

And he was asleep, just like that. The kid had an on-off switch that Adam would have killed for. He turned off the table lamp, which barely made a dent in the brightness given the glow of all the night lights.

It didn't matter. Adam was wide awake, watching his thoughts do laps around the over-bright room.

He had kept his word. On Thursday night Adam had made his dad drive him back home even though it was so late. Sweetie's tests hadn't ended until 11:41 p.m., and Adam didn't get back to his house and through the door until 1:03 a.m. Even with his mom asleep and the darkness shrouding the mess, 97 Chatsworth was smothering.

So he couldn't sleep there either. But when it came right down to it, he'd rather be awake in the glaring light with Sweetie hogging all his blankets than alone in the claustrophobic darkness of his own home. The truth made him sick.

Adam had not once asked his mother about the letter, but it was clear that she had received another one. Her eyes were hollow. It was probably why she'd gone berserk at the hospital, but he couldn't very well explain that to Dad and Brenda, and he couldn't make himself ask about the letter. Adam didn't ask over breakfast, or after school the next day. There was lots of time. He just couldn't bear the answer.

She was trying *so* hard. His mother had made cinnamon pancakes for breakfast on Saturday and they'd eaten at a newly reclaimed rectangle on the kitchen counter.

"Will you be okay? Not too lonely?" he asked while waiting for Brenda to pick him up.

"No, honey," she said in the bright chipped voice she'd been using all morning. "Didn't you notice? I've taken out five big trash bags this week and still you can't tell, so this weekend I'm going to tackle the kitchen area for sure! And, well, let's face it: that's going to be a massive job. Just wait until you come home, though! You won't recognize the place!"

"That'll be real nice, Mom." Adam smiled at her, stuffing down nausea with his pancakes and maple syrup. She had said the same thing two weeks ago, before his last weekend at Brenda's, and two weeks before that. "It would be good for you to do that, real good. But I want to help."

"Sure, baby, sure, and you will, as soon as I break the back of it. I just have to get it going and get a bit more organized, and I have to do my sorting or it will be impossible."

She clutched Adam to her when she heard the horn. It was a clumsy hug because he was so much taller now and neither of them was quite used to how the new parts fit. She ended up kissing the back of his ear.

"As soon as I just get the worst over with, I promise you can help and then we'll get our house back! How great would that be?"

Brenda honked again.

"Yeah, great." He grabbed his things. "That would be great."

His mother stayed rooted to the kitchen, wearing his father's fraying cable-knit sweater and holding a green garbage bag.

"Uh, I hope that Sweetie is . . . Tell them . . . well, say that I . . ."

"I will, Mom. Don't worry, I'll make them understand." He shut the door as fast as he could.

Each time he left for *them*, he felt he was abandoning *her*.

At 1:39 a.m., Adam blinked at the brightness and then at a sleeping Sweetie. The cast alone took up most of the bed. Sweetie's accident—that was a close one. Too close. He was doing a crappy job all around.

Adam got up carefully, stretched and began. He paced in concentric rectangles while tapping into his left hand. This kind of pacing required tapping. Ninety-seven sets. Adam tapped to thirty-three and then started again.

And again.

At 3:17 a.m., Adam sat down on Sweetie's bed, watching his little brother breathe. He guarded him while not breaking pattern. *Seventeen, nineteen, twenty-one* . . . He could *not* mess up again; the consequences were too dire, and already those he loved were paying the price. It still didn't feel "just right," so Adam had to focus hard on a few more rounds. This required seventeen sets of fast tapping and two rounds slow into the one-elevens. Sweetie loved one hundred and eleven. But Adam was tiring and he'd get muddled and have to start all over again.

At 4:57 a.m., Adam unplugged all of the night lights. "It was all my fault, little guy." He smooshed Sweetie up tight just the way he liked before climbing into the sliver of bed that was left for him.

"It won't happen again," he promised the dawn.

And at 5:03 a.m., Adam Spencer Ross finally fell asleep.

CHAPTER THIRTY-THREE

"**N**ice to see you, Adam." Chuck directed him to the overstuffed armchair and pulled up his own across the little coffee table from Adam. He clicked on a recorder, a Zoom H2 Handy Portable Stereo Recorder. Chuck cleared his throat.

"March 2, 5:35 p.m., with Adam Ross."

This was new.

"Hope you don't mind—all the best shrinks have been recording since the Stone Age. I'm a little late to the party." Chuck tapped the tiny black box. "I think it's on, but I'm not sure, so I'm still going to take notes if you don't mind."

Adam nodded and looked around the office as if he had never seen it before. Chuck's office, like all psychiatric offices in the Queensway Hospital, was in the basement. The room was smothered in beige on beige on beige. Each shade fought to be more muted than the next. It was a fight to the death. Chuck stood against this in a riot of colour. Today he had on his favourite Jamaican Olympic bobsled team jersey plus red skinny jeans. It was hard for Adam to take his eyes off the therapist in all that super-subdued nothing.

Probably what Chuck had in mind to begin with.

"The last time . . ." Chuck riffled through his file. "Ah, found it—it was the impromptu appointment. It's been a while, right?"

Adam nodded. He actually had little to no memory of that session. He remembered being agitated. But then, he was always agitated. He needed some sleep. Adam had taken to swallowing Advil PMs each night, having convinced himself that this was way preferred to upping the Ativan dosage any more. Besides, he was out and he couldn't ask Chuck for another prescription. The Advils didn't work.

"Adam?"

"Sorry, I'm not sleeping much." What were they talking about? "I'm kind of up and down and up and . . . And yeah, so my immediate response to all my fear and anxiety stuff is still to count and . . . well, I may not have been clear about this in Group, but the counting is escalating and becoming more involved with patterns, grouping and speeds."

"Including right now."

It wasn't a question. Adam felt caught out. He *was* counting and he wasn't even aware of it. "Including now," he admitted. "In my head."

"In an effort to neutralize the anxiety of being here?"

"Little bit."

"Okay, don't concern yourself about that. It's okay, Adam. I know you're worried about the escalation, but you've also grown so much in the months since Group began." The therapist smiled at him. "Literally and figuratively."

Five quick breaths. "Look, I know you're all keen on starting the ERP thing . . ."

Chuck nodded. "We will commence with the exposure

response and prevention therapy. We'll tackle and take down each one of your maladaptive coping strategies, one by one. Documenting, challenging and grading them. It's the only way, Adam. Whether your condition is genetic or environmental, or some combination of the two, I believe that ERP with the right combination of meds is the gold standard for this thing."

Adam nodded but he didn't buy it. He sucked at sticking to stuff like that. He couldn't even remember to do the List. The List! Damn, he'd forgotten to do the List. Maybe Chuck had forgotten too.

"You are ready, or I wouldn't have suggested it."

"And I want to, sort of. Look, I *do* want to get better, actually. But I'm in a godawful hurry . . . I can't right this—"

"I don't mean today. Relax. Today we talk, get caught up." Chuck started writing.

Okay, Adam knew how this went. This he could do, no sweat. He exhaled and stopped counting heartbeats.

"Let's begin at the beginning. How are things at home, er, homes?"

"Uh, complex."

"It's extremely stressful to be in a shared-custody situation, even in the most ideal circumstances, but you layer in OCD and your mother's, uh, coping techniques, and that is a recipe for disaster."

"Welcome to my nightmare."

Adam caught Chuck up on Sweetie's broken arm and the increasing hostility between the two houses. He glossed over his mom's hoarding.

Chuck asked about the letters.

You are an abortion.

"I can't, sorry." Warning shots rang out from the deepest part of him. "I promised her. I can't talk about her letters. They're supposed to be a secret and I blew it by blabbing in Group."

The therapist was quiet for a long time. How would that sound when he hit play on his fancy new machine? "But the letters are a serious factor, Adam, and they affect you directly. It may well be time for action. I want you to check in on that after every Group session. Let me know if there's a new one."

"There hasn't been a new one in a long time." Adam tried to keep the fear—the lie—out of his voice. Would the machine hear it?

"But if there is, it may be time to call in the proper authorities. We have to get to the bottom of this. I believe your recovery is tied to this."

And there you have it! His mother had warned him, pleaded with him, but he had to open his big fat freaky mouth, and now . . .

"We need to talk about the letters and their effect on you next session. I can almost guarantee that it will help." Chuck glanced back to his notes. "How about the threshold issues? You talked about the church door, I believe, and your own? Are the thresholds escalating?"

Jesus, what a whack-job list. When they went through them—his *things*—that way, there was nowhere to hide. He was the opposite of fixed; he was broken and getting brokener.

"Yeah." Adam slumped lower in the chair. "Lots of them, actually. There's the church and tons of classrooms at school, but especially the large biology lab. Three subway entrances. The side door to Brenda's and, like, four random store-type places. Robyn's front door, although she doesn't know that yet. I just walked by a couple of times in the last week."

"And . . ."

Adam wrapped his right foot behind his left and tapped. "And the worst is my house. Next thing you know, I'll be wearing a tinfoil hat." He shook his head. "My own house. It's escalating."

Chuck didn't seem to be impressed. "Front or side or back door?"

"All of them, but the front is the real problem, and to tell you the truth, I don't think you could get in through the side or back doors anymore."

"How involved?"

"The quickest I can now do is twenty-seven minutes."

Chuck let out a long, slow exhale. "That's a tough one, but again I want to assure you that it is entirely normal and within the scope of this disorder that a progressive deterioration might occur. You are *not* crazy and I need you to stop calling yourself that in your head. I know you do that. At the root, as you know, is fear, dread, anxiety. I personally believe that OCD has more of a neurobiological than a psychological basis, although one's emotional environment is critical to the presentation. And bear in mind that most threshold issues present most prominently at the patient's principal abode."

"Yeah, whatever." Adam crossed and recrossed his legs. This was going nowhere. Chuck didn't understand, wasn't getting it. "But I *have* to get fixed, like *totally* this time, right? Like, counting actual things and the Internet scrolling went away, and now I've got all this crap and it's worse. Look, I know *cure* isn't in the cards, but control— that's possible, isn't it? You said so that one time. So I'll do that exposure thing. I will. I'll do it all, whatever it takes." Adam couldn't stop shivering. "You've seen my Lists, the old ones. I have to get better for Robyn. I have to protect her and . . . well, Robyn and me . . ."

Chuck put down his notepad and his pen, and smiled. Nobody smiled like Chuck. "You have strong feelings for her."

"Well, yeah, that's putting it mildly." Adam stared at the blinking recording machine. "But it's like she's way ahead of me in this race. I can feel it. She seems . . . so much better."

Chuck pressed pause on the machine.

"She is, Adam."

She is?

"She is." He nodded solemnly. "I am not her attending thera-pist, so this is only a theory, only hypothetical, but I think Robyn is struggling to accept that. It's for her attending to call the shots. But you see, sometimes participants have trouble letting go, even when it is in their best interests."

"Huh?"

"OCD symptoms can, as we know, fluctuate over time." Chuck leaned forward, closing the distance between himself and Adam. "And in five to ten percent of all cases, patients experience a spontaneous and complete remission of all their OCD symp-toms. Some believe it might have a hormonal link, but"—he removed his glasses—"we don't know."

Remission. Adam did not hear a single word after "remission." That was like *cure*, right? They never talked about cure with him. *Never.* Here *he* was, going to hang his guts out to dry for a chance at *controlling* his symptoms. And *she* was fixed!

"In my experience, it can be an episodic remission, meaning it *can* return, months or years later, but every day would be—"

"A day in heaven," Adam whispered. What *would* that be like? To wake up one morning and be *normal?* To not bite down and parcel out each second of each day. To not wrestle and negotiate with your obsessions. To not have thoughts that ran you into the ground.

To have a quiet mind.

A quiet mind.

Quiet.

Shh.

But *he* was keeping her in hell, with him, watching him, fretting over him.

"The remission, uh, how long has it . . . ?"

Chuck didn't answer directly. "Again, academically speaking, I believe that a person experiencing said remission should continue with her attending therapist, but that an OCD group may be more of a hindrance than a helping element, especially if a person like that were vulnerable to a co-morbidity, the most common of which is depression. I believe that is where the focus should be concentrated."

Adam's stomach gnarled itself into ever-tighter knots. He said nothing.

"Adam." Chuck leaned closer to him. "You will reach that point too. I know it. You will do the work. You will no longer need us, me." *Blah, blah, blah, blah.*

One, three, five, seven, nine, eleven . . .

They spent the last fifteen minutes reviewing and reality-checking. Chuck offered a couple of good suggestions about the doors, but later Adam couldn't remember them because he hadn't been paying attention. Still, whatever it was he said, Chuck's soft, warm voice calmed his chattering heart.

Temporarily.

The dread came charging back as soon as the hour was up.

"Adam? One more quick thing." Chuck took off his glasses and rubbed his eyes. "Do you ever cry? I mean lately. I know you haven't in the past few years, but recently, with all the upheaval and turmoil. Do you ever cry?"

The question surprised him. He had to think about it. "Uh, okay, I'm not much of a guy, I'll grant you, but I am a guy, so, no, I don't cry, and no, I haven't been crying lately."

"Never?"

"Never."

"It might be a good thing, a healthy thing, if you did, if you could. We'll note it to talk about and explore in—"

Adam was already heading for the doors.

He rode up and down the hospital elevators. "Shit!" he yelled as he pressed all the odd numbers. He didn't care if anyone heard; he was leaving the shrink floor. They'd all be used to twitchy psychos muttering to themselves. "Batman my ass. Some protector I am!"

Robyn's Batman had not come to save her. She was doing just fine until Batman came into her life.

And *now* she was in danger.

Because of him.

He reached the ground floor and pressed all the odd numbers up to seventeen again and again and again. He disgusted himself. After thirty-seven minutes, Adam emerged from the elevator.

He *had* to get better. He promised himself. He just *had* to.

And then he got worse.

CHAPTER THIRTY-FOUR

When Adam finally emerged from the hospital elevator he headed straight for the cemetery. He had to jump the fence because it was already dark and the gates were closed. Once in, he made his way to the massive black granite headstone that he had first encountered just over six months ago. He stopped, genuflected in the muddy ground and made the sign of the cross. Adam apologized profusely to Jennifer Roehampton, May 7, 1971–October 14, 2008, and asked for her forgiveness for almost crippling her daughter.

He swore that he would make it right, and that he would keep on coming no matter what, to pay his respects, to atone.

Even in the dark Adam could see the black varicose veins of the willow's trunk. The old tree had protected them, hidden them. He had propped Robyn against it on Monday, and for at least a while, time had stopped, they had so been lost in the taste and wonder of each other. Now he wanted to climb inside of it and stay there. Instead, he jumped the south fence and made his way out.

And then he got home.

And then he couldn't get in.

At all.

Adam gave up after forty-one minutes of trying. The door to his very own home was impenetrable. He couldn't clear it. At 9:07, Adam crossed the street and knocked on Mrs. Polanski's door. She answered it instantly, having no doubt been a front-row spectator to this theatre of the absurd.

"Hi, Mrs. Polanski, how are you?"

"Adam, are you okay?"

"Yes, ma'am. I mean, no, ma'am. I, uh, I can't get into my house and my mom's on night shifts this week."

"Oh, my dear." She frowned but opened the door wide. "Well, our houses are practically the same."

And then he saw it.

"And my boys knew how to jiggle both the back and side door locks in a certain way that would get them to open. Or they'd use credit cards. Do you want to try with my credit card, dear?" She started to turn.

"No, no, ma'am. I can't. Those doors, they, uh, they can't be opened." He was hypnotized by the house, *his* house, or at least a mirror image of it from a long ago time. There was the sheer expanse of the welcoming hallway, leading off to a spotless bright kitchen. Adam was pierced by a memory of his house being welcoming, breathable, clean. To his horror, tears sprang to the back of his eyes, but thank God they stayed there.

"There, there, dear. Pay no attention to me, I'm just a prattling old thing. Come in, come in. What would you like to do, dear?"

"I'd like to . . . uh, could I borrow your phone, please, and call my dad to pick me up?"

"Of course! Come into the kitchen. That's where I keep my

phone and it's actually attached to the wall, I'm afraid. The boys are always on me, but I would just lose something that's not attached, don't you think?"

He hoped he was smiling at her.

Mrs. Polanski's kitchen had escaped any attempts at a reno or "freshening" over the years, but it was gleaming and ready for action. The cupboards were painted a snowy white and the blue counters were immaculate and free of anything, save a toaster and a bowl of green apples. Adam never wanted to leave. It was like the best memory of the best day in his own house . . . before.

Before everything.

Mrs. Polanski put on a teakettle and placed a mammoth piece of apple strudel in front of him as he reached for the phone.

"Sweetie? Is Dad there?"

"Batman! Are you coming home? Come home, okay?"

"Yeah, yeah, I will, but put Dad on, okay?"

"Now? Are you coming now? Come now!"

"Yeah, I'm coming. I promise. Now go get Dad."

The phone was dropped and Adam heard Sweetie tearing around the house yelling for his dad. "Daaad, Batman's coming home. Dad!"

"Adam? Hi, son. What's up?"

"Dad?" His heart settled as soon as he heard his father's voice. "Could you come and get me? I'm at Mrs. Polanski's."

"Did something happen?"

"No, sir."

"Are you okay? Is it your mother?"

"No, not . . . um, I can't get into the house. I cannot *enter.*" He glanced at Mrs. Polanski. "I had that appointment and then I went, uh . . ." She was busy making the tea at the far end of the kitchen and trying to look like she couldn't hear. "Then I did an errand and came back and . . . was not able to get in."

"Does your mother—"

"No, sir. Could you call her and tell her at work?"

"Is she on late shift?"

"Yes, sir. Tonight and tomorrow until midnight. And could you tell her that I'll be staying for a few days?"

"Adam, you know how she—"

"I know it's not your weekend."

Mrs. Polanski bustled over with teacups, a sugar bowl, milk and Godiva chocolates that had to be at least forty years old. Adam nodded and smiled a thank-you to her.

"Tell her that I am the one that asked."

Now she was slicing some bologna and cheese. It was like a reverse dinner.

"No, tell her"—he cupped the mouthpiece with his hand— "tell her that Chuck suggested it. She'll buy that and he'll back me up."

"Adam, are you really telling me that you can't get through your own—"

"No." It had come to this. How? "I can't, Dad. No."

"I'll be right there. Tell Mrs. Polanski thanks from me."

"Yeah, okay." The room seemed to sway in relief. "I will for sure. Bye."

He turned to Mrs. Polanski. "He says to thank you very much and we all apologize for the inconvenience and—"

She caught Adam in her cushiony arms in two strides. Hugging him hard, surprising them both. Miraculously, he "fit" well into her short dumpling body.

"We often hurt the ones we love, dear."

Adam exhaled. "It's what I do best, Mrs. Polanski."

"I doubt that, dear. You're a good boy. I'm old and I've seen a lot." Mrs. Polanski sighed, returning to the bologna. "And remember what a busybody I am. Not much escapes me." Now that she'd sliced enough meat for a squadron, she continued to fuss about with the dishes and silverware.

"Sometimes it's actually necessary to hurt the ones you love. You can check that out with your fancy-pants doctor, or whoever you go to every Monday." She patted his hand. "Letting go, Adam. It's the really hard part of growing up. You're ready."

She was right.

It was time.

But how?

"Now, do you like mustard or ketchup with your bologna?"

CHAPTER THIRTY-FIVE

There was no getting rid of Sweetie, of course. He was on Adam like a suction cup. "You're here! You came! I'll be good and I won't pest you, I promise!"

By "good," Sweetie meant that he wouldn't bother Adam while he was on the phone with Robyn, *not* that he would *leave him alone* while he was on the phone with Robyn. Over the next couple of weeks, Sweetie's routine would be to sit quietly on the other side of his bed, pretending to play with his ever-growing empire of Tonka trucks while Adam whispered to Robyn.

Adam always closed his eyes and let Robyn's satiny voice cover him. Tonight she talked about how her dad had actually booked off an entire week for spring break. They were going to go skiing in Whistler and bring her baking friend. Robyn was going to take lessons. "If only you could come instead of Jody, it would be perfect. Imagine us in all that snow."

He missed her already, ached for her. But she sounded so surprised and happy about her father arranging it all.

Adam had hoped that they would see each other every single

day during break. He needed to kiss her. As they talked, he would disappear into the movie of them. Scenes of them leaning against Marnie Wetherall or sitting on the cold hard winter grass as grimy icicles dripped off the willow. Scenes of them kissing and holding each other against the raw stone, touching each other, exploring shyly. "I love you, Adam." "I love you more, Robyn." They were always warm together in the cold. Good thing too. He couldn't bring her to his house, and she didn't ask him back to hers. So, protected by Marnie or the willow, he replayed every kiss, every touch and every caress—until he remembered to return to the conversation.

"So it's kind of a 'who do I think I am' thing. I've never even been to a single drama club meeting and now I want to try out for the lead."

"What's the play?"

"*One Flew Over the Cuckoo's Nest.*"

"Really? Really, Robyn? You doubt for a single second that you'd nail the role of Nurse Ratched? You could do it on life experience alone, never mind brilliant acting talent. Watch the movie, it's superior."

"You are impossible *and* adorable, you know."

"No, I'm not," he mumbled. *I so am not.* "It's true, that word, about you—*adorable*, I mean."

"How do you do that? How do you make me feel this way? I don't even know what it is. Wait, that's a lie, I do know. I've known from the beginning, from when you took the stairs that first time because of Wonder Woman. You are so *good*. It's like I feel safe with you, safer than with anyone else in the whole world."

He felt like he'd swallowed a tray of ice cubes. "Really?"

"It's true. I didn't know it was true until I said it, but it's true."

She was smiling. He could always tell by the timbre of her voice. And that hurt even more. He couldn't take it. Adam explained that he wouldn't be calling over the next few days, that privacy at Brenda's was simply not an option and it was killing him.

He needed time to sort it out.

Everybody lies.

"I'll miss your voice. I can't wait to meet him—your Sweetie, I mean."

"Yeah," Adam whispered. "Yeah."

Unable to contain himself a second longer, that same Sweetie erupted into exploding cannonballs, bouncing from one bed to the other the whole time that the two engaged in their mandatory marathon closing.

"Well, good night, fair queen. I'll hold on to you while you hang up."

"No, dear prince, I will hold on while you let go."

"Hang on a sec." Adam covered the receiver. "Sweetie, quit bopping around before I break your other arm."

Instead, Sweetie burst into giggles and bounced with greater abandon.

"I think I see what you mean." Robyn laughed.

"Yeah, well, there you go. So, dear angel, you hang up while I hold on to you."

"No, dear angel, you hang up," Sweetie parroted.

So much for "not pesting." Adam picked his brother up and held on to him until Robyn finally hung up first.

He was drained by the time Sweetie regained his freedom. "Goof!"

"Now?" said Sweetie. "*Now* can we be us?"

"Not yet. I just have a bit of homework to do first, okay?"

Sweetie sighed hugely and dragged himself back to his Tonkas, contenting himself with crashing them into ear-splitting pileups.

Adam went to the desk and retrieved a piece of paper. He had promised Chuck that he'd bring in the List for their next session. Maybe if he brought in the List, he could put off the ERP discussion some more.

March 9	**THE LIST**	Adam Spencer Ross

Meds: Ativan (I need a new prescription)
Anafranil 25 mg 3 x per day (need a new scrip there too)

1. I believe that Robyn Isobel Plummer is my one true love, my first love, and that I will never ever love anyone like I love her.
2. I believe that getting fixed is pretty much the most important thing in the world.
3. I believe that I will for sure start the exposure thing and do everything I need to do this time (including these stupid lists).
4. I believe that I don't know what to do about my mom.
5. I believe that my mom, my dad, Brenda, Sweetie and Robyn all actually love me. I no longer believe that is enough to fix me.
6. I believe that I lie when I have to and that everybody lies. Deal with it.
7. I believe that even numbers are a bitch.
8. I believe that the threshold and door stuff is serious and getting worse.

9. I believe that all of the superheroes (maybe even Wolverine) are my friends and that I am theirs. This is important in a way I haven't figured out yet.

10. I believe that I am unclean and will harm those I care about the most and that there is too much noise in my head and that I am so goddamned tired.

Adam folded the paper, slowly got up and reached for his PJs. Sweetie was like a golden retriever on steroids. "*Now* can we play Batman? Can I be Robin, just for pretend? I know you have a Robin, even though she's a girl, but can I be Robin and we can kill the Joker to death? Huh?"

He was hollowed out, couldn't even smile at his brother. It would cost too much.

Robyn.

There were also times when they didn't kiss and roam non-stop. The in-between times. That's when they just held each other and whispered. Marnie, of course, heard it all. Adam would try to make Robyn laugh, and she would, whether it was funny or not. She would tease him and he would tell her what it was like *before*. And they talked about what it would be like *after*. It was as if they were two normal kids in love, sitting on a sofa in a warm living room, telling each other almost everything and sorting out the world with someone's mom puttering annoyingly in the background. Except, of course, they weren't two normal kids. Would never be.

"No, sorry, little guy. I can't. I'm just so . . ." He got into his bed and lay on his side.

"Did she make you sad? You're sad. Did she make you sad?"

"No, no, she didn't. It's not like that, it's . . . Look, I'm too tired, Sweetie, okay?" He girded himself for the onslaught of pleas and pushes. It didn't come.

"Okay," Sweetie whispered. He turned off the table lamp and even unplugged two of the four night lights. He padded back to Adam and tucked him in properly, smooshing the covers just so and knocking him about with his cast in the process. Finally satisfied with the tucking, Sweetie climbed up and sat beside Adam, propping himself against the headboard.

"I'll stand on guard, okay?" He yawned. "I will keep you safe."

Adam nodded. He couldn't trust his voice.

"Would you like to borrow my one hundred and eleven number? I'll give it to you. That's a one and a one and a one."

Adam nodded again, too tired to speak, using all that was left of his strength to stop the tears before they started.

CHAPTER THIRTY-SIX

Wonder Woman's chair sat aggressively empty. Nobody said anything. It gnawed at him. She was AWOL again. Wonder Woman was the only one of them who had missed any sessions. The rest of the superheroes scored a perfect attendance record. They were crazy, but keenly so.

Adam surveyed the room, stopped at Wolverine.

Damn. Wolverine looked good. He always looked good, but lately he was looking alarmingly good. Was Wolverine getting better? That would be seriously *unendurable*. Adam listened carefully as Wolverine droned on about his deadly disease du jour; he had moved on from heart ailments to critical blood cancers. "Do you even know the symptoms of multiple myeloma? I have been lethargic for five days now. I'm going for tests . . ."

Naw, he was still nuts. Green Lantern, however, seemed to be making progress, and Adam, no matter how bent out of shape he was, could not begrudge the green guy his victories.

"So I'm trying to follow that OCD manual by the letter, but I'm probably still calling Chuck way too much."

Chuck smiled and shook his head.

It struck Adam at that moment that Chuck had a lot of them as private patients as well, and that they must all call him. And then he realized that he had tons of other private patients who must also call and cry and whinge. So when did the therapist chill or BBQ with his family? Did he have a family? Chuck sat quietly while still managing to nudge and cheer them on like there was nowhere else he'd rather be. The guy should get a medal or a car or something. Adam wasn't sure why he was getting these blinding little insights, but lately he'd started to notice the world around him a bit more. Just how much Chuck, Brenda and his father had to put up with. Adam noticed it and it sucked that he noticed.

It was hard enough when he didn't notice.

"So you're not rewinding at all?" asked Snooki. Everyone in Group knew that one of Green Lantern's "things" was revisiting the scene of his latest imagined catastrophe, whether physically or in his head.

"Well, yeah, a bit," admitted Green Lantern. "But I've mapped it all out as per page 147, and I'm rating each compulsion like it says. And, I don't know, just doing that actually cuts it down a pile."

"Wow," said Adam. "That's impressive, man. I've got to get my butt in on the exposure stuff, but it's scaring the crap out of me and I haven't even opened the stupid manual."

Green Lantern tried hard not to look pleased with himself.

Adam could tell that his breakthrough impressed the hell out everyone except for maybe Thor. He couldn't see Thor making maps of his rituals and compulsions and whatever else he had going on—which, let's face it, had to be higher on the *I am crazy* scale than on the regular OCD one. Adam turned to Thor. The big guy had been unusually quiet. Okay, he was always quiet, except for the growling, but today and last time he seemed too—what? Placid? When Adam finally caught his eye, there was barely a response.

It made Adam unbearably sad.

He held Thor's eyes as he jumped back into the fray.

"Yeah, well, at the other end of the scale—I've hit a new high or low or whatever. I can't go home," he said. "I can't get through the door at all."

That got everyone's attention. Thor stayed on him, cloudy-eyed but on him.

"I couldn't get in one night—just couldn't break through—and I haven't been back since. I have enough stuff at my step-mother's to get me by, you know?"

"What the hell?" snapped Wolverine. "What kind of pussy are you? Your old lady is being stalked by a psycho-turd and you take off on her?"

You could smell the indignation. Everyone sat up straighter. Robyn and Snooki glared at Wolverine, and Thor even roused himself out of his fog enough to emit a decent approximation of a growl.

Wolverine was right, though. "I agree." Adam nodded. "It's total candy-ass." Snooki's hand shot to his knee. She was patting energetically. "But I'm a mess and the house situation and the situation with"—*careful, careful*—"my mom and the letters, and not being able to breach the threshold . . . Aargh! I *do* worry for her. I make myself puke. That I can't just snap out of this and take care of—"

"Nobody here is judging you, Batman," interrupted Iron Man. "Nobody. That's too much. You do what you got to do." Thor *grrrr*-ed in agreement. "But no one's judging you, man." He eye-balled Wolverine.

"Yeah," said Snooki. "Like, you are so here for everyone in here, all the time. I don't think it even registers with you how much you carry. You worry about too many people, *like* your mom, *and* your fat friend, *and* your little brother, *and*"—she shot Robyn a look—"and God only knows who else. Cut yourself some slack, Batman."

He'd talked about Stones to them?

"She's right," whispered Robyn. "She's right."

"Yeah, man," said Captain America and Green Lantern in unison.

"No crap, man. Too much is too much." Iron Man was shaking his head.

"No, see, Wolverine actually nailed it when—"

"Excuse me, Batman." Chuck rarely inserted himself into the conversation, so it was always an event when he piped up. "But how about you let those comments wash over you for a bit. Let them sit for a while. Let them challenge what you perceive to be the truth. Maybe they're valid observations. *Maybe* you can trust them."

Adam exhaled before speaking. "Thanks, guys," he said to his feet. "I mean it." His feet were still. His breath was even. No single part of Adam was counting, until the end.

At 4:51 p.m., Chuck cleared his throat. "Uh, you've all no doubt noticed Wonder Woman's, uh, Connie's absence." *Connie? Why had Wonder Woman become Connie again?* "We—that is, Connie and her family—have decided that it would be best for her to continue her treatment by entering the residential program in Houston."

Residential. The word swirled around the circle menacingly and landed with a thud.

Residential.

Shit.

No one breathed, let alone said anything. Chuck looked taken aback by the silence.

"Whoa, guys!" said Robyn. "It's not a death sentence. It's the best thing for Con— er, Wonder Woman. We all know she's been sliding. Look, residential was a massive piece in my being able to function and put one foot in front of the other."

Residential.

"I honest to God don't know where I'd be without it, *or* without you guys." She looked directly at Adam.

"Robyn is right." Chuck nodded. "This is an extremely positive step for Connie and she will join us all again in a few weeks. I'll update you as best I can, and we'll talk about getting in touch next session, okay? So until then, try to remember that this is the very best thing for her." He glanced at his watch. "Okay, superheroes, good work today. Class dismissed."

Snooki got up and left without saying a word.

While they were stacking chairs, Adam whispered to Robyn that he'd meet her at the gates.

"You got it." And she kissed him, long and hard.

Everyone had left except for Chuck and Thor, but they saw. And they looked sad.

When Thor clomped out, Adam ran to keep up with him. Thor always took the stairs, not because he was claustrophobic but—Wait a minute. Thor might be claustrophobic. Thor might be a thousand things. Adam didn't know. What Adam did know was that the guy was in a lot of pain. It wafted off him in waves. The waves had struck Adam from the very first session. It was familiar.

"Thor, wait!"

The big guy turned unsteadily in the stairwell.

Adam's nerve was quickly evaporating. Again, even though he was two steps lower than him, the mighty Thor was taller, larger, more substantial in every way.

"Look, Thor, something's up. It's none of my business, but are you okay? I mean, meds and meds adjustments can mess you up almost as much as the OCD can. Believe me, I know." It was like trying to converse with a mountain. "So I just want to know if you're okay, okay? The thing with Wonder Woman, you know, it can spook a person."

Thor tried unsuccessfully to focus on Adam. Zombie eyes. Adam recognized the effort, remembered the trial and error, the weeks and weeks of side effects, thick tongue, exhaustion and body tremors until they arrived at a manageable meds combo and dosage.

"Hey, remember how we all wrote down our phone numbers that first session?"

Thor was still struggling to aim his eyes.

"Well, you're probably more of a text guy, but I'm not allowed anything like that, right?"

Thor nodded, or he wanted to, Adam was sure of it, and sure as well that a decent guy was trapped in there somewhere.

"Well, Brenda, my stepmom, her number is on that list too, okay? You can call me there anytime, man. And once they get your meds squared up, I bet you'd go for a wicked game of Warhammer, eh?"

No response.

"Hell, you look fiercer than the fiercest Orc. Ben—that's my fat friend that Snooki was referring to—well, Stones would get a real kick out of you, and you'd like him, I guarantee it!"

Thor lifted his big beefy arm, placed it on Adam's wiry shoulder and looked in his general direction. "I got you covered."

Okay, so not exactly what Adam was going for.

"Well, thanks. But I mean it about calling, anytime."

Thor sighed as he turned. And the two walked down the rest of the stairs in a companionable if confused silence.

CHAPTER THIRTY-SEVEN

"**Y**ou were great in there, in Group." She kissed his cheek. "But look, I know you tried to talk to Thor." Robyn slipped her arm through his, as she always did, and they walked like this to the cemetery. She kissed him again. "You know you can't save everybody, right?"

"What?"

"It's part of your problem, like Snooki was saying as she was gripping your knee. Once in a while, even that over-toasted air-head stumbles onto something."

"What do you mean?"

"Thor," she said. "You forget, I've been through a lot more programs, therapists and hospital groups than you. And . . . well, you learn to recognize the Thors. The Thors of this world tend not to make it through, Adam."

Spoken like someone who has.

"No, I, uh, just think that he's on the wrong meds combo. The poor guy could be too heavy into the old-school bennies. Clonazepam could do that, or even Anafranil. The guy could hardly move, you know. I actually think he's lots better."

Robyn cocked her head.

"Except for lately."

"You just *have* to save the world, don't you." She squeezed him to her. He was heading straight for a Sister Mary-Margaret intervention. "It's one of the seventy-three thousand reasons I love you."

He wanted to grab her and pull her into him and never let go. They would freeze into a headstone, forever linked and together.

They were almost at the weeping willow.

"But really, my very own Batman, you've got to let go of all those distractions, all those extra worries, and concentrate on yourself." Robyn looked uncomfortable. "I mean it. You've got to home in on just you. Please. Please just get yourself better first." She kissed him again and gently extricated herself to go to her mother's grave.

The black headstone devoured what was left of the weakening sun.

Adam reacquainted himself with the neighbours, the monuments and the stone angels. He remembered how all those months ago he had tried to puzzle out which one she was visiting. He greeted young Lieutenant Archibald-Lewis, all those who were engraved into the base of the two soaring obelisks, and their favourite, Marnie Wetherall, 1935–1939. Adam offered up a quick prayer for their souls and a longer one begging for strength.

Robyn executed a round of the rosary. After she'd made her final sign of the cross she turned to him. "Did I tell you that I contacted Father Rick and he put me in touch with Father Steven at St. Bonaventure, which is apparently my parish church?"

Adam didn't say anything. It was so clear.

"So I'm going to start their 'I Wannabe a Catholic' classes on April 27!"

Even from this distance he could feel that she was centred, whole.

"Cool, eh?" Robyn frowned when he still didn't respond. "Isn't that great?"

She didn't even need him for the God stuff. There was no value added with him whatsoever, just distraction and detraction. Adam held her back in a place where she no longer belonged. He couldn't lie to himself anymore. He was a prisoner. She was free.

"Hey, earth to Adam!" Robyn waved both arms in the air. "What's up, Batman?" She started towards him. "Something's up. The past couple of weeks, at Group, on the phone . . . I know you've got a ton of stuff with your mom, but that's not it, is it?"

"No," he said.

She hugged herself.

He couldn't do it. "I lied to you."

She nodded, waiting.

"I don't live in your neighbourhood. I live at almost the opposite end of the city from you. I've been doubling back all these months. And my dad's place is even farther north."

"Oh, that!" Robyn said, relief clearly washing over her. "I know about that."

"What!"

"I've known almost from the beginning." She waved her hand. "I asked my cousin, who's a senior at St. Mary's, to get me your PTA list. She's a bitch, but she did it. Your address is in there— 97 Chatsworth." She smiled, and he heard his heart crack open.

"Why didn't you say anything? I feel even more like a jerk."

"No, don't! I thought it was so incredibly sweet that you were pretending to live nearby just to walk home with me, just to be with me. Even in here, in this place."

Adam nodded to his shoes.

"Then it sort of got too late to say anything and I didn't know . . ."

"Yeah, same," he said. "I felt crappy about it, but I didn't know how to undo it. I couldn't stand thinking what you might think." Adam shook his head. "Everybody lies."

Robyn joined him on the path. She stood in front of him. Her smile vanished. "But that's not it, is it?"

Adam raised his eyes to meet hers. "No."

She swayed a bit.

"You're better. I am not."

"Not true!" She grabbed his arms. "And even if it was, who cares? You'll get better and fast. What does—?"

Adam put his finger to her mouth. "I'm a hell of a long way from better. I can't even see the finish line anymore." He stopped and searched for that one good breath. "I know that you shouldn't even be in Group at all. My hunch is that your therapist is warning you off it, and off me too. This—we, *us*—is not good for you, Robyn."

"Shut up!" She threw her arms around him. "You, Adam, are the best thing that has ever happened to me. Ever! You've helped me so much." She clung to him. "You helped me face my stuff and tell the truth. You make me brave. *You* do that! And once you get going on the ERP—"

"Like you said, you've been through a lot more programs and therapists and groups, Robyn. You *know* I'm worse." Adam kissed her forehead and then her face over and over again, memorizing the salt-and-peach taste of her. "I've been reading all about spontaneous remissions—what you have. It's like a miracle, but it could come back. In the meantime, you have to get clear while you can. Robyn, you have to celebrate, not feel guilty because I can't get myself under control. You have to use this time right now to get stronger every day, so that if it does come back, you can be powerful enough—"

"I'm not some kind of warrior in one of your fantasy games! I need you!"

"You so *are* a warrior. Don't you see?" He pulled her into him and kissed her hair. "You *don't* need me. I just made you believe that because I love you so, so much, Robyn Plummer."

"But I love you more, Adam Spencer Ross! It's what makes me strong, I swear!"

"No! You're strong because you're you." He swallowed the hurt before it swallowed him. He was gutless. "Robyn, you deserve—"

She tried to hug him again, but he held her arms tight. The cemetery was eerily still. They seemed entombed in the silence.

"You are the bravest person I have ever, or will ever, meet."

"I sweat terror, Robyn! I'm scared every single second about every single goddamned thing. I worry obsessively about being buried under an avalanche of fear. Jesus, Robyn, I'm scared like only the truly crazy can be."

"But *that*, you dope, is the definition of courage: you go on *despite* the fear." She pulled back and hugged herself. "And it's just a matter of time, a short time, before—" The darkening sky joined in on their bewilderment and started to drizzle.

"You're not listening," he said. "Whatever I've got or not got, it's exactly the wrong thing for you to be around. It's bad for you. Your housekeeper sensed it. Chuck knows it. I'm sure your therapist has warned you."

"They are all so full of—"

"And you know it too." He stroked her cheek. "Look at me. Have you ever told your father about me, like you said you would?"

Her eyes glistened. "I . . . the thing is—"

"See? Part of you—the best part of you—knows. Trust that part, Robyn. It's the part that will keep you well."

She was crying now. It was an ugly cry, snot soaked, heaving, and he loved her more.

"Adam, I can't . . . It's because I lied so much, and then I told you too much about how awful I—"

"No! Stop, stop. It's none of that. I was"—he scrambled in a panic for the word—"I was *honoured*. It made me feel important."

"Because you *are*, damn it! Listen to me, Adam!"

"Shh, you know I'm right. And even if you didn't"—he leaned into her and whispered—"it wouldn't matter. Nothing could change my mind. Nothing. You have to go now." As he scrambled, he remembered Mrs. Polanski's advice. *It's time to leave. It's the really hard part of growing up—knowing when to leave.*

"Who's doing the leaving, Adam? Who the hell is doing the leaving? Answer me that! I can't be brave without you."

"Yes, you can. It's time. You have to be with *normal* people now." She looked like she was going to erupt. "With normal*er* people. This is what you need. You know I'm right, Robyn. Don't make this harder. I can't take it."

"Good. I hate you! I hate your crazy guts and it should be hard!" she spat. But she drew herself back into him. "God, I didn't mean that. I'm sorry, I'm sorry. But I won't let you go. I can't, Adam. Don't make me."

He was weakening. The coward in him, the hunger, would win. "I need you to go now." He held her as tight as any human being could hold another. "I need to concentrate only on me. I'm falling apart, Robyn. You can't save me. You're making it worse."

Everybody lies.

That did it.

"Oh, Adam, damn! Oh God, this hurts. I can't . . ."

He kissed her hard, almost wanting to hurt her more. They hugged, heartbroken and wretched. Robyn crying and Adam mourning, even as he held her. Each trying to find a way in, to memorize the feel of the other. They clung to each other right up until they were interrupted by the flashing high beams of a car. Again, a door slammed. Again, a flashlight turned on them.

"Get a room, guys. It's past closing, for God's sake!"

They turned to the security guard, who looked startled to see them. "You two again! What is it with you? You never have enough sense to get in out of the rain!" Then he paused. "And you look like a couple of train wrecks," he muttered as he turned back to his car. "I'll keep both the south and north gates open for another five minutes, but that's it." The door slammed and his vehicle rolled away.

"We better go." Robyn reached for Adam's hand and began walking towards the south gate.

"No, Robyn. I don't live over there and we're not pretending anymore. I'm going back through the north gates."

They were soaked to the bone and still they didn't move.

"Okay," she finally said. "You turn around and go first. I'll watch and keep you safe."

"No, it's my job to keep you safe."

"Go! It's pouring, and we're going to drown. Go!" She pushed him. "Adam, let *me* take care of you, just this once."

He shoved his hands deep into his pockets and shook his head. "No, Robyn. Please. Let me do this one thing, this one more time. Please."

Fresh tears streamed down her face and mingled with the rain. Adam was spent, his heart so full of grief there wasn't room for coherent thought. Robyn turned and began to walk away. He watched her go, holding her deep inside him, until she was just about to disappear around the bend.

"I will always love you, Robyn Plummer," he whispered.

And just as she disappeared, he distinctly heard it.

"And I will always love you more, Adam Spencer Ross."

CHAPTER THIRTY-EIGHT

When Adam got to the north gate he turned left rather than right, heading towards 97 Chatsworth. It wasn't a conscious thing. His mind was too pockmarked and punctured for a deliberate decision, but even when he realized that he wasn't headed for his dad's, he did not turn back. Adam wanted to go home.

Minutes—or was it hours?—later, when he got to the foot of his path, Adam glanced over at Mrs. Polanski's. No lights. She wasn't home. Mrs. Polanski wouldn't be there to save him. *That's okay*, he told himself. *Mom's home.* Carmella had been on double shift all last week and had been home the past four days.

All he had to do was get in.

The closer Adam got to the door, the more it felt like he was walking through a net of razor blades. It would have been an 11 out of 10 on the OCD mapping scale, if he had ever mapped, if he had ever done anything in the damn manual. But there was never any time. His life kept getting in the way.

When he stepped on the landing dripping with rain, he could sense the force field surrounding the threshold. The razors nicked him. And even though he knew better, Adam checked for signs of blood. *These thoughts are not reality; they are mere thoughts.* He faced the door with a raggedy breath. The field around it shimmered.

No way.

His courage dissolved into the fog. Robyn was wrong. He *was* gutless.

And then he smelled it.

Unmistakable. He had lived with the terror of this possibility for years.

It was coming from inside the house.

"Mom! Mom! Open up, Mom!" He extended his arm to begin the ritual, the clearing, but there was no time. *It's all a lie, it's not real! Just go through!*

Adam reached into his pocket, but he was bathed in sweat by the time he pulled out the key.

She would die if he touched the door unclean.

She would die if he *didn't* touch the door.

He was shaking uncontrollably. As he raised the hand that held the key, the world spun, whipping around faster and faster. His stomach pitched. Nausea erupted and he just barely managed to turn his head in time. He threw up and then turned the key in the lock.

"Mom!"

He shoved open the door, except that he couldn't. There was too much stuff in the way on the other side. It was jammed! "Mom! Jesus!" Adam threw his shoulder into the door. He could see in just enough to confirm that smoke was billowing out of the kitchen. "Mom, please!" Just as he readied to throw himself into the door again, he heard steps pounding behind him, gaining, and then the door exploded. It opened another six inches.

"Again! Let's go again, Batman! Together! On three. *One . . .*"

"Thor! What the hell . . . how?"

"*Two . . .*"

"Thor?"

"*Three!*"

The boys threw themselves at the door, forcing it another three inches. Still not enough.

"I'll push, you squeeze in," Thor grunted.

Within seconds, Adam had wedged himself through and was leap-frogging over junk on his way to the kitchen. "Mom! Mom!"

He saw her immediately. His mother was slumped on the floor in front of the island that divided the kitchen from the dining room. A winter boot lay awkwardly under her foot. Had she tripped? Carmella's eyes were closed, but she winced, moved. An egg-sized lump had already developed on her forehead. A glue stick fell out of her hand when she tried to right herself.

"MOM!"

Adam threw himself into the kitchen and at the stove. Angry smoke rushed out of a lone pot. There was no fire, but the pot was purging itself of burnt soup and a plastic ladle. Miraculously, he had the presence of mind to turn off the gas burner rather than grab the pot handle.

Adam was dimly aware that Thor was now in the hall. Somehow he had made it in. "Thor, call 9-1-1!" yelled Adam as he reached for his mother.

Carmella's eyes flew open. "Adam? Adam, no!" she coughed. "They can't come. Stop him!"

Adam tried to help her up. She clung to him in a panic.

"He was here!" Carmella's voice was hoarse. "We fought. It was terrible, horrible. He is so evil. He wouldn't have come if you'd been here. He said that. That's what he said. We fought. See, he hit me! He hit me, Adam." His mother touched her forehead and winced. She started to cry but without tears. "He could have killed me, baby."

Adam took in the glass on the counter, the vodka bottle beside it, the magazine, the ripped-out pages on top of the other mess. "Let me help you up, Mom. Can you get up?"

"Yes, of course. I'm fine. Call them off, I'm fine!" But she didn't get up and she didn't let go of him. "He was the devil himself." Her eyes were over-bright, desperate. "Oh, Adam, it was awful—thank God you came. Thank you, Lord!" She clasped her hands as if in prayer. "Now, stop that man this instant, before they come. Say it was a mistake." She grabbed his coat again. "You know *they* can't come here. *They* can't see . . . Adam, *you know*."

"Oh, Mom." All the fight leaked out of him. There was nothing left. They both heard Thor rummaging in the hall, shoving, piling.

"Thor?" Adam called.

"I'm clearing a path for the ambulance guys!"

"Make him stop!" Panic played across his mother's face. "Stop him right now! Adam, please!"

Adam gently pried her hands off him. His mother was still in her scrubs, even though she hadn't been to work in days. Still in Dad's sweater. Her lipstick was smeared, her dark hair dishevelled, and the egg on her forehead was already turning a pinkish mauve. Yet she was still lovely. People always said so and there it was. Indisputable.

And he looked like his mother. He was so much *like* his mother. *Jesus.*

"Adam, baby, now!" She ran her fingers through her hair. "He said if we told anyone, he'd come back. He'd get me. He'll kill me, Adam. He was even worse than in the letters, Adam, and you *know* how bad the letters are. I know you saw."

He heard sirens faintly, far away. He stopped to listen, to breathe, but he couldn't. He felt like he had been run over.

"Mom, listen, I've known almost from the beginning."

"There were more letters, baby. Lots. I didn't want to worry you. I decided not to worry you. He said that—"

"Stop, Mom." He leaned close to her ear. "Stop. Please stop now. I know that there is no *he*." He reached for her, but she leaned away from him. "I know it was you. I *know* you've been writing those letters to yourself." He picked up the glue stick and put it on top of the torn magazine pages.

"No, no. That's not . . . you don't understand. See . . ."

The sirens were closer now.

"Thor?" Adam called. Thor had all the numbers. "Call Chuck. I'm going to need Chuck—"

"No, baby, please!"

"And then call my dad."

They could both hear Thor carrying out Adam's instructions. They were the most sustained conversations that Thor had executed in years. But he did it.

His mother stopped protesting and fell into a steady silent sob in Adam's arms.

And that's how it was.

Until it wasn't.

Within seconds, it seemed, the house was filled with people. Radios crackled, men in steel-toed boots and uniforms sporting glow-in-the-dark strips of tape were followed by ambulance people pushing a gurney on wheels and carrying what seemed to be coolers full of stuff. All of them stepping on the stray junk, cursing quietly under their breath.

The truth came barging in with them.

And then Adam saw, really saw. He looked at his house as if through their eyes. He and his mom might as well have been living in a building in the Bronx with boarded-up windows. They were like squatters who had taken up residence in charred, garbage-filled rooms. When had this happened? How? A box of cutlery narrowly missed one of the firefighters as it fell from its perch atop a mountain of clothes and shoes and empty boxes of Glade Automatic Spray Freshener. The first responders stepped on cookbooks, on bags full of other bags, on orphaned bird and hamster cages, and on stacks of *National Geographic* magazines that had toppled from piles that were taller than they were. That's why he hadn't been able to get in, because of the toppling. How had she even got them up that high, and why hadn't he noticed before?

The kitchen floor was littered with puzzle pieces of Tupperware containers, aluminum roasting pans and five-pound bags of Uncle Ben's rice. Carmella herself was tucked between packages of toilet paper, hundreds of wooden stir spoons and what looked to be all of Adam's baby clothes. CDs and empty spice containers crunched under their feet.

"I was sorting," she whispered raggedly to Adam. "Tell them about the garbage bags. I was sorting, organizing it all. Tell them!"

Adam saw a stack of *Sentinels* teetering on the counter. There had to be a hundred of them. He pushed it over and watched them slide to the floor of what had once been the dining room. They were all yesterday's date.

A voice, calm and in command: "Don't attempt it, but do you think you are able to stand, ma'am?" Carmella didn't say anything. Then the firefighter, with all the grace of a guardian angel, knelt beside her and gently took her hand in his. "That's a nasty bump, ma'am. Do you think you've broken anything?"

Carmella was asked many, many questions, but she retreated, burrowing deeper into Adam, not comprehending—or pretending she couldn't. And she was asked the same questions again by the paramedics. Stethoscopes appeared, blood-pressure cuffs, an oxygen mask ... and all the while the firefighters trampled through the main floor. One of them found the smoke alarm, which Carmella had disembowelled years ago.

"How many fingers am I waving, Mrs. Ross?"

The other firefighters started for the upstairs and his mother began wailing in earnest. "No, no, please don't ..."

Thor stood guard at the door, directing traffic, but Adam could see the crying was getting to him too. And then, thank God, Chuck appeared.

And then his father.

And that's when Adam collapsed inside.

His mom clung to him even as the paramedics insisted that she let go. They would have to examine *ma'am*. They would have to take *ma'am* to the hospital. "Just for x-rays, ma'am, to rule out a concussion."

She did not go willingly. She did not want to let go of Adam. She promised and pleaded with him, with the paramedics, with Chuck, with Adam's dad. "Don't! Don't let them, Adam! You know what will happen—they'll put me in a place. You're my baby! You don't want to do this to me. You will *never* forgive yourself!"

"I'm doing this *for you*, Mom," Adam said, or thought he did.

Chuck stepped in and extricated mother from son, murmuring official doctor-type words.

Adam's father shook with rage as he took in the detritus filling his old home. He stared open-mouthed at the carnage that had once been his kitchen. It was unrecognizable. All of it.

"Oh, son, I am *so* sorry. I should have known. I should have. God, I'm sorry." He grabbed the boy into his arms, smothering him. "I'm sorry." The son was as tall as the father.

And then she was gone. They had taken her.

Chuck got into the ambulance too. Lots and lots more words were spoken, but Adam was too tired to listen. He had to lie down now. Even though the rain had stopped, his dad wanted to drive Thor home. Hell, his dad wanted to give Thor a small country to run. Thor politely refused both.

Before he got into the car with his father, Adam used the last of his strength to reach up and hug Thor, catching him off guard. "Thank you! Thank you!" He hugged the startled Thor harder. "How did you know?"

"I've been watching her for weeks," Thor rumbled, and he threw his tree-trunk arms around Adam. "I told you I'd nail the prick. I . . . I . . . I'm sorry."

Adam shook his head. "No, you're incredible. If you hadn't . . ."

Thor snorted. "You, kid, are the real goddamned deal." He turned back to 97 Chatsworth and shook his head. "You're a super-hero. Deal with it."

Then Thor smiled.

What the hell?

On the ugliest night of his life, Adam had made the mighty Viking smile. If he could have smiled back, he would have.

CHAPTER THIRTY-NINE

A dam stayed away from school for the rest of the week. He would have stayed away longer, but track tryouts were in the first week of April and there was no way he was going blow his chance at making the team. He had to have something to show for all that running around the cemetery.

He saw Chuck twice. They didn't start in on the exposure and response prevention, not yet, but he was well and truly committed to it. Really. Chuck spent the time trying to unravel what Adam had really been carrying around all these months. It was a killer List.

Funny thing, but "thresholds" was no longer on it. Of course, Adam didn't know for sure about the big biology lab at school or the south doors, or even Robyn's front door, but all the others were cool, including 97 Chatsworth. He knew because he had been back. The house reeked of burnt soup and plastic, even on the outside stoop, but he had no issues walking through the door.

"Trial by fire," he told Chuck. "They should put that in the manual."

On Thursday, Adam met up with Father Rick and a social

worker who was supposedly on his mother's "care" team. They met
at the house at three o'clock sharp. The social worker was attached
to a clipboard, a BlackBerry and a camera. She tried to behave as if
she had seen a thousand houses like 97 Chatsworth, but it was clear
from her pursed lips and googly eyes that she had never seen anything remotely like it. This was especially so since the first responders
had left new layers of scarring and chaos in their wake.

Father Rick held himself in the middle of the hallway sur-
veying the slaughter. "Shit," he muttered, not quite under his
breath. The social worker took pictures, drew plans and generally ignored Adam. She deigned to answer a question from
Father Rick, however, about what she was doing. "This process
will aid in formulating a coherently comprehensible plan of
action for supported sorting and purging, when and if Mrs. Ross
is ready to participate in her recovery."

What did that mean?

Everything that woman said sounded like she'd recited it from
a manual. Adam knew from manuals; he'd actually cracked the
book open that week. The social worker moved through the
rubble, taking notes and speaking into her phone importantly.

Adam left Father Rick to deal with her and went up to his
room to feed his fish. Was Steven pregnant again? He also wanted
to call Stones to fill him in as best he could without Sweetie glued
to him as he always was at Brenda's. He picked up and put down
the phone eleven times.

"Dude, that is such major sucking suckage. I don't even know
what to say! It's a soul-sucking tragedy! What can I do, dude?"

While they talked, Adam started filling up one of the four
boxes he had brought along. He told Ben that his Orcs and all his
warriors were coming to live at the Stones' garage forever.

"No way!"

"Way!"

"Way?"

"Way."

"Are you thinking of offing yourself?" asked Ben.

"What? No! What the hell?"

"It's one of the seven signs or ten tips or some crap like that of when you might be thinking of jumping off a cliff."

"How the hell would you know?"

After a pause that threatened to break their record for "awkward long Ben–Adam phone pauses," Ben said, "Okay, dude, thing is, I been googling OCD crap and, like, depression is a real morbid possibility."

"Co-morbidity," said Adam.

"Yeah, that too."

"How long? How long have you been googling it?"

"Years, dude. Are ya pissed?"

"No, man, you're probably more up on it than me. I just opened up my OCD manual on Wednesday."

"So you still nuts?"

"*Nutser.* You still fat?"

"*F-a-t-t-e-r*! But I'm firming! Hey, what do you want for the collection?"

"Nothing, man. Well, maybe, could we have a friend of mine from Group come and chill with us a couple times when we're playing? The guy I was telling you about? You'll like him. He's fierce but quiet." One box was full. Adam reached for another.

"Anything, dude! You can bring him and the all-girls choir from My Lady of the Perpetual Virgin or whatever your damn school is called. Wait, that's not a bad idea. We should definitely get some dudettes interested in the game. And you're free now, so it's a new world."

Adam groaned. "Stones, I want to be very clear: I am *so* not trolling for girls." He was charged by a lightning strike of feelings. He had to sit down. *Robyn, Robyn, Robyn* . . . "OCD is a walk in the park compared to girls."

"Bad, eh?

"Brutal bad."

"Yeah, but now you've got the taste, you've lifted the lid! You're gone. I'll give you a minute for grieving time, but hell, I need you, dude! You're so pretty, they'll go for you and I'll swoop in for the leftovers!"

There could never be anyone but Robyn. Adam held his head with one hand. "That's a helluva plan, Stan."

"But we'll stay away from the older ones for a bit."

"Yeah, yeah, for sure."

The boys rambled on for another few minutes, thereby smashing another record, this one for prolonged phone banter. Adam promised to spend Saturday over at Ben's, when his dad would drive him over with the figurines. It was such a *normal* conversation in the midst of such, such . . . Adam couldn't even find the words to describe the last few days. Thing was, after the hurricane, life went on. You had to buy milk, fix the broken windows, play some Warhammer, discuss some girls. Wow!

"Adam, you okay?" It was Father Rick. He leaned into the door jamb.

"Yes, Father. That was Ben I was talking to."

"Ah." He nodded. "Good kid, good friend."

"Yeah, he really is. Is the, uh, social worker . . . ?"

Father Rick rolled his eyes heavenward. "Yes, she and her

mighty clipboard are ready to leave the building. I'm driving her back to the clinic—but can I take you home first?" He shook his head. "I'm going to pray that they've got better than that at the hospital. Have you seen your mother yet?"

"Mom? No. It's no family for a month."

"Makes sense, I guess. Are you okay with that?"

"I'm kind of relieved, actually." Adam felt his face redden. "Sorry, Father, that's lame."

"Adam Ross, I grant you official holy dispensation regarding any feelings of guilt or lameness. Of all the people I come across in my flock, young man, you probably have the least reason to regret your actions about anything."

Adam mentally whipped through his most recent checklist of lies, tics, betrayals, cowardice and wants—there was Robyn, and all those driving, overwhelming wants. "Oh, Father, *you* have no idea."

"Oh, Adam"—Father Rick shook his head, smiling—"I think even *I* remember being fifteen." He extended his arm. "Come on, let's grab what you need and get out of here. I spoke to your Mrs. Polanski—she'll feed your fish until we figure out how to bring them over."

"Sure, Father. Could we drive through the cemetery, though? I want to pay my respects—it'll just take a second."

"Are you gentlemen ready up there?" called the social worker. "I have an enormous paperwork burden to sort through and a 4:47 meeting. Chop, chop."

"You bet, son." Father Rick put his arm around him. "I'll take you wherever you want to go, and you take as long as you need."

CHAPTER FORTY

A dam could barely drag himself out of Father Rick's car and into the house. Lately he slept like the dead and still he was so tired he sometimes shook with exhaustion. Brenda said it was because he was catching up on months of sleep deprivation.

Clearly, Brenda and Dad had read the riot act to Sweetie about a great many things, but mainly about not heaving himself into Adam as soon as he opened the door. Mr. and Mrs. Ross were measured and achingly thoughtful. Sweetie's version of thoughtful was that he didn't pepper his brother with non-stop demands for attention. But he still shadowed Adam from the moment he came into the house until they both went to bed, terrified that his big brother would disappear again into the bad place.

"Hello, Adam." Brenda brushed his forehead with a kiss. "How did it go? Was it bearable?"

Adam nodded, not sure whether it was or not. He wasn't sure how he felt about a lot of things. It seemed to take him days to sort out whatever thing had just happened, let alone the whole . . . well, everything. "It's a protective shock," Chuck had explained.

Whatever it was, you'd think it would protect him from the rest of his compulsions, but no. Although he'd broken through the threshold thing, Adam was still counting in an endless series of patterns. That didn't seem to rattle Chuck. "It's just the leftover, Adam. No biggie. The ERP will nail it. You have tremendous resources. You, Adam, are going to be *fine!*"

"Were Father Rick and that woman from the hospital there too?" asked Brenda.

"Yeah, they both dropped me off. She's a piece of work. I hope she doesn't get anywhere near my mom." Adam grabbed a biscotti from the cooling rack and saluted Brenda with it before heading to his room, Sweetie hot on his heels.

Their room was lit up like a Christmas tree. Sweetie had decided that his brother would be much comforted by an extremely bright room. All the lights were on—the table lamps, all four night lights, the overhead. Sweetie had snagged their father's desk lamp, which now illuminated the floor beside the garbage can. And to add to the festive holiday air, Brenda's Christmas candlestick lights twinkled merrily from the windowsill. You could have shot a movie in there. Sweetie trotted over to the far side of his bed and pretended to be absorbed in his latest Tonka truck acquisitions.

With a shaking hand, Adam reached into his pocket for the handmade card that he had found peeking from under a flat white stone in front of Marnie Wetherall, 1935–1939. He hadn't trusted himself to open it while the priest and social worker were waiting. He knew it was from her, of course. They loved Marnie best and Marnie loved them. Adam had taken the folded creamy paper and replaced it with the $6.99 Batman ring that Snooki and Wonder Woman had given him.

Now, on his bed, Adam stared at her perfect rendering of the Batman insignia. His heart beat in his throat as he opened the note.

I heard about your mom. About all of it. You were right, though, and that song you always sing for Sweetie was also right:

"A dragon lives forever but not so little boys."

You, Adam Spencer Ross, are a man, and will forever and always be my Batman.

I miss you. And I will love you,

Until . . .

Robyn

He sat on the edge of his bed for a long time, blinking in the brightness. Finally, with his hand still shaking, he put the card back in his pocket.

"You can talk to me, you know. I won't fall apart or anything."

Sweetie shot over like a bullet almost before Adam could finish the sentence, and clambered into his lap.

"Batman?"

"Yeah?"

"Do I still have to take care of you?"

And Adam wondered for the hundred millionth time, *Just how does this kid's mind work?*

"No, Sweetie."

"Good! I like it better when you have to take care of me all the time."

He turfed his brother off his lap. "You're too big for lap-sitting, goof!"

"No!" Sweetie's lip quivered. "They said I was too little, a shrimp. On the monkey bars, the big boys said . . . they said . . ."

"If they say it again, point 'em out and I'll nail 'em for you. Besides, you're not too, *too* little." He messed up Sweetie's hair. "We, you and me, are what they call late bloomers."

"Late bloomers," Sweetie said, repeating and storing. He hopped back onto his brother's lap. "And you're going to stay here with us forever, right, Batman?"

"Geez, little guy, things like that are mucho-hyper-complicated."

"No, they're not," said Sweetie. "Our dad and Mrs. Brenda Ross love you more than Mrs. Carmella Ross does. And I love you more than all of them, so we win and get to keep you!" He looked delighted with himself.

"Sweetie, that's not fair. My mom . . . well, she *does* love me. She loves me a lot."

"Okay," Sweetie conceded. "But she's very, *very* crazy, so she can't do a good job."

Adam turfed him off again. "Hey, any of us Ross men calling anybody else crazy is just the pot calling the kettle black."

Sweetie frowned, trying to wrestle some meaning out of talking pots and black kettles. "Is *Daddy* crazy?" That seemed to be his takeaway.

"No! Dad's a bit of a workaholic is all. Chuck—that's the doctor guy I go see—says that's how Dad deals with his anxiety."

"Anxiety," Sweetie repeated, waiting semi-patiently for more.

"Anxiety is like being afraid."

"Ohh . . ." Sweetie was instantly sympathetic. *This* he understood. "Is Mrs. Brenda Ross anxiety too?"

"No. Well . . ." Adam whipped another pillow at him. "Your mom is . . . like, your mom is just a little sensitive. She kind of sees things and feels things about people."

"Like you, 'cept you're really, really sensitive, right?"

"No, I'm—" *Wait! Was it true?* "Uh, okay, maybe you're right, Sweetie. Maybe I *can* recognize when people are hurting or sort of lost, more than other people."

"And that's why you can fix me when I'm bad-scared?"

"Maybe."

"But you're not very, *very* crazy, right?"

Everybody lies.

Well, hell, maybe everybody has damn good reasons to lie. Maybe we all just lie to hide the hurt or to fake being strong until we can be strong. That's not so bad, is it?

Is it?

"No, not *very*, very, I guess." Adam could almost see the wheels turning as Sweetie tried to sort all this out.

"But Mrs. Carmella Ross is," he said brightly. "So you have to do the rest of your growing up here!"

"Aaargh! I give up! Yeah, maybe, probably, mostly." Adam sat back down on the edge of his bed.

Sweetie sat on his own bed, mirroring Adam movement for movement, except that the cast kept getting in the way. "I'm never going to break my arm again," he announced, folding his hands in his lap when Adam did.

"Good call."

"I've been thinking."

"Uh-oh."

"Thinking and thinking and thinking and thinking and—"

"Okay, *what* already?"

"You're still the Batman, right?"

"Yeah. I'm still part of Group, and so yeah, I'm still Batman."

"But you lost your Robin?"

My Robyn. Adam's throat closed. He got up, sat down, got up again and started to pace.

Sweetie got up too. "She's gone, right?"

"Yeah, yeah, I lost her." *One, three, five, seven, nine, eleven . . .*

"Okay, good." Sweetie started pacing with Adam.

It was crowded. The room wasn't big enough for two simultaneous pacers, but they continued nonetheless.

"So can I be your new Robin, and you won't have to call me Sweetie anymore, ever? Mrs. Brenda Ross said exactly, 'Robin is, I *suppose*, rather marginally better than Sweetie.' And our dad said exactly, 'Well, there might be more hope of him not getting the crap beat out of him every other day if he's a Robin.' So can I be your Robin, huh? I asked everybody. Robin should be a boy anyway. I asked everybody, and *everybody* said so. I'll be the best Robin in the world and I won't ever pest you again in my whole life, promise."

Adam wondered who would have been included in Sweetie's extensive polling group.

"Please, Batman! Please!"

The kid was nuts.

They were both nuts.

He reached into his pocket and clasped the note.

A dragon lives forever but not so little boys.

A sweet, hard hurt threatened to crush him.

"Sure." Adam threw his arm around his crime-fighting partner. "Okay, Robin, go tell Mrs. Brenda Ross about your new identity."

"Yay!" His brother shot out of the room screaming. "Holy name change, Batman. Mom! Mom! Guess what, Mom!"

As soon as Sweetie left, Adam took out the note again. He exhaled, inhaled. The weight was unbearable. *One, three, five . . . No!* He opened the note and traced the words with his finger. *You, Adam Spencer Ross, are a man.* A man?

And then, for the first time since that man was a boy, Adam Spencer Ross sat on the very edge of his bed, in that very bright room, and wept.

ACKNOWLEDGMENTS

It takes a lot of work by a lot of people to turn what I write into a novel. I am grateful to the following purveyors of courage and encouragement—in other words, my first readers: my family, Nikki, Ken and Sasha Toten; the indefatigable Marie Campbell; and my writing group, Susan Adach, Ann Goldring, Nancy Hartry and Loris Lesynski.

I received generous advice and inspiration from every practitioner and young adult I met at the 19th International OCD Foundation Conference in 2012. My story was shaped and shaded by their stories. I also thank Friar Rick Riccioli, OSM Conv.; Albert Ottoni; Geoffrey Pearson; and Jenn Coward for their counsel and honesty, as well as Dr. Peggy Richter, who pointed me in the right direction. If I veered off course or drove into a ditch, it is entirely my own doing.

I am grateful beyond words to the patient and talented team at Doubleday Canada: Amy Black, Allyson Latta and especially Janice Weaver, who managed somehow to both embolden me *and* save me from myself.

Finally, I am indebted to all those who cannot be named but whose courage and determined hope drove me to write this book. You are not alone.

TEN QUESTIONS FOR TERESA TOTEN

1. Where did you get the idea for this book?

This book has been in my head for years. I watched so many of the young adults who were in or near my life struggle with OCD and debilitating anxiety. Their courage was both breathtaking and fascinating. I became haunted by the question of what it would be like to be them, to cope and carry on in the world with this invisible burden.

2. So is Adam based on someone you really know? He seems like such a genuine character.

Ah, bear with me here. My Adam is a composite of a few young men I've had the good luck to know. I stole their gentleness, intelligence and fierce protectiveness, and I gave those pieces to Adam. He became real and whole very fast. That first scene—when he falls in love with Robyn before she even shuts the door—was in my head for years. Yet after I'd finished the first full draft of the novel, I worried that Adam was too good, too sweet, too decent in the face of the enormous weight he had to carry.

Then I went to an international conference on OCD in Chicago, and it was there that I met him: a young man about Adam's age, strikingly attractive, sensitive, smart and funny. I watched him as he posed questions to the experts. This young man vibrated with confusion and pain, not only for himself but also for the people who loved him. In his soft southern accent, he asked expert after expert when he would "hit bottom with all this," and if he'd recognize it when he got there. He'd deal with it, but he wanted to know how much further down he and his family had to go. I'd found him. This was *my* Adam.

The next day, I noticed him standing alone and I went up to tell him that he had inspired me. I told him that I was writing a book and had been fretting about the "hero" being too amazing. And now, because I had met him, I knew there was no such thing as too amazing. I thanked him, and he—understandably bewildered—thanked me. And then, to my everlasting regret, I ran off before he could say anything else, because like a fool, I was crying.

3. What about Robyn? Is she also based on someone you know?

Robyn is probably me. I inserted myself into her reality and took her story where I would likely have taken mine if I were her. I would absolutely have fallen in love with an Adam.

4. I love the way the kids' alter egos reflect aspects of their personalities. What made you choose superheroes?

When I was a kid, I loved, loved, loved comic books! I confess that I still line up for all the superhero movies. While my girlfriends read about Archie, I read their older brothers' stash of superhero comics and got into heated, never-ending debates about Marvel versus DC. Marvel had the character edge for me overall, but I always loved Batman best.

5. Your portrayal of obsessive-compulsive disorder is so true to life. What kind of research did you do when you were writing the book?

It was a long road. I certainly know quite a few young people and adults who have OCD. That was my starting point. Then I read dozens of books, memoirs, self-help guides and research papers. I had the benefit of good advice from generous professionals like Dr. Peggy Richter at the Frederick W. Thompson Anxiety Disorders Centre in Toronto, and as I mentioned, I went to that wonderful international conference in Chicago, where I spent a few days questioning and observing everyone I met, and snuck into as many teen panels and workshops as I could.

6. Was there a particular message you were trying to get across with the novel?

No. I honestly wouldn't know how to do that with any skill. My characters move through their drama while handicapped by a disorder, but the novel's not *about* the disorder. All of us have experienced, to varying degrees, moments of debilitating anxiety and depression, and even obsessive thoughts. That is part of being human, and it is certainly a hallmark of being a young adult. To me, *The Unlikely Hero* is about first love, making friends and struggling with yourself. If my readers have done any of that, hopefully they'll feel just a little less alone when they pick up the book.

7. If readers see themselves in Adam or Robyn, or any of the other kids of Room 13B, are there places they can turn for help?

There are some excellent resources for both teens and educators on the web, and people can go to those out of interest or need. I've posted links to the most helpful sites on my website, teresatoten. com, and we've also provided a list of resources in this book.

8. The book tackles some serious issues, but it's still so funny and heartfelt. Was it hard to strike that balance?

Thank you. I am clearly drawn to dark things and heartache, but I also have a finely honed sense of the absurd. It's helped me a lot with the dark bits in my own life. And like so many readers, I *always* respond when a book makes me laugh and cry at the same time.

9. I think we've all experienced those moments of laughter
mixed with despair. Can you tell us some of your favourite
books for that?

It's like writing on a knife-edge, trying to pull off the despair/
funny card trick. Even so, dozens of those books line my shelves,
and I am a certified fan of so many more. I'd have to say that
memoirs seem to play with that balance the best. My favourite is
Mary Karr's *The Liar's Club*, followed closely by Catherine
Gildiner's *Too Close to the Falls*. A couple of exceptionally funny
and heartbreaking OCD memoirs are Jennifer Traig's *Devil in the
Details* and Fletcher Wortmann's *Triggered*. In YA literature, the
"Sues" (Susan Juby and Susin Nielsen) finesse humour and hurt
each time out, as do the amazing John Green and Libba Bray.
Stephen Chbosky's *The Perks of Being a Wallflower* also holds a
special place in my heart. And finally, although he writes for a
slightly younger crowd, the wonderful Brian Doyle showed me
what to aspire to in just about everything he ever wrote.

10. What are you working on now? Will we ever get to find
out what happens to Adam and Robyn?

I leave the fate of Adam and Robyn with my readers. I genuinely
look forward to hearing what they think will happen to them. My
next book is called *Slightly Damaged*. It's a psychological thriller
about two beautiful, emotionally injured young women who
somehow become entangled in a murder.

You Are Not Alone:

Places to Find Information and Help for
Young People, Parents and Educators

The Canadian Mental Health Association:
www.cmha.ca/mental_health/obsessive-compulsive-disorder/
#.UV3iNhlgPE4

The Canadian OCD Network:
canadianocdnetwork.com/

The Children's Hospital of Eastern Ontario:
www.cheo.on.ca/en/mentalhealthtopicsandconditionsAZ

The International OCD Foundation:
www.ocfoundation.org/whatisocd.aspx

The Jack Project:
www.thejackproject.org/

Kids Help Phone:
www.kidshelpphone.ca/Teens/InfoBooth/Emotional
-Health/Anxiety/Obsessive-compulsive-disorder.aspx

Mind Your Mind:
mindyourmind.ca

The National Institute of Mental Health:
www.nimh.nih.gov/health/topics/obsessive-compulsive
-disorder-ocd/index.shtml

Teen Mental Health:
www.teenmentalhealth.org/